The Alkoryn Chronicles

Part I

Scripture from the Past

T0159448

The Alkoryn Chronicles

Part I
Scripture from the Past

C. J. Gleave

COSMIC
EGG
BOOKS

Winchester, UK
Washington, USA

First published by Cosmic Egg Books, 2015
Cosmic Egg Books is an imprint of John Hunt Publishing Ltd., Laurel House, Station Approach,
Alresford, Hants, SO24 9JH, UK
office1@jhpbooks.net
www.johnhuntpublishing.com

For distributor details and how to order please visit the 'Ordering' section on our website.

ISBN: 978 1 78279 838 5
Library of Congress Control Number: 2014945520

A CIP catalogue record for this book is available from the British Library.

Design: Stuart Davies

Printed in the USA by Edwards Brothers Malloy

We operate a distinctive and ethical publishing philosophy in all
areas of our business, from our global network of authors to
production and worldwide distribution.

I'd like to thank

The greatest muse a writer could have, Ian Cannon, who has encouraged my writing from the very start.

And

Nicklas Lindeborg, who has supported me strongly with writing this book.

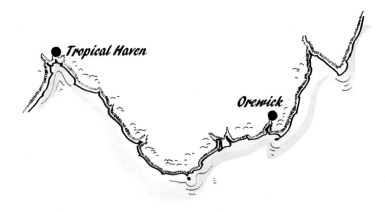

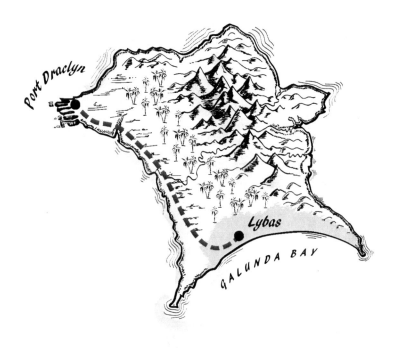

Port Draclyn

Lybas

GALUNDA BAY

N
W E
S

1

Mystical Words

The figure lay face-down in the clear ocean water, the waves licking at its naked feet. The skin was pale, almost translucent. The vast bay was covered in fine white sand, and scattered with small speckled pebbles and shells. The sand was scorching, yet the form did not move, seeming oblivious to the burning sun. As the water drifted back and forth, the head sank further into the sand. A sun-dried hood hid its face and its limbs lay helplessly by its side. The body wore armour, from under which tattered clothes could be seen peeking out – these looked oddly unscathed despite its journey across the seas. The strong bindings still held, in defiance of the pressure they were under from the bloated carcass.

The incoming tide slowly pushed the body further up the shore, where it lay, waiting...

* * *

The tide was once again coming in as Daimeh finished his daily routine of delivering various commodities to the people of Alkoryn, his people. Although his profession was regarded as an important one, he always referred to himself as 'the delivery boy'. As the grandson of the sovereign, he did not have to work, but he felt a personal obligation to contribute to the economy of his village, Lybas.

Carelessly, he strolled barefoot across the warm sands, a slim, athletic, young man, dressed in loose-fitting, beige clothes, crafted for him by his mother. She was the village tailor and was incredibly talented at her profession. After a day's work his attire was somewhat in need of a wash; however, this did not worry

Daimeh and, feeling quite content, he enjoyed the fresh-smelling sea breeze which tugged and played with his ear length, dark auburn hair.

As he beachcombed, his skimming walk left odd-shaped footprints in the moist sand: a shallow elongated imprint, then a firmly pushed-down one. Daimeh would usually take a relaxing stroll along the Galunda Bay after his work and collect kelp and shells. He had already found a few pieces and placed them in his hip pouch. As he lazily walked, sand stuck to his soles. Suddenly, he felt a jolt of pain from his foot. Daimeh yelped and hastily lifted the offending limb. He hopped on the spot as the sharp pain quickly became a numbing throb. Realising he had stumped his toe on a jutting, solid object, he peered down at the cause of his discomfort and noticed a particularly beautiful shell, washed-up by the tide and half-cemented in the sticky sand; a polished pearly husk poking upwards. The pain in his foot was instantly forgotten as he stared at the lovely object before bending to quickly dislodge the large, spindle-shaped shell with agile fingers and hold it in his hand. After brushing away the excess sand, an opalescent, perfectly smooth surface was revealed, adorned with swirling marbled markings. He'll be very happy with this one, he thought, opening his hip pouch and removing some kelp. He carefully wrapped it around the shell before placing it with the others and continuing on his way...

* * *

With every wave more fresh sand washed ashore and Daimeh's feet sank deeper. He gazed out along the shoreline in contemplation, then looked out to the hazy horizon, he had always questioned what was over the seas and had often thought about acquiring his own boat for an expedition. Yet, as he had been taught from a young age by Alkoryn scholars, the lands beyond Alkoryn were impassable.

Closing his oval, peridot-green eyes, relaxing his jaw and letting out a weighty sigh, Daimeh tossed his head back and ran his hands through his hair. He stood still for a moment, appreciating the invigorating sea air tickling his nasal canals. Daimeh had almost reached a meditative state when he suddenly noticed a nauseating smell of decomposition commingling with the natural fragrance of the ocean. He immediately awoke from his trance-like state and the brilliance of the sun pierced his eyes. He reached his hand up to block it out and used his other to cover his softly pointed nose. Stunned and squinting, he surveyed the immediate vicinity; there was nothing. He looked out further along the shore, and after a short while, an unusual glint caught his eye. He could see instantly that it did not come from a shell but from something unnatural. A foul smell and something that glinted unnaturally in the afternoon sun, two strange things on his familiar beach. It came to Daimeh that both things could be related. Without another thought, he sped through the warm shallows, bursting with curiosity. He wiped the sweat from his brow, his gaze fixed on the glinting object as its shine brightened. He wondered, as he neared it, if it was armour. Alkoryn was free of conflict and Daimeh thought back to the rhymes of war he had heard in his childhood. One fable he remembered particularly well was "The Winged Giant";

The day was pure,
And the skies were clear,
When the giant soared,
Above us he roared,
Blue was its colour,
With claws to sever,
As it dived towards Alkoryn.
Our people scattered and ran,
Some of us wore armour,
Yet our minds were sombre,

3

But, with swords by our sides,
We fought and we died,
As our numbers were great,
We battled with weight.
Then the giant let out a mighty yell.
And from the sky it thunderously fell.

Daimeh recited the rhyme as he ran, and before long he was within reaching distance of the anomaly. The sickly aroma had intensified and with his dirty tunic held to his nose, Daimeh flopped to his knees, staring ahead, his mind blank.

A calm tide was washing against the muscular body, but it did not move. It was huge. Curious, Daimeh reached out and brushed away the few grains of sand that were clinging to the glossed armour, like flour to sticky dough. Cautiously, he gripped the smooth edge of the chest-piece. The metal was boiling hot from the sun. He tried to release the armour from the body, but was unable to endure the heat; instead he grabbed the cadaver's swollen arm. It felt sticky and also warmed by the sun. Daimeh was determined to turn the body over, so he held it with both hands, letting his beige tunic fall from his nose as he did so. The stench was now even worse than before. He lifted the arm with effort, then quickly wedged one hand underneath. He heaved with all his strength, his feet digging into the sand. The body had absorbed a lot of water and was twice Daimeh's size, but still he persisted. He was stronger than he looked and he managed to slowly roll the corpse across the sand until it slumped onto its back with a dull thud.

Catching a glimpse of the uncovered body, Daimeh recoiled. "What the...?" He had never laid eyes upon such a brute; it lay motionless and clad in sand covered armour, a sword sheathed at its hip. A dark hood still hid the face – inviting him to reveal who was under it. Using only the tips of his fingers, Daimeh carefully lifted the soggy cloth.

4

He jumped back, shrieking, fighting the desire to flee. The thing's wretched, lifeless eyes were locked on Daimeh's; it was as if they had already known where he would be. They protruded slightly from the sockets, which made them seem even closer than they were. Breathing quickly, he gradually gained the mental strength needed to examine the horror in more detail.

The black centres of the eyes were clouded, as if they had been steamed from the inside and the white of the eyes rippled with veins. After the initial shock had subsided, Daimeh examined more closely its most striking features: two blunt tusks protruding from its chin. He frowned with curiosity before looking over the rest of its freakish face. The flesh between the nose and mouth was decayed: just two small holes were left, flat against a blanched, leathery face.

The jaw had been dislocated and the mouth laid wide open, exposing large teeth, obviously intended for grinding. Thick, bloodless lips sagged below the gum line and its tongue lay slumped to one side – inked by a touch of crimson.

Daimeh placed his palm on the coal-pigmented armour, lukewarm to the touch, facing the sand as it had. He noticed the faint outline of an embossed symbol, covered in sand. He wondered what it meant. Then he slowly bounced his palm on the chest piece. He was expecting it to squeeze against the body, but instead, found that it was solidly in place, as if something was under it. Daimeh removed his clam knife from his calf strap and began to tear at the bindings. They were tough, but he persisted, and eventually they broke. He tucked his hands under the plate and peeled it towards himself. It felt lighter than he expected. Dirty, damp garments were exposed, brownish in colour and stained with the ocean moisture. He noticed a shrouded oblong shape and tugged away the limp cloth covering it. A flare of sun caught his eyes, and he saw, bound to its torso, a sleek tablet, made from incredibly polished stone and with a flawless surface. Breaking the straps, he released the oblong stone. Daimeh lifted it up more forcefully than was necessary and noticed how light it was, like the chest-guard. How so, he thought, rubbing the perfectly curved edge and turning it over, continuing to run his hands over the glassy, satin finish. When he reached the centre of the stone, the pigmentation of deep obsidian dissolved, revealing a translucent surface shining with an inner light, as if it had been activated in some way.

Daimeh noticed a glowing, metallic, golden fluid, which was pulsing upwards from the centre of the stone and filling narrow etches to create writing. The glyphs looked exotic and mysterious to Daimeh and he could not make any sense of them.

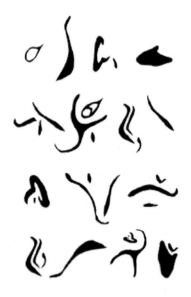

He turned the stone over and gleams emerged from the other side. It was Alkoryn. His geographic knowledge was limited: he recognised the Alkoryn islands, but the lands further away were unknown to him. As he turned back to look at the strange symbols again, they intensified in colour, and at the same time he became conscious of a delicate woman's voice whispering in his head. He heard her say to him, "Share the script; hide the magic."

He felt an uncontrollable urge to take the tablet with him.

He was unclear about what to do with the body and stood for a few moments deep in thought. "Maybe I should leave it here for someone else to find?" he muttered.

He knew that would be irresponsible, but he wanted to take the easy way out, rather than having to deal with this burden.

Standing up, he tucked the tablet under his belt, but its warmth against his belly was not pleasant on such a hot day. Pulling his light top over it, he prepared to head towards home. Just as he turned, he glanced at the sword and paused. He contemplated taking it, then decided he must. He dropped to his knees again and grabbed the black corded hilt. It was smooth and simply designed, yet was easy to grip. He was able to slide it from its sheath without any difficulty. He had expected it to be light, and it was. What is it he asked himself, some kind of knife? A lengthy, thin knife? No it was not quite a knife. But what? He had never wielded such a blade, and this one was clearly much too big for him. Daimeh held the sword at arm's length, surprised by his own agility. He began to swing it around as if fighting. The marbled, ebon surface, glinted in the sunlight.

Daimeh carefully ran his fingers along the contoured edge. It was clean and very sharp, and the outer edge was serrated. He looked at the sheath and decided he should also take it, for his own safety. Breaking the straps, he tore the sheath away from its belt and lowered the sword into it. It was thin enough that he could hide it under his clothing.

Daimeh suddenly felt waves splashing against his lower legs and realised it was time for him to head back. Before leaving, he paused again in contemplation, watching the tide rising over the body's knees. What he needed to do was suddenly clear to him. He knew he couldn't just leave it and decided to drag the body to the dunes, away from the water's edge. Hastily, he grabbed the discarded belt and strapped it around the carcass's wrists. Confident it would hold, Daimeh pulled the hefty arms up over the head and found himself a firm dragging position. He knew a challenge awaited him as the body was so sizably brawny.

Tensing his muscles, he began to haul it away from the incoming tide and towards the closest dunes, leaving deep trails in the sand as they went.

The sun had by now sunk lower in the tropical, azure sky. Alkoryn never fell into darkness, the sun never set and the land was eternally sunny. When Daimeh was finally almost at his destination, he stopped for a moment and sat down. His muscles were beginning to seize with cramp, and after all the events of the evening, he needed a bit of respite. Admiring the beauty of the tufted clouds high above, peacefully flowing across the horizon, he sensed that the air pressure had dropped. He knew it was late evening. The distinctive sound of the dyak cliff bats calling loudly to each other confirmed his suspicion. On any other evening, Daimeh would have enjoyed the salty, dry scent from the baked sand and crisp kelp, but that evening his lungs were still filled with sickness from the decomposing cadaver that lay behind him. He continued heaving the corpse along the beach.

He saw small sprouts of grass poking through the sand and he knew he was nearly there. Eventually he reached the dunes, and, exhausted, he dropped the belted body behind them. After he had relaxed his back and arms, he gathered a few pieces of dried foliage and scattered them over the body, making sure to cover its bulging eyes first.

Once it was completely hidden, he strolled back to Lybas thinking about the strange stone slab, wondering where it came from and how it got there? Who should he tell? He knew his mother should know, then the words "hide the magic" came to mind and he realised that no one should know about the tablet. He decided he would make a copy and show her that.

* * *

Daimeh arrived at the outskirts of Lybas as the sun was approaching its lowest point in the sky. The village of Lybas lay on Bayhaven, one of the eastern islands of Alkoryn, and was predominately a fishing colony, providing protein rich sustenance to the islands.

The earlier clouds had dissipated, leaving a warm, golden-orange hue. Daimeh approached the first Lybas bay-house, a humble home built on stilts; the sunlight bounced of each curved, vertical plank. He could see Bermel, a middle-aged fisherman, and his dusky silhouette. He was peacefully fishing from his exquisite balcony.

Bermel, looking completely tranquil, reeled in his line and glanced over to the returning young man. Taking his ivory pipe out of his mouth, he waved to Daimeh. "You're late today," he called, in a deep, husky voice. The smoke from his pipe rising in gentle wisps.

Daimeh ran his hand through his sweaty hair and nervously checked that his bounty was discretely hidden before replying, "Fete soon, Bermie. Just wanted to stay out a few more hours. Lost track of time though, but I did find the most beautiful shell." He smiled to himself, feeling guilty about not disclosing his other finds but knowing he must keep his secrets a while yet.

"Heh, you're a hard worker, it's good to see around here, just make sure you have time for yourself too."

Bermel sat back down in his sturdy, well-made chair, returned his pipe to his lips and cast his line back out to sea.

Before he disappeared behind the wooden wall, Daimeh shouted, "Not much time for that Bermie, but I'll try." He waved then continued past the chestnut house.

Daimeh calmly walked along the seafront, feeling his toes digging into the warm sand. He passed four more bay-houses, each with their own fishing boat, gracefully bobbing on the tide. Daimeh admired the small, colourful, potted plants on the balconies. They finished the look perfectly.

Once he reached Lybas, the stone path began. The souls of his feet brushed sand over the smooth, well-sculpted engravings; the sensation always gave him that relaxing feeling of being home.

* * *

As he walked towards the elegant houses, arranged in circular rows like a ripple, he caught a scent of sun-dried fish – the village delicacy – and realising that he had not eaten since the afternoon, headed in the direction of the smell. Fish lay baking on the stone ground, the pavement's decorative carvings acting as a makeshift grill; the juices running through the cracks. After consuming the largest fish he could find, he rummaged in his pouch and picked out a petite cream shell and placed it where the fish had been: an adequate payment to the village chef. He then continued his stroll through the village.

A small gust of wind blew smoke from kelp weed towards him. The weed was dried, then mixed with a concoction of herbs before being rolled inside a thin reed and smoked. Although Daimeh had heard people say that it "calmed the evil of the soul", he found the pungent, burnt algae smoke rather disgusting and always refused when it was offered to him. He looked towards where the kelp smoke was coming from and saw, without surprise, the usual drunk crowd babbling outside The Fish's Flask. From within the alehouse he heard muffled melodies, and, not wanting to rouse any attention, he briskly walked towards the second row of houses, past the central canopies.

After a few moments, he arrived in front of a set of wooden steps which led up to an elaborate front door. A perk from his coming of age was being allocated his own residence, modest but comfortable. He lived alone and spent most of his days foraging, although he always set aside some time for a bit of adventuring as well.

He nimbly hopped up the etched stairs and opened the door to his house.

Daimeh closed the timbered door behind him and immediately lifted up his baggy top. He removed the small stone slab and placed it on his simple kitchen table before removing the sword from his belt and resting it against the wall.

The scripture and maps lit up again when he touched them; the words "share the script, hide the magic" continued to repeat in Daimeh's mind. He walked through an arched doorway into his cosy living room. Opening a vine-thatched cupboard, he took out a single sheet of parchment made from pulped locyan-palm; the most abundant tree in the vicinity, a thick-trunked tree with parasitic vines. He picked up a feathered quill, taken from the light-blue ryndia bird; a large native parrot with exquisite feathers. Finally, he sought out a small pot of black ink.

Returning to the kitchen, he sat down and settled the parchment on the surface of the flat stone. The symbols were so bright that they shone straight through it. He allowed the quill to soak with ink before carefully tracing the markings as accurately as he could. When the last symbol had been copied and its ink had dried, he turned it over and copied the map. As soon as he had finished, the mysterious glowing fluid began to flow back into the tablet, as if a plug had been removed. Its smooth face remained as inscrutable as it had been when Daimeh first held it.

He rolled up the parchment and tying it with a thin leather bind, placed it on the table. As he did so, the second half of the verse repeated in his mind: "hide the magic". At that, he looked around for somewhere to store everything. Perfect, he thought, focusing on the sturdy larder door. He opened the door and an aroma of spices and fish gusted towards him, overwhelming his senses. It was a pleasant smell in Daimeh's opinion. He proceeded to bury the items amongst his provisions.

After closing the pantry door, he gently tossed his full hip pouch onto a highly-glossed bench and glanced out of the window. The sun was at its lowest point in the sky, just above the trees, meaning that it was currently the middle of the evening.

He had managed just five hours sleep the night before, and his exhaustion finally caught up with him. Reaching the stairs, he shuffled up the steps, sliding his hand up the banister. At the top of the wooden stairs a luxurious carpet greeted him; it was an indulgence for his toes. He tiredly walked into his cosy bedroom and towards his low bed, the cream, woven sheets left unmade that morning.

Daimeh lifted his grimy top up and over his head, then dropped it carelessly onto the carpet. Without disrobing any further he stumbled over to his bed, flopping chest down onto the wool-filled mattress, leaving his arm hanging over the edge.

The yellow-orange evening light shone through the opaque window. It was so tranquil, and Daimeh was so tired, that in no time at all he was fast asleep.

2

Naivety Has Its Advantages

Bright, blazing sunlight beamed through Daimeh's window. Almost white, with a hint of yellow, it glared down on his lightly tanned face. He had not moved at all during the evening; his body still lay in the same position as it had the moment he had dropped onto the supple, leather mattress.

He was woken by the sound of knocking. At first it was very distant, but became increasingly loud as he slowly awoke. Still fuddled with sleep, he moved his head from side to side, but the banging only became louder still. It had slipped his mind to close the weaved curtains, and the room was full of sunshine.

He drowsily opened his eyes, which watered a little from the bright sunlight. Thud, thud. Daimeh, still confused, opened his eyes fully.

"Daimeh!" A female voice was calling him.

He quickly realised it was his aunt and that he must be late. He jumped out of bed, instantly alert and awake. Hastily he checked the sun's position, and saw that it was at its highest point. His stomach sank; it was midday – the hottest time of the day. Without even putting a top on, he rushed downstairs to open the front door.

"Have you just woken up? What is wrong with you, Daimeh?" His aunt was silhouetted by the bright sunshine. "Get dressed and come on." Her voice was stern.

"I'm so sorry, Aunt Cresa," he replied as he quickly picked up his hip pouch from the kitchen bench. "I stayed out late, but it was worth it." Opening the pouch, he unwrapped the shell and passed it to his aunt. "Look at its beauty; Grandfather will love this one, I'm sure."

Cresadir took the shell and turned towards the sun, holding it in the light. Her butterscotch-golden hair caught the wind and shimmered as she turned.

"Hmm. It certainly is a very special specimen," she said, twisting it around to examine it properly, noting its impeccable shine and the sleek surface without a single scratch. The shell glimmered in the sunlight, a dappled, turquoise violet hue.

"This is evidently a remnant of the elusive monea snail, a rare deep sea snail," she said, turning the shell. "See the elongation of the base? This is because the monea have a small sucking pad for a head, which they use to grip to the seabed, allowing their shelled bodies to just drift on the current. Amazing that you found this, Daimeh."

Cresadir smiled forgivingly behind her loosely curled hair, which was now blowing across her face.

"All right, I can forgive your short lie-in, now get your clothes on and help me with this packing. You know how much I dislike being the last to arrive."

Daimeh ran his fingers through his hair, using them as a makeshift brush. "I know aunt," he said. "I'll hurry, just give me a few minutes to get my things in order."

He shut the door, feeling a little anxious. He had to get back to the body at Galunda Bay. He couldn't do that alone, and wasn't quite sure when he would be able to leave the village. His thoughts interfered: maybe he could just tell her, everyone was going to know at some point. He couldn't tell them, they'd just panic. His mother would know what to do. After considering the matter for a short while, Daimeh bounced up his stairs and picked up his dirty top from the day before. It smelt musty, but this did not bother him and he put it on anyway. Once downstairs, he went straight to the kitchen larder and picked up the closest full basket, which was loaded with dried, peppered, thinly carved meat. He carried it out with difficulty, leaving the door open to make the return trip easier.

The young man hauled the vine-woven basket as hastily as he

could through the narrow alley outside his house, in the direction of the centre of the village. As he passed his parents' house a warm breeze wafted the delightful smell of peppery, spicy, seasoning up Daimeh's nostrils; a pleasant beginning to his day.

He exited the alley and, in the shade of the front steps he saw his father, Halgar, hard at work preserving young palm leaves with oil squeezed from the avopalto, a fatty fruit that has a variety of uses, from sealing leaves, to varnish, ink and paint. To Halgar's left there were leaves drying, their lush green colour decoratively preserved. To his right, were thatched leaves ready for roofing.

Halgar looked up at his son with his friendly, deep-set eyes. "There you are boy," he said in a carefree tone. "Your mother and Aunt Cresa have been working so hard. Tell them to take a rest, would you? They don't listen to me. You know what they're like." He nodded abruptly. "Well that looks heavy, go drop it under the canopy and see your mother at the barn."

"M-hm," Daimeh replied, hauling the basket into a comfy position and walking off.

He was quite close to his father, who had taught him the basics of village life, and the responsibilities the villagers bore towards one another. He was mature at forty-four, a little younger than Bermel, and his hair was beginning to grey slightly.

Daimeh felt the weight of his basket as he shuffled towards the busy canopied centre. The stalls were adjoined, creating an almost market-like appearance. Young children weaved between the banisters, rolling a small wheel with sticks. Daimeh admired the enthusiasm of his people, actively hustling with crates and sorting through them. They were pretty cramped under there, shading themselves from the radiance of the sun. Others sat on fabricated rugs in front of their houses, arranging decorative flowers.

Daimeh was so tall that he had to duck slightly before

entering.

"Where do you want this?" he asked.

"Oh." An elderly woman tilted her head towards him. "Just put it down here." She smiled pleasantly as she spoke.

Daimeh carefully placed the basket down next to a collection of other baskets, all filled to the brim with vegetables, seafood and shells.

"Thank you, dear."

He grinned in response.

The barn stood opposite, and by it he could see his mother, Miah, with her older sister. His mother was a few years younger than his father and she was more active, always busy with things. Behind her, deep inside the barn, was a well-constructed cart. As Daimeh approached, he saw that his mother had become irritated by a stray hair that had blown loose from her ponytail. She put her heavy basket to one side and tucked the cinnamon-coloured strand behind her ear. She hadn't noticed Daimeh.

"Hello, Mother, anything I can do?" he asked, strolling into the barn.

She glanced at him with her honest, arctic-blue eyes.

"Oh, Daimeh, about time you turned up."

Cresadir interrupted. "I was knocking at his door at midday. He'd only just woken up!"

"Oh, come on, Cresa. I showed you the shell."

"Shell?" Miah queried.

"Outstanding find, a monea shell. I think it'll be the nicest gift Father will get this year."

Daimeh joined in. "What? Better than what Uncle Alfrit will bring?"

"I believe so," Cresadir chuckled.

"That would be a nice..." Miah began, but then her fine, straight, hair suddenly blew completely free from the ponytail. "Damn." She preferred things to be fuss-free.

"Anyway, can you pack those crates onto the cart?" She

pointed to the stacked boxes in the corner. "We want all the carts loaded before tomorrow morning," she continued, holding her hair back and retying the ponytail.

"Sure. What time do we leave?"

"At the first high sun hour."

Daimeh walked across the straw-covered floor over to the boxes in the corner. He picked up the first crate, which was full of shells, all equally-sized; the villagers had sifted them prior to packing. He dumped it onto the cart, and tucked it at the back against the high wooden barrier.

The second crate held quaint wooden ornaments with shells embedded into them. He pushed the crate next to the first, moving it back and forth to make them as compact as possible.

* * *

An hour had passed.

"I'm done here."

"Go on." Miah swept her hand, waving her son to get more goods. "Get the rest."

Since she was his mother, Daimeh had little choice but to obey her orders, but he was often reluctant to do so and sometimes felt angst-ridden about his situation.

"Yes, Mother." Daimeh's unwillingness was all too clear to Miah and she crossed her arms. He meandered towards the canopies to collect the first woven basket. All he could think about was the body at the bay.

* * *

The dry straw crunched as Daimeh wearily dumped the last basket onto the barn floor. He saw his mother still shuffling the baskets about like she was doing a puzzle. She was diligent as always; she had the attitude that everything must be right.

Daimeh rested a moment, then addressed Miah. "Mother, I need to do something before evening. I found something at the bay yesterday." Regardless of how tired he was, he knew his day was not over.

"I know, your aunt has showed it to me already," she replied, whilst securing the goods with a vine rope.

"Not the shell," Daimeh said, nervously exhaling, and looking at his feet. He needed to tell her.

"You're making me worry, Daimeh; what is it?" Miah asked, looking at him with concern.

After a few moments of contemplation, he decided that the direct approach was best.

"Erm, a body washed ashore... Like nothing I've seen before... I hid it in the dunes."

"A body?" Her teardrop shaped eyes immediately opened wide with surprise. Daimeh had her attention. "Why didn't you tell me about this earlier?" she asked, tucking wayward loose hairs behind her ears.

Daimeh's shamefaced expression explained enough.

"The fete – and you know how Cresa gets," he began, glancing to his right, thinking quickly. "And it's not a good time to be alarming everyone."

Miah checked around in case there were any eavesdroppers before whispering to her son, "Look, don't you think Cresa would want to know about this too?" Although she was speaking quietly, the anger in her voice was apparent. "And what do you mean, it's like nothing you've seen before?"

"It's not Alkoryn."

"What? All right, I can understand you didn't want to scare anyone, but you should have told me and definitely your aunt Cre..."

"I've told you now," he interrupted

"Never mind. We'll keep this quiet. I don't want any villagers to know." She placed her hand on his shoulder, trying to reassure him. "Get your cousin to help – he's feeding the glennies – then bring it up to Cresa's. Don't let anyone see you."

He nodded compliantly, relieved.

Glennies were herd animals with large clumsy looking ears and soft protruding snouts. Alkoryn's bred three breeds of glenny, one known as the 'kashi' with lush, thick, soft wool, the 'saable' bred purely for milk and the 'moxo' used as a pack animal and for quality meat and leathers. They stood just short of a man, with sturdy hooves and a fluffy short tail. They were most commonly cream in colour.

Each Alkoryn child was given a glenny to teach responsibility.

* * *

As Daimeh walked towards the open fields behind the barn, he was met by a gentle breeze and the smell of fresh straw. He ran his hand along the wood of the adjoining fence as he walked. Oeradon, Daimeh's cousin, was tipping grain into a wooden trough, snuffling his nose as the dust irritated him. The sound of falling grain excited the maize-shaded glennies. The herd strutted towards the troughs – one specially lacquered to hold water – and started munching, each one competing for the freshest food. One glenny in particular, a moxo with creamier, shorter wool, broke away from the herd, seeming even more excited by the sight of Daimeh than by a full trough. As she got closer, she couldn't contain her delight and started bouncing on her strong hooves.

"Popley." Daimeh was just as happy to see her and held out his hand, allowing her to lick him. "Awww girl, sorry I didn't see you yesterday." She appeared not to mind – as long as she could lick his hand, she was content. He tickled her behind her ear and she snorted as he scooped up a handful of grain for her.

Oeradon, who was a few years his senior, interrupted the affectionate exchange. "What's up?" he asked, still pouring grain.

"Oh," Daimeh said, suddenly coming to; he sometimes lost himself in thought, "er, I need your help."

"Yeah." Oeradon scratched his nose as he answered his cousin. "With what?" A curious look came into his pale blue eyes and he smirked. "Ooh, I know... You want me to put in a good word with Karalyn?" This lightened the tone and he grinned, Oeradon had a wide, attractive smile.

"No..." Daimeh realised he must have seen him looking at Karalyn and threw a handful of grain at his slim cousin.

"Oi," the older cousin shouted, shaking the kernels from his taupe clothing and then composing himself.

"It's important – you'll see why when we get there," Daimeh said, brushing the remaining husks from his hands. He knew he had to keep his reasons mysterious for the moment. "We need to bring Popley too." Knowing that his cousin had a cowardly disposition, Daimeh chose discretion and beckoned to his glenny, opening the fence clasp as he did so. Popley trotted through the small, open gate and patiently waited for her master to saddle her. This was a routine she was familiar with.

"Er... all right. You got me interested."

* * *

It was Miah's turn to sweep the dried leaves off the barn floor. It had to be cleaned daily and a rota was the fairest way of organising it. She was just about finished when she heard the clop of hooves on the stone pavement.

Miah looked up, and saw Daimeh, Oeradon and Popley. "Remember what I said... keep it 'shh' and go around the back."

Oeradon's curiosity increased.

"What's this about, Daimeh? Some secret surprise for the fete?"

"Unfortunately no, nothing like that." There was sadness in

Daimeh's eyes: he knew what his cousin was about to see, and he felt guilty about keeping it from him. As they went past the central canopies, Daimeh bent down and picked up two thick pieces of cloth from one of the tables. He handed one to his elder cousin. "Here, you'll need this too."

* * *

The afternoon sun was still high; it beamed down on them from a cloudless sapphire sky. Collecting a body wasn't going to be nice on a day like this.

As they strolled past Bermel's house and out of the village, Daimeh quickened the pace. Popley pranced next to him excitedly. Oeradon noticed his worried expression and his suspicion increased, causing a lump in his chest. The eldest cousin continued to follow Daimeh until they arrived at the western dunes.

"Not far, just over the next dune," Daimeh said. They were close to the hiding spot and for a moment he thought – out of habit – about doing some shell-hunting. But he quickly remembered the real reason he was at the beach: to retrieve the unknown body.

Popley was the first to react to the smell of decay. She halted and made snorting noises in disgust, stamping her front hooves. The covering heap of leaves had blown around a little during the low-sun hours, but they still completely concealed the body.

"Here it is."

Daimeh pointed at the mound.

"Leaves? And, what's that smell? It's horrible." His cousin reached for the cloth in his pocket.

"Not leaves... And, yes, you might want to cover your nose now." Daimeh felt it was polite to at least give his cousin some warning. He scuffled at the browned, desiccated leaves, brushing them away from the creature's face. Once the foliage had been cleared away, the creature stared rigidly up at them. It was evident that the natural decomposition process had progressed: a few attentive insects were flying in circular motions around the tear in its jaw.

"What the…?" Gasping in shock, Oeradon took a step or two back. His initial reaction wasn't too dissimilar from what Daimeh's had been. "It's grotesque… and the stench! This cloth isn't enough," his disgusted eyes peered over the cloth mask, whilst still holding it as firmly as he could to his face.

The odour had become richer since the day before, but Daimeh's previous lengthy exposure to it meant that he was able to stomach it more easily than his cousin. But he still tied the facial cloth around his head so that it covered his nose and mouth, more for reasons of hygiene than anything else.

The corpse's arms were where Daimeh had left them, above its head. After they had swept the final leaves away, Daimeh tried to move the body.

"I've got the wrists." He knelt down and held the corpse's wrists firmly. They were stickier than they had been the day before and the skin felt slimy against his hands; Daimeh felt overwhelmed with feelings of disgust. He coughed.

"You take the ankles."

Oeradon almost choked. "Are you serious? I'm not touching that thing," he said, then secured the cloth in its previous position.

"I'm deadly serious. Now take the ankles!"

Oeradon was a little startled – Daimeh was never this assertive. It must be serious, he thought. He leant over and firmly grasped the sticky ankles.

"Now, let's turn it over." Daimeh said, once he was sure they both had a good hold.

As they heaved the body onto its front, Oeradon noticed the creature's large, dry nails and leathery skin, and was struck by the sheer size of its feet.

"Oh, Popley. I know it smells bad, but we need you, girl," Daimeh said in a soft voice, trying to reassure her. She remained unimpressed and cautiously stepped backwards. The cousins tried to lift the body onto Popley's back, but she continued moving away.

"C'mon, girl – I hate this too," Oeradon coaxed, fully sharing her repulsion.

They laid the body down on the grainy sand and Daimeh walked over to Popley. Whispering her name, he gently rubbed the soft mane under her chin. He rubbed his fingers along her cheeks and stroked between her ears. Daimeh waited until she had settled before he returned to the body. The two cousins lifted it up, then laid it on the glenny's back, its arms dangling over one side and its legs over the other. Continuing to reassure Popley, Daimeh knotted a rope under her belly and firmly tied the corpse's hands to its feet.

"Seems secure," Daimeh asserted. He gave his glenny an affectionate stroke, then tugged the thin reins, indicating it was time to leave. "Let's head back to Cresa's."

As they came closer to Lybas, the sands beneath their feet were replaced by lush flourishing grassland. They walked through pastures which harboured wide leaved, deep-green plants; a few were in flower, with an almost luminescent fuchsia and olive hue, others were a vivid yellow. But it was difficult for Daimeh and Oeradon to smell the aroma of these beautiful plants over the stench of the deteriorating corpse. The festering odour was so strong that they kept their noses covered for the whole journey.

The dense forest to their right always made Daimeh's chest drop. He could never forget the time in childhood when he had got lost in the forest and injured his foot quite badly.

Beyond the fields was a small hill; Cresadir's manor stood atop it. It could be seen from quite a distance away. After an hour's walk through the green fields, the two cousins arrived at the rustic pebbled walkway that sloped upwards to Cresadir's house.

As they started to ascend, Popley suddenly stopped and peered down. Leaning forward, she started munching on a small shrub planted in a scooped-out wooden pot. "No, Popley, they're Cresa's." He pulled on the cord and she slowly looked up, with a guilty expression, still chewing on a flower.

Daimeh giggled at her. "C'mon girl."

She continued with them.

* * *

As they approached the superbly constructed porch, they saw Cresadir. She waved as she jogged down to meet them. Her sister remained at the door watching them; she looked anxious.

"Bring it round the back and I'll take a look," Cresadir said, directing them to the gardens. "It's quieter and away from nosy eyes."

Miah went inside, shutting the grand double doors behind her. Daimeh and Oeradon walked around to the garden gates where they were greeted by tall locyan-palms, adorned with lavish hanging shells. Cresadir hurried ahead, opening the gates inwards so Popley could easily fit through. As they made their way over the turfed grass, they saw Miah was already waiting for them. She was stood in front of the large pond, next to an exquisitely carved statue of a young Alkoryn man; he was on one knee, arm outstretched and looking upwards; water trickled through his fingers.

Daimeh led the abomination through the gardens, feeling regretful: it seemed that by bringing it here he was somehow dishonouring this enticing place.

Miah approached the convoy and immediately doubled over. "Oh, uuurrrgh... ouugh... caauugh." The stench was too much for her and she ran, spluttering, towards the grass. Daimeh rushed over to give her his cloth towel, which she pressed to her mouth to contain the vomit.

"It's all right, Mother; you'll get used to it," he said, placing his hand on her back reassuringly.

"She won't need to; we'll be embalming it soon," Cresadir said, cutting the tying cords. She seemed completely unbothered by the smell.

Daimeh looked at his cousin and grabbed the corpse's wrists. "Help me lift it again," he ordered Oeradon. His cousin took hold of the ankles as before and together they hoisted it off Popley's back and dropped it in front of Cresadir. It made a thud as it slumped onto the lawn, causing Miah to shudder with surprise. As soon as Oeradon had let go, he strolled towards the pond feature and sat on a short stool. With his tall lanky legs he was clearly too big for it, but at least he was surrounded by the beautiful shrubs and flowers.

Cresadir and her nephew turned the corpse onto its back and the full grotesqueness of the creature was revealed.

"I'm... going... inside," Miah mumbled, still tightly holding the cloth to her mouth. Shaking her head, she went into the manor. Once she was gone, her sister knelt down to examine the body.

She gently touched and prodded the rotting face. "I've not seen anything like it."

"There was some armour too."

"Armour?"

"Yes."

"Clearly civilised in some way," Cresadir commented.

"It's probably buried in the sand by now," Daimeh said, then paused, unsure whether to continue. He knew he should tell his aunt about the tablet, but he decided to obey the message he had heard earlier: *hide the magic.*

"I wasn't able to retrieve it."

This deliberate deception left him feeling a little conflicted.

He showed her the writing instead.

"This was also on the body."

She took the parchment and untied the binding. She flicked it a little to straighten it before inspecting it. "Interesting. The language I don't understand, but the map of Alkoryn is intriguing. My father must see this; his knowledge is far greater than mine." She rolled the paper up and retied it before passing it back to Daimeh.

"What now?" He glanced up at his aunt. "We embalm?"

"Yes, we can't take it to Aelston like this. The smell would alert too many people." She looked at the sky, checking the position of the sun. "We don't have much time; best hurry." She shouted over to her son, "Oeradon, I'm going to need your help."

Oeradon nodded and got up from the wooden stool.

"I'll need some bottled astringent fluids and thin grass stalks – you know where they are."

"The cupboard with the stained glass door."

"Yes, and from the drawer above get me a sharp scalpel, it must be the one with the curved edge." She glanced quickly at her nephew before continuing. "Daimeh, get some large linens from your mother. The bed sheets will do." Daimeh bobbed his head in compliance and ran off.

Before Oeradon had reached the manor, she called to him, "Wait, help me get this thing inside first." She held it just under its sticky knees.

"Really?"

"Come on – grow up, Oeradon."

He awkwardly took hold of the body, holding it under its armpits and together they shuffled the corpse towards the house.

3

Somebody Has To Do It

The corpse lay on white sheets, its wide, lifeless eyes staring up at the mosaic ceiling.

Cresadir paced up and down then stood still and peered over the body. She had taught herself biology, and had some rudimentary ideas about evolution. Deaths were rare in Alkoryn, but being the village physician, she had seen many dead bodies. Cresadir was the daughter of the monarch and regarded her royal status as something natural and fitting, yet she didn't consider herself superior to anyone.

The creature had decayed quite a bit. Its stomach had sunk into its ribcage, its skin had become dehydrated and wrinkled, and its face had started to putrefy. Cresadir poured water into a glass bowl and rinsed her hands, she soaked a sponge.

"Come over here, boys; you might learn something."

"I've seen enough of that thing," Oeradon said, wearing a disgusted expression. "I'm going to help Aunt Miah with the packing." With that, he promptly left the hall.

"Daimeh, then, come on." She beckoned to him.

Hesitantly, he walked towards her. He had seen the body several times now, but was still not quite prepared for what he was about to witness.

"We need to remove its clothes before we can prepare it for the internal autopsy," Cresadir began, pulling the hood fully off its head and revealing straggly black hair plastered to its face. Cresadir tucked the gluey strands behind its ears.

"Tubular, narrower at the base, opening wide at the tip – interesting." Stray strands of hair were stuck to its earlobes. She twisted the ears a little.

"They're flexible and look as if they can move in different

angles." A hunted species, perhaps? With acute hearing, Cresadir thought before saying, "All right, let's remove the rest of the clothes."

* * *

"Now to clean him."

Cresadir wiped the sponge down the corpse's chest.

"He's clearly a male" Squeezing the excess water from the sponge, she began to wipe the grime of his face. As she did so, the rotting lower jaw dislodged further and dangled loose. She was unfazed and firmly held the jaw in place before closing his mouth; she lifted his lips and ground the teeth together, making it look as if he were eating.

"You can see the teeth are flat, wide and worn down. These teeth are for grinding, so as fierce as he appears, this 'man' did not evolve from a predator."

Whilst holding the jaw, Cresadir gripped one of the short, thick horns with her other hand.

"These are very striking, however – artificially blunt," she said, stroking the horn, "grainy, possibly sanded."

She released the jaw and let it flop down once more until it dangled like a pendulum. Reaching down, she opened a small drawer. Pulling out a sheet of papyrus and a chunk of charcoal, she said, "I'd like you to take notes."

Daimeh took the makeshift notepad and gave Cresadir his complete attention.

"Will do."

"My conclusion is these 'people' are not dangerous. I believe the horns are not intended for fighting, but instead are simply a facial feature of the male of this species."

She turned the body's head from one side to the other.

"Look at the size of these eyes, and look at how wide apart they are," she instructed, moving her fingers up to his temples.

"Notice that the pupil and iris are black in colour and also relatively large compared to ours and much more spherical in shape. This eye position supports my suspicion that the creature is non-predatory and their size and shape indicate that this mortal, whoever he was, came from a very dark place."

"How's that so?" Daimeh was confused; he had never experienced darkness before.

"There are many things you don't know about this world, Daimeh," Cresadir said, rubbing her fingers over the corpse's flat nose. "The nostrils are very small, and protrude slightly forward. Smell is clearly not his strongest sense." She prodded at the decomposition under the nose. "Typical decay around the mouth and nose from increased bacteria in these areas."

"Still taking notes?"

"Yes."

She opened the next drawer down, took out a frightening-looking saw and placed it onto the tray. She then picked up the curved, pointed scalpel.

"You may want to prepare yourself for this."

Cresadir positioned the pointed end of the scalpel over the broad neck, at the base of the throat. From there, she began to slice down towards the cadaver's chest in a staggered motion, as if skinning an animal. The incredibly firm skin, perhaps two inches thick, meant that cutting took some time. As she dissected the lower torso, a repulsive odour started to emanate from the abdomen. Cresadir was unfazed by the smell but Daimeh immediately keeled over, covering his mouth. The nauseous young man couldn't hold back and vomited uncontrollably onto the polished timber floor.

"Don't worry; it happened to me," Cresadir said calmly. She looked over and passed him a flannel. "Now wipe your mouth and lay that over the floor"

Daimeh was unable to reply but did as she asked.

His aunt passed him a glass of water. "Here"

"Thanks." He tipped his head back, sloshing water into his mouth whilst staring upwards through tear-filled eyes. The ceiling was so blurry to him that he could only just make out the naked, kneeling man in the mosaic.

"Are you ready?"

"M-hm."

She carried on carving through the corpse's white flesh, slashing the blade through the hypodermis which connected the skin to the rib cage. "Acutely pale skin, most unusual. Very thick and blubbery." Maybe to keep warm, she thought. While the skin was a greyish white, the creature's blood, revealed by the deeper incisions, was just as red as their own. Having opened a gash in the corpse, Cresadir tugged at the skin from both directions, revealing the rib cage beneath. With precision, she aimed the blade at the sternum, just under the right collar bone, and stabbed firmly into the ribs, chopping through the first bone with difficulty; then, using the saw, she carved through the rest with comparative ease.

She pulled the rib cage upwards, making a cracking noise. Daimeh was having trouble focusing on the examination and Cresadir noticed that he seemed unsteady on his feet.

"Daimeh?"

"I'm fine."

Holding the ribcage up, she began carving into the bloody membrane under the bones, she then chopped through an adjoining bone, enabling her to remove it.

"Now we'll see what's inside," she said, placing the saw and bone onto the side bench.

Looking down at the exposed lungs, she plunged her hand into the cold, squelchy cavity in the corpse's chest. She grabbed the copious right lung, which was around twice as large as an Alkoryn lung. It was grey in colour, and pink emanated from deep inside. It was so large she had to clutch it with both hands.

"Cut this loose, would you?"

"Must I?" Daimeh answered, his face visibly blanched. He felt light-headed and there were patches of sweat showing through his top.

"Our time is limited, Daimeh; I can't do this without you." Her eyes were insistent. "Just take the knife and cut the connecting stem bronchulus under there." She turned the lung over, and it flopped around in her palms like a fluid-filled sack. She indicated the designated area, then stretched the adjoining tube upwards. Daimeh took up the scalpel, but hesitated before making an incision. He could see where he had to cut, but was unwilling to slice through the fibrous membrane. He took a deep breath and pressed the curved blade down on the tube. Sea water spurted out of the dissected lung, splashing into the cavity below it.

"Urggh," he cried, covering his mouth with his free hand.

"That's good, you've done well."

Cresadir smiled proudly at Daimeh.

"Now write this down."

She paused for a moment to drop the oversized lung into the glass bowl, which it filled completely.

"Water in the lungs tells me that this 'man' definitely drowned getting to us. Also note that the lung capacity is enormous – this was a powerful creature."

A confused look came over Cresadir's face as she stared down at what had been revealed.

"A heart on the right side, intriguing. An abnormally large heart at that. We're going to need another bowl."

Daimeh took that as his cue, and hurried off.

Once he returned, he assisted Cresadir with removing the left lung in the same way they had taken out the other. Daimeh found it more bearable the second time round.

"Two hearts," Cresadir observed with a startled expression. "I've no explanation for this. I've never seen or heard of anything like this."

The hearts were deep red in colour and of similar size, roughly the width of two hands.

The lower abdomen revealed further anomalies.

"Two connected stomachs." Where is our friend from, she thought, before continuing her dissection, slashing through the outer membrane.

"Let's see what he eats," she said, spilling the stomachs' contents into a metallic tray. "Hmm, there are stalks, grass and tree bark in the first, and the remains of vegetables, fruits and seeds in the second." A grazer, supported by its grinding teeth, she surmised.

The rest of the autopsy was relatively straightforward. The remaining innards were very similar to what Cresadir was used to from Alkoryns, although they were substantially bigger. Once the chest and abdominal cavity had been emptied, Cresadir performed one final examination of the hands and feet. She held the creature's wrist and twisted the joint back and forth, moving it in all possible ways.

"Gigantic hands with opposable thumbs and a very strong grip. Thick, grey skin, leathery and tough. The fingers are long and wide with very thick fingernails."

She glanced down to its feet and noted to herself that the skin there was also thick.

"Pass me the notes please," Cresadir asked Daimeh. She wanted to review what had been written, as well as add her own comments.

After reading through the notes, she walked outside to check the sun's position.

"One hour until low-sun," she said, re-entering the hall. "Let's start embalming, shall we? The draining will take two hours at least."

Cresadir handed the notepad back to Daimeh then removed a bulky key from her pocket.

An enormous, expensive-looking cabinet stood grandly in the

corner of the hall, its doors extending up to the ceiling. Daimeh had never been sure of its purpose, and had seen the deep, beautiful carvings so many times that he no longer appreciated them. But he hoped that now his questions would be answered. Can't be anything nice, he thought.

Cresadir rattled the key around in the lock, then slowly opened the immense, creaking doors.

"Wow."

Daimeh gasped. Inside, he saw two pulleys, part of a gigantic and ingenious-looking device impressively constructed from wood and metal. It was securely bolted to the cabinet and a slate-grey ceramic bowl stood below.

"Not many know of this, Daimeh. You must be discreet. All my embalming takes place here, in this hall. It's the only place in the village suitable for it."

The hall was customarily used for village meetings and discussions.

"How does it work?" Daimeh asked, appearing more interested in the machine than in preserving the body.

"We secure those cuffs around the ankles of the deceased," Cresadir said, pointing to a couple of chunky leather bindings which were buckled and studded to ensure a tighter grip. "You can see they're attached to the lower pulley." She motioned her fingers down to the mechanical system, then pointed to the side. "Grab that rope."

Daimeh untangled a braided leather rope from its bolted hook and slid it between his palms. At the same time, Cresadir reached up and grasped the restraints as they lowered down.

"The lower pulley comes down with the restraints and the rope connects the two together, so bodies can be lifted with ease." She released the clasps and pulled the connecting rope through the system, then walked over the corpse. She bound its ankles, and signalled to Daimeh.

"Pull now. I'll hold the arms until we get him in place."

Her nephew took a deep breath and hoisted the rope downwards, as if he was ringing church bells. As he did so, Cresadir shuffled the body closer to the draining device, moving the cadaver into position with surprising ease. Daimeh secured the twisted rope to its hook. Both aunt and nephew stared up at the hulk of a body.

"Before we start can you make sure that cork is firmly plugged?"

Daimeh reached down and pulled out the hand-sized cork from the ceramic bowl, as he pushed it back in, he bashed it with the palm of his hand. "It's secure."

"This bit isn't nice either."

He could guess what was going to happen next.

Cresadir picked up the scalpel with the curved cutting edge and aimed it at the dangling body's neck. She sliced downwards through the tough muscle of the primary neck artery. Burgundy-coloured fluid immediately oozed, gurgling, from the slash. It dribbled slowly down the creature's face, spilling over its chin and flowing, like deep-red honey, down its cheek and over its eyeballs, finally clotting on the crown of its head and dripping into the cold stone bowl below. She made two further descending incisions in the forearms, slicing through the arteries in the wrists. Semi-clotted blood, dark, almost black in colour, leaked from the large hands and trickled over the hardy, cracked nails. The thick deep-red plasma drizzled into the grey bowl.

"Now, we wait," Cresadir said, shutting and locking the creaking cabinet doors. "Go home, Daimeh and rest. I'll come and get you before we embalm."

Daimeh looked relieved. "Yes, Aunt Cresa." He was in need of a nap after his long ordeal.

* * *

Two hours had passed and it was now evening. Cresadir knocked on Daimeh's door as she had earlier that day, but this time her nephew answered promptly. He had changed his clothes, and was now wearing a finely stitched shirt with a laced-up front. "I'm ready,." he said, re-energised and smiling.

* * *

They walked back to the grand manor hall, which was now looking even more beautiful than earlier. They entered the building and immediately went to the room they were in before. The lowered sun shone through the stained-glass windows, creating criss-crossing geometric patterns of pastel green and violet across the floor-boards. Cresadir briskly walked towards the towering corner cabinet, throwing the patterns into shadow. She removed the key from her pocket and unlocked the creaking doors, and as she did, Daimeh took a moment to appreciate the familiar engravings that stretched across both doors. A kneeling man reaching up towards a robed woman stood next to him.

The doors opened and the smell of curdled blood wafted out from inside. The ghastly white body was still hanging in the same position although blood was no longer draining from it.

"Lower the pulley and I'll take the arms," Cresadir immediately instructed. "Help me with the legs when he's down."

"M-hm." The corpse wasn't as heavy now and it was lowered relatively effortlessly.

"We need him back onto the table," Cresadir said.

As they shuffled towards it, she nodded towards an unusual-looking device hanging on the opposite wall. "Would you pass me the syringe, please?"

"Yes, what is it?" Daimeh asked. He examined the item before passing it to her.

"It's made from the bladder of a glenny and a pygmy gidar's quill and…" she stopped to squeeze the air out of the sack, "glued together with palm resin." Cresadir dipped the sharpened quill from the small, turkey like pygmy gidar, into an alcohol-filled bottle and pumped the elastic syringe allowing ethanol to be sucked into the bag. She filled it completely, then felt inside the wrist wound, and, taking the now-drained artery between her fingers, she expertly inserted the syringe into the hollow opening. Holding the incision area firmly, she compressed the bag, forcing the astringent solution into the artery

"We're going to need more bottles," she told Daimeh. One bottle would not go very far.

"I'll get some."

As he ran up the stairs, she yelled after him, "Bring me the bag of herbs and salts as well!"

* * *

The pleasant spiced aroma of the local phoro plant followed Daimeh back to the embalming table. The phoro plant being a herb usually wound into incense, they were used primarily for their aroma. He placed the large basket of dried leaves on the bench, along with a rudimentary glass jar filled with sea salt.

"Now you can start filling the cavity with salt," Cresadir said, popping the rubber seal off the jar. She delved inside, then began sprinkling salt into the crevice. "Make sure you push it every-where, even the mouth."

Daimeh followed his aunt's guidance and began pressing salt into the corpse.

"Now compress the phora on top of the salts – this will minimise the unpleasant odour."

* * *

By late evening the body was just about ready. Cresadir neatly stitched up the gash using thin sinew thread and a strong bone needle. She took the edges of the blanket and wrapped it around the corpse, tucking it under each side. Removing some leather ropes from the first drawer down, she tied them tightly around the body.

They had just completed the embalming process when there was a knock at the door. Oeradon entered the room cautiously, not wanting to see anything gruesome.

"Just in time," Cresadir said, smiling.

"We're finished out there. I've parked a cart out the back for… *that*. You can take it to the barn after." Oeradon glanced at the motionless mummified body and immediately recoiled.

"We could use another pair of hands to get him outside," his mother replied hopefully, opening the doors to the garden.

Oeradon hesitantly walked towards the table, his face pale.

"Er, I see."

He hung back, hesitantly reaching out one hand.

"Oh never mind," Cresadir said in a quiet, wavering voice. She flapped her hands at him.

"Just clean up then."

She lifted the corpse's shoulders and Daimeh held the lower body. They shuffled towards the rear of the hall and went out through the double doors into the glowing yellow luminescence of the low-sun. The wrapped body was now emitting a surprisingly pleasant fragrance. They hoisted it onto the wooden cart and the aroma became more intense.

Oeradon's glenny stood before the cart. She sniffed the breeze and fidgeted a little while they loaded the strange cargo. Her master watched as he reluctantly cleaned congealed blood off the bench.

They made sure to conceal the body under the side panel, and Cresadir stacked thatched baskets of phora leaves around it, hoping to further mask the smell. She took a chunky leather cover from the porch, pulled it over the load and bound it firmly. She checked all around the cart, making sure that the body was completely hidden. "Take the cart down to the village and park it next to the others."

"Will do."

Cresadir raised her voice. "Everything's ready for our departure tomorrow, I hope?"

Oeradon called back, "Yes, Mother. We're all set."

"Well, time for us to rest then. We have quite the day ahead of us." She tapped on the rear of the cart and Daimeh led the glenny down the gravel path.

4

Recollection

It was the first hour of high-sun and the village of Lybas was already bustling with people. The vivid crystal blue sky was perfectly clear and the village was drenched in brilliant sunlight. Outside of the shaded areas the light was eye-scorchingly bright. Daimeh had awoken early and gone out to sit on the front steps of his parent's house. From his shady seat, he quietly observed his fellow villagers running their final errands before the leaving party: some fed the glennies in the barn; others were busy packing the last of the commodities. The festivities would last a few weeks and, to Alkoryns, marked the dawning of a new year and the commencement of drawing up the yearly trade plans. They were a particularly gregarious community and saw both work and chores as opportunities for a social gathering.

Other villagers were busy decorating Lybas in preparation for the local celebrations, placing fluorescent coloured plants, small trees and dyed cloth banners between the houses. The centre canopy was adorned with colourful silken banners, and candles had been placed on the shaded tables.

Daimeh travelled to the capital every year, since he was a chosen relative. As Cresadir was the island head, she always chose her closest family members. Daimeh usually hated going, but recent events meant that he now had a reason of his own for visiting.

Still sitting on the steps, Daimeh watched his aunt and cousin at the village entrance, tying their glennies to the full carts. They were talking and laughing at each other; from what he could see it seemed that Oeradon did not know how to fasten a glenny securely and so his glenny kept wandering off. Daimeh smirked to himself; Oeradon never had got the hang of those knots.

Cresadir's lustrous hair flowed down her back; it was so feathery and wavy that when she laughed, it bounced. She reached inside her leather pouch and pulled out a hair tie which she used for plaiting her hair. The day was very hot, and she wore no more than a pale, flax vest and close-fitting, hide trousers. As Cresadir was plaiting her hair, Oeradon's glenny wandered off again and he was forced to run off in pursuit. After chasing the glenny for a few minutes he managed to grab the lead and pulled him back to the cart.

"I got it this time," he said with confidence.

The inexperienced Oeradon then tried, for a third time, to tie up his glenny. After a few minutes, still fumbling with the leather noose, he stepped back. He raised his hands from the knot and tapped the glenny on her hind-leg. The animal pulled forward, jolting the cart. Oeradon clapped with pride.

"Told you. Hah."

"Good going, it took you all of fifteen years to learn," Daimeh said, approaching his aunt and cousin.

He grinned at Oeradon.

"Hehehe, I'm just playing."

"Yeah, yeah." The older cousin took one of the reins in his hand and formed a loop with it, doing a hangman impression, much to his mother's displeasure; Oeradon may have been the eldest of the two cousins, but he certainly didn't act like it.

While the cousins were bantering, a short, squat villager came into view, clumsily carrying a basket of fish so big that it obscured his field of vision. He wobbled, as if drunk, towards where they were standing. Just as Daimeh was about to intervene, the man walked into the cart and fell backwards. The fish scattered across the stone ground.

"Woah, are you all right?" Daimeh asked concerned, holding out his hand.

"Oops. Yes, yes, I'm fine," he hastily responded. He seemed amused by what had happened.

After helping the small, stocky man to his feet, Daimeh said, "I'll get those," and pointed to the spilled fish.

"Thank you, thank you. I'll go get another."

"Er, maybe a smaller basket this time."

Daimeh felt obliged to give his advice, even though the dedicated, but blundering man had already walked away.

"Yes, yes, of course," he said, speaking very fast and in a friendly manner as he walked, raising his hand and waving.

Daimeh collected the fish and put the basket onto the cart. He noticed the hidden body, he checked it was fully concealed and made sure the sword was tucked by its side, before covering them up. "She's good to go," said Daimeh as a signal. Oeradon jumped up onto the back of the large-wheeled wagon. This was his favourite way of travelling.

Two other carts were waiting at the entrance closest to the ocean.

Daimeh had almost forgotten about the rolled-up parchment.

"Wait, forgot... er." He looked at his feet, and saw that he had no travelling sandals "...My sandals." He rushed back to hishouse.

* * *

First Daimeh got his sandals, then he went into the larder, retrieved the parchment and hid it in his satchel. He hopped back, putting his sandals on as he went, and on the way he noticed Cresadir pushing Theo, her husband, from the manor to the cart in his wheelchair. He was catatonic and so was unable to show his feelings, but she knew that the fete was good for him anyway. Some part of her believed that he was aware of what was happening.

Daimeh ran up the path to meet her.

"How is he?" he asked when he reached them.

"I sense he knows that we're leaving for the fete today."

She smiled and stroked his hair. "You know, since our routine is a bit different."

Daimeh looked into her eyes and smiled.

* * *

Miah and Oeradon were waiting in the carts for the last three travellers to board. Miah was to be the driver of the first cart which carried the leather, clothes and wool. Surrounded by such material, Oeradon found it easy to get comfortable. He settled, then rolled some weed, all the while whistling his new tune. His lute lay beside him; he was an aspiring musician and viewed the annual visit to Aelston as both a good opportunity for sight-seeing and a chance to do a bit of strumming.

Cresadir drove the second cart, her husband secured amongst the cargo, together with the spices and shell ornaments. On these trips, she always put a shell in his hand; she liked to think that he could feel the textures as they travelled. Daimeh drove the third cart, the one in which the corpse was being transported in, along with all the seafood delicacies and phoro filled baskets.

The glenny's started to move, and the journey began. The travellers slowly exited the village, the locals sending them on their way with goodbye waves.

"Bye, enjoy the celebrations. See you all soon," Oeradon shouted, waving back.

* * *

Oeradon watched Lybas getting smaller and smaller; smoke could be seen drifting upwards from the village. The sounds of home were increasingly drowned out by the noise of the cart's wheels.

The sun was high in the sky as they travelled west towards the chalk cliffs. After a while, Daimeh began to feel thirsty, he took a swig from his hide water-flask, wiping the sweat off his face as he drank. He leaned over to the back of the cart and finding his flat cap, placed it on his head, shading his eyes.

The white cliffs gradually came into view and the party followed a gravel path which led up to the cliff tops. Oeradon had to hold on tight as they ascended and slipped a little towards the back of the cart. He could see pebbles and dust being kicked up as the glennies strained to pull the cargo. Cresadir was behind and was forced to cover her face against the flying debris. As soon as the dust cloud subsided enough, she checked on her husband; he was fidgeting with his shell, apparently completely unaware of the bumpiness of the ride. If he hadn't been securely strapped in, he would by then have been lying by the side of the road.

Miah's cart reached a meandering road and the ascent became less strenuous. The wind was noticeably stronger and the air was warmer atop the cliffs. She stopped her cart and looked over to the savannah meadows visible to her right. Jungle could be seen in the distance. Oeradon gazed at the ocean below until he was distracted by a nearby flock of forest birds fluttering their wings.

Cresadir was the next to reach the top, and Daimeh followed soon afterwards. They all rested at the top, watching the wild glennies running through the pastures. These were somewhat smaller than their domesticated cousins, especially the moxos, with short, fluffy fleeces. They all watched as a single, dominant male grunted in a low tone, then shook his head, swaying his spectacular antlers from side to side. He led the herd of females to a new feeding ground, the lambs bouncing after their mothers.

* * *

The intense beauty of the ocean always filled Daimeh with wonder. From where he stood, he could hear the waves crashing against the base of the cliff. In the hazy distance, Daimeh could see the neighbouring island of Spiritmist. This was the isle furthest away from the mainland and was the Alkoryn religious centre. Squinting his eyes, he could see the monastery towers and tall monuments to the deity: wonders of craftsmanship built from stone. These outstanding statues could not be seen from Lybas as they were obscured by the cliffs. The monks' contributions to the fete were art, jewellery and religious rock sculptures.

Miah was looking in the other direction: over the lush fields to the dense forest beyond. They always reminded her of Daimeh's childhood and that time when he had gone missing. When she thought about how her brother-in-law and her son had gone missing that day, she still felt terrified. She lost herself in the disturbing thoughts.

Her desperate calls could be heard across the fields.

"Daimeh!"

The moist grass squeezed between her toes; she flicked dewy soil as she went. Her pained calls seemed in vain, consumed by the wind and fed to the leafy rustle of the dense forest ahead – in her exhausted and confused state, it seemed like an impassable green wall.

Please don't be taken.

She ran further away from the village, feeling more drained with every passing second; her steps faltered as her body was overtaken by fatigue. She coughed, trying to gather just enough strength to jog onwards, sweat dripping from her clingy hair.

Miah's ankle-length tunic flapped against her body. The thin, cream fabric was useless against the oncoming wind but she advanced heedlessly towards the fringes of the forest. She was still crying and shouting; her mouth grew drier all the time, but she continued calling to her son. Fighting to overcome her exhaustion, she entered the forest feeling even more determined.

Through the trees, she heard the distant growls of a forest dwelling tygrisa pack. These slender reptilian predators, similar in appearance to a big cat, however with scaly deep green skin, stood at about the height of a child and hunted cooperatively by skulking through the undergrowth with strong legs built for pouncing on prey and razor spiked teeth, with protruding canines. Their eyes were big, bright orange and side slanted, adapted to the lower light of the dim forest thicket, they were positioned front-facing for more effective hunting. Tygrisa could open their mouths particularly wide and were always awaiting their next meal. Miah recognised the deep gurgling sound they made, which sounded as though water was boiling in their larynx. *Daimeh.* Her only concern was for her son's safety. Yet, her silent sobbing and the slight shaking of her hands showed that she already feared the worst – that her son was already gone; that her beautiful boy had met his fate in the jaws of some beast.

Daimeh watched his mother gaze into the forest. She did the same thing every year, as though she always wanted to remind herself of when she had nearly lost him. Daimeh also found himself drifting into memories of that time.

The trees were so tall to a boy of his age and the leafy canopy was so compact that time eluded him. But he was not deterred by the limited sunlight and trampled over mangled roots, alert and determined. The leeching vines erratically twisted up stocky trunks, hoping to find more nutrients there. His feet were cushioned by the mossy uneven ground. As he made his way through the humid forest, intertwined branches grabbed at his arms, wafting the earthy scent of droppings and rotting wood towards him.

What was that, he wondered? The boy stopped in his stride. He heard piercing shrieks. He'd never heard anything like that before. Buzzing insects took this opportunity to irritate his skin. He frantically swatted them away and stumbled backwards.

"Ah-ouch."

A single upright stalk, as tough as bamboo, had stabbed the underside of his foot. The sole was still soft, not yet hardened by the Alkoryns' customary bare-foot walking. He straightened himself, then limped over to the nearest protruding rock. Its mossy surface gave him little comfort and the bugs tickled his calves, which only increased his anxiety.

With a quick, jolting movement, Daimeh yanked the hollow stalk from his foot and blood began to leak from the small puncture. Ripping at the lush foliage, he pulled a large leaf from the vegetation; it was poetic revenge, he thought. Remembering what his aunt had taught him, he enveloped his foot with the flat leaf, securing it with a soft vine. The resourceful boy shrugged off his injury and persevered with his search, hobbling on one leg. Although the jungle chatter had quietened for a moment, all was not peaceful among the wild palms.

Daimeh heard his mother's voice, coming from the high, overhanging leaves. He looked upward, relieved, but also somewhat disappointed that his brave search had to come to an end.

"Muma! This way!"

He shouted as loudly as he could, propelling the air from his lungs. He decided to stay where he was and lay down on a fallen tree-trunk.

Miah looked at Daimeh and he nodded back to her; they both recalled the events of that terrible day.

Having pinpointed which direction Daimeh's voice was coming from, Miah ran through the thicket, her dress laden with moisture, in constant danger of tripping over. The sound of gurgling started before she had even passed the first vine-coiled tree. She knew they were close. She heard the sound of a tygrisa hissing, and it was quickly joined by others; Miah was being stalked from three directions. She fearfully looked around her, darting her eyes in all directions, especially behind her. One particular bamboo stalk caught her eye; it was the longest she could see. Preparing herself for an imminent attack, she kicked the stalk firmly until it broke, then grabbed it, making sure that the shattered spike was pointing away from her. Despite the hissing, her heartbeat was still drumming in her ears as she turned jerkily from side to side. The gurgling ceased, and then only the beat of her heart could be heard. It was time for her to move.

She swept the giant leaves aside; stray branches punished her frenzied progress. Their thorny twigs scratched through her tunic, leaving rags of blood-soaked cloth. She had to keep going, her son was in peril.

The leaves of the bushes ahead ruffled. Daimeh braced himself, and glared in the direction of the disturbance. After a few moments, Miah emerged from the overgrown shrubs, whacking at the vines with her makeshift baton. Forgetting for a moment about his injured foot, the elated boy jumped forward and called to his mother, but toppled over as his foot touched the ground. Miah sharply inhaled before speaking.

"What've you done?"

Dropping the stalk, she rushed to his side, her badly scraped knees, smeared by the undergrowth, pale in comparison to Daimeh's swollen foot, its bandage straining under the pressure. Miah cradled her son.

"Please, Daimeh, let the adults deal with this," she said, lovingly kissing his head. "It's too dangerous here, remember what I told you about the bad animals?"

She looked at his feet.

"You're not even wearing forest shoes."

"I..." His broken voice was muffled by his mother's arms tightening around him. "I didn't find him." His tears soaked the cloth.

"Let us..." Miah began, but was interrupted by low growling, followed by hissing.

She bent down.

"Quiet, don't worry."

Her voice trembled as she whispered in his ear, "I want you to be a brave boy, all right?"

"I can be…"

A branch cracked and the gurgle ceased for a moment. Daimeh's voice was so quiet that she had to interpret his words from his lip movements.

"I can be brave."

That is what he said, but his shaking body told a different story as he pressed his fingers against her clammy back.

Miah searched desperately for her bamboo spike. She had dropped it next to her, yet in her panicked state of mind she could not remember where it was now. Running her hands through the prickly undergrowth, she managed to find the ridged surface of her weapon. She used it to push herself off the forest floor, and, clutching her son, she helped him to his feet. He wobbled slightly, but she steadied him until he got his balance. They both stood as still as they could. Miah closed her eyes and consciously synced her breathing with Daimeh's, tuning out her other senses. The sounds of passing claws were heard and high-pitched hissing followed, similar in rhythm to a civilised language. She remained in that position for a few seconds but when she opened her eyes, reality hit her and she began breathing in terrified rasps again. She indecisively stepped in one direction, then the next, unable to make a clear decision.

"Over there," Daimeh said, hopping towards the closest tree, pulling his mother's hand. "Here, Muma." Wide, creeper roots clung to the enormous trunk. "I can climb this tree."

"You sure?"

At that, he limped closer to the spiky vines and took a firm hold. "Just push me up."

Miah lifted her son up, making sure he was stable before letting go. He clung on as best he could and endured the pain in his foot, still feeling unable to put much pressure on it. He needed to use the strength in his arms, but the spiky vines were digging into his palms and his feet were scrambling frantically among the creepers. Using his toes, he managed to push himself up to the first sturdy branch and clung to it tightly.

There was complete silence, just the ambient noise of the forest: rustling wind through leaves, chirping birds and insects. Miah slowed her breathing and stayed absolutely still. She sniffed the air, looking for any kind of hint of where the tygrisa were. Carefully removing her bamboo weapon from where she had tucked it, she looked up at her injured son. Daimeh had been surveying the area and had seen no sign of the predators. He slowly nodded his head to indicate it was clear. Miah prepared herself for the climb.

Just then, a sudden clicking arose out of the stillness and an intense tremor ran through the bushes. A hungry tygrisa pounced out of the wild foliage, its claws extended and its mouth opened to its widest extent. Miah screamed in panic, forced back to the soggy thicket. Watery mud dampened her clothes and she flayed her legs in frenzied confusion, kicking her forest shoes into the air in terror. Her feet dug into the moist soil as she tried to back away from the predator. It hurtled towards her. Miah thrust her stalk weapon sideways into its mouth. It growled intensely at her; she could feel its warm breath on her face and could smell its last, semi-digested meal. She shrieked and began kicking its belly, but the tygrisa did not flinch. The growls of two others could be heard behind her. Miah wrestled with the beast, but she was becoming aware of the fate that lay ahead of her. Her fight-or-flight response had been triggered and she persisted with the struggle, managing to knee the vicious animal in its tender thorax. The tygrisa yelped and ceased its attack. Miah took this as an opportunity to pull the sharp bamboo stick out of its mouth and thrust it upwards just under its lower jaw. She aimed the stalk at the vulnerable throat area, and it penetrated the creature's head. The tygrisa let out a very short, extremely high-pitched squeal. Miah had been aiming for its brain and judging by its sudden limpness and glazed eyes, she had been successful. The tygrisa flopped lifelessly on top of her, still breathing for a few moments before its body ceased to function. The other two beasts were now within striking distance of Miah, hissing intently, fury in their eyes. She knew they would continue the attack if she did not move quickly. She hauled the deceased animal off and looked behind her. Scrambling to her feet, she took a firm hold of the bamboo stick and lifted the heavy body. She mustered all her remaining strength and threw the still-bleeding body towards the other two. They were just about to make their next move when their dead pack member tumbled into them. Tygrisa may be loyal to each other, but when a meal dropped in front of them, they took advantage of the easily obtained sustenance, no matter what its origin. The fresh, gory wound captivated them and they were unable to resist and began tearing at the scaly skin, ripping the flesh with their claws and teeth.

Miah stared at them for a few seconds, consumed by both fascination and fear. Daimeh's terrified yells broke her daze and she immediately turned around and dashed towards the tree, leaping up it with such force that the thorny vines cut through her hands. Despite this, she still managed to clamber up the tree trunk. Daimeh reached down and clutched her fingers, Miah's blood-covered hands making the grip feel sticky. He aided her up to a branch where they could both safely perch.

Miah embraced her son and held him tightly against her. They were both ragged, filthy and tired, but relieved to still be alive and together. She loosened her grip and put her gashed hands on either side of Daimeh's face, unintentionally smearing her blood onto his skin. She stroked his clammy hair away from his forehead and gently kissed it, smiling as she quietly spoke to him.

"We're all right."

She kissed his forehead a second time, then looked down at his tightly bandaged foot.

"Let me take a look at that."

She lightly removed the vine wrapping and peeled off the shredded leaf.

"It hurts so bad," Daimeh said, recoiling as she removed the covering. His foot was badly inflamed, the insertion wound was swollen and deep in colour; clotted blood filled the hole and clearly the foot had been contaminated with whatever bacteria had been on the stalk.

His mother tried to comfort him.

"Don't worry, Daimeh, Aunty Cresa will fix this up for you... when we get home."

She stroked his cheek.

"We'll stay here, until the tygrisa have gone."

"Yes, Muma." Daimeh replied, nodding.

Miah looked above her, trying to gauge the time, but it was difficult to even estimate from their settled position. The light was dim, but an intermittent orange glow could be seen shining through between branches and leaves. Distant hooting and whistling could be heard.

"It's low sun, I can tell that much," she observed.

Miah's arm was around Daimeh's shoulder and his head was snuggled against her chest. They weren't relaxed but at least they felt safer. The two tygrisa had appreciated their free meal and were completely unaware that Miah and her son were watching them, thankful for their narrow escape.

The fiery, radiant sunlight gleamed off the smooth leaves and reflected white sunlight into Miah's eyes. She was looking up at the jungle birds, which were yellow and cream with fluffy feathers. She did not know what species they were, but it was one source of joy in a terror-filled day and she appreciated it. Daimeh laid his head on Miah's lap; he closed his eyes while Miah gently stroked his arm.

She checked on the tygrisas, which had by now removed just about all the flesh from the carcass and were now lying on their bellies licking their retractable claws. Miah knew that soon she and Daimeh would be able to make a move.

After some time, one beast gurgled and then stood up. It began to walk away from where Daimeh and Miah were hidden; shortly afterwards, the second tygrisa also rose to its feet. It sniffed the corpse one final time, then followed its pack member into the jungle thicket.

Miah nudged Daimeh, but he wasn't sleeping and immediately opened his eyes.

"It's time to move," she said assertively.

Miah descended first, using the same footholds that she had used before, but holding the vines less tightly this time as her hands were still bleeding from the ascent. Daimeh followed. Once Miah had reached the base of the tree, she held her hands up and lifted Daimeh down. She cradled her exhausted son.

"I'll carry you home, Daimeh; you rest." She looked at her son.

Daimeh saw the love in her eyes, and relaxed in her arms, feeling safe.

The forest now appeared calmer than earlier: there weren't as many stinging insects and the animal calls were soothing and tranquil. Miah trampled through the mossy bushes, but this time she was vigilant, taking care where she put her bare feet and making sure she avoided all the broken stalks and aimed her feet only at the lush grassy areas. The island breezes could not reach the deep forest, and so, as the low-sun hours proceeded, the jungle air became more stagnant and humid. Miah could taste the earthy, warm air more with each breath, and could smell the saturated, musty odour; the forest would only begin to freshen once the high-sun hours had begun.

The edge of the forest was now within sight; rays of light were streaming between the thinning branches and Miah could see the quiet pastures ahead of her. She exhaled heavily and an exhausted smile covered her face. She finally reached the outer fields, and looking at the sky, felt the sun on her face; it was now late afternoon. She awoke the sleeping Daimeh and went straight to Cresadir's manor.

Cresadir jerked the reins. She knew what Miah and Daimeh were thinking about and gave them a moment.

"It's time to move again… Miah! Daimeh!"

"Oh," Miah said, suddenly returning to the present moment. "Coming."

As they continued along the cliff tops, another outstanding statue came into view.

"Oh, that's new." Daimeh did not remember it from the previous year. "Hey, look at that," he said, pointing to the monument.

Cresadir shielded her eyes from the sun. "Oh, fantastic. Their grandest so far." She was absolutely awestruck by the white marble, female deity.

"It's marvellous," Miah replied, seeming less interested than the other two.

Oeradon was snoring with his head tucked into a sack of wool.

They rode on.

* * *

Four hours had passed and evening was now upon them. The air had become close and damp. They approached newer pastures: large areas of green with countless distinctive mounds scattered throughout. There were lagus burrows scuffling with activity. Dozens of the big legged animals were out, illuminated by the sky's orange glow. They were as high as a man's waist and lived in mound hills. They tended to be territorially aggressive and had two sharp incisor teeth and ears too large for their heads, giving them a cartoon appearance. The silhouettes of five baby lagus bouncing and playing on top of their burrow were a delight to observe.

A few clouds had gathered as they approached the western peninsula.

"Slightly grey under the white tops. We may have a little rain soon."

"Aunt Cresa, I think it has already started over there." Daimeh pointed to vertical clouds massed over Ridgemead, the volcanic mid-isles: a ridge formed between two land masses.

As they travelled further west, the diverse geology of the isles became increasingly apparent. An erupting volcano could be seen in the distance. That particular volcano, the tallest one, was active all year round and formed its own island. The populated area was surrounded by stretches of fertile agricultural fields. The islands were renowned for their exquisite ales and wines, and most trained apothecaries used the local herbs for health remedies and medicines. Unsurprisingly, their contributions to the fete were alcoholic brews and medicinal remedies

The faint sulphurous smell of lava, mingled with fermenting alcohol, drifted across the ocean. This was a smell they had become familiar with over the years.

Oeradon turned around and sniffed the air. "Mmmm, ale, I know what I'm doing first," he said, grinning.

"Why can't you be more like your cousin, Oeradon?" his mother asked.

"As in sensible."

But despite her words she had accepted that her son was a bit foolish and didn't take many things he said seriously.

"Hey, Mom, what can I say? Two sides, same coin." He smirked. "You know it's true."

"I think that's a compliment, Daimeh," Cresadir said, glancing over to him.

Her nephew just laughed in reply; the conversation soon ended and they continued their trek to Port Draclyn.

5

Port Draclyn

It was late evening when the party began to descend into the port. The town was positioned specifically to catch the wind and this provided a natural form of air conditioning. Port Draclyn also had a centralised drainage system, which used gravity to carry waste.

The glennies trotted along, pulling the carts over the small ridge, and the travellers were met by an awe-inspiring view of the harbour. The entirety of the town could be seen from atop the cliff, and even from that distance they were still able to see the activity in the centre. Dozens of grand, square-sailed ships were docked in the port, and others were waiting further out at sea. The tall ones were the most impressive, and the smaller fishing vessels, which were similar to those in Lybas, wove between the bulky cargo ships. The road sloped down for a mile or so and the houses were built on sloping roads.

They cautiously began their descent through the outskirts. The houses were cramped, many in shade, with a few families living in each building. They were very basic by design, shanties of type, but well-crafted, as would be expected from Alkoryns. The people here formed a self-sufficient community with their own markets and means of recreation. The population was made up of immigrants from the islands hoping to find prosperity, or the village 'bad blood', as well as hopeful, ambitious, young Alkoryns. The outskirts of the harbour didn't have the rural beauty of Lybas however, trees were scarce in these overflow areas, although a few dwellers had placed plants in their windows.

The streets weren't clean and there was a slight stench of urine and manure; dry foliage blew across the gravel.

"Hygiene is difficult to maintain up here. They don't have the water resources," Cresadir said, looking at some small children who were playing in dirty clothes.

"Come here!" Miah called to them and the three girls came running. She reached into the cart and pulled out a few folded tunics. "Take these back to your families," she said, smiling and ruffling one of the girls' hair.

"Wow, thanks lady," the children answered, and with that they ran off to their homes.

* * *

As they continued through the streets and down the hillside, the dirt road gradually turned into a cobbled path. The dwellings increased in size and the unclean stench was replaced by the smell of homemade cooking. Here it was one family per house, and the two-storey houses were similar in their design to those in Lybas.

They dismounted and continued on foot, pulling on the reins to guide their glennies. There were people hanging out clothes; one woman sat weaving, and across the street from her was a man relaxing in the low-sun, exhaling weed smoke. Other than that, the streets weren't very busy.

They were still quite high above the populated centre and continued their descent. The ship sails began to be obscured by taller buildings. The cobbles were gradually replaced by sculpted paths with raised pavements.

The party remounted their glennies and proceeded down the road. Sunlight beamed through the gaps in the buildings and scattered through the streets. They rode past the first shops, which all had dwellings above them where the shopkeepers' families lived. Women held their children's hands as they peered through the windows; as every year, the shops were already closed. Only the shine of lamps could be seen through the neat glass windows with adorned wooden frames.

There were a few nicely dressed townspeople walking towards the nearest gambling den. Miah's cart was the first to pass the public house and from his vantage point, Oeradon was able to peek through the windows.

Ogling an attractive young patron, he asked, "Can I get off here?" His sense of humour always wound his mother up, so he tried it on Miah.

She waved her hand. 'Pfft."

* * *

The carts travelled along a gradual curved road, which slowly levelled out. They arrived at a junction and noticed something they hadn't seen before. An elaborate garden had come into view; there were yellow-headed stalks poking out from the grass, a few dark green bushes and a circular marble fountain.

"Lovely," Miah commented.

They turned left at the junction and were met by a long, straight road which led directly to the harbour. The travellers felt a sense of melancholy watching the gleaming sun illuminating the uniform brick edges of tall townhouses on both sides of the road. The buildings were three storeys high, with steps in front leading up to a lacquered front door with pillars on either side. All the houses had small gardens fenced by dark iron railings. They had now been travelling for half a day, but there was just one street still to go.

As they approached the outstandingly constructed harbour that occupied the whole bay, they noticed the precisely laid planks and the highly-glossed railings sculpted from brass. Even the cranes had intricate carvings on their shafts. A well-dressed man stood on the pavement corner and waved to them.

"Hey, travellers from Lybas, I'm Annard. I'm sorry to say we've had to change the location of your rooms. There's been a fire in your usual lodge."

He was very welcoming, despite the disappointing news.

The man's calm demeanour convinced Cresadir that the fire hadn't been serious, but she said nonetheless, "Oh my, I hope no one was hurt?"

"No, no, don't worry, madam. The high-sun caught a misplaced pair of glasses, and well, you can guess the rest. But only the lobby was damaged, nothing serious."

"Well, I do hope the refurbishment goes well," Cresadir replied, relief in her voice. "So... where are we to stay?"

"You'd be very welcome to stay here at my establishment." The gentleman smiled and gestured for them to enter his hotel.

"Thank you, looks very inviting," Cresadir said, smiling warmly at the young man.

"There are stables around the back, just down that alley."

He pointed to a shaded cobbled path.

Miah shook the reins gently and led the way down the path towards the stables.

* * *

Miah and Cresadir jumped down first and guided the glennies into the stable, which was really more of a large barn. They detached the carts to give themselves more comfort, then tied them close to the trough. Oeradon stepped off Miah's cart and immediately began scuffing his feet on the pebbles like a child. Daimeh was the last to ride through the alley; he stopped the cart next to his mother. He helped her lift Theo off the back and into his wheelchair again, but as usual, his uncle's expression was unchanging and he looked right through them.

"Take him inside; I'll check on – *you know*," Cresadir whispered.

Daimeh nodded and followed the polite man to the back door of the hotel. Miah and Oeradon followed suit.

Lifting the covering cloth, Cresadir examined the body, which was dry to the touch and smelled of spices, as she had expected. Satisfied that everything was in order, she joined the rest of her family.

* * *

The rear lobby was rather upmarket, with a high ceiling and carved wooden walls – a fitting place for a monarch's family. Windows were limited, but there were doors in each wall, their architraves carved. A finely woven rug lay across the floor, the wooden floor planks showing through only at the edges. Annard guided them through the next door, and invited them into the main lobby area.

Two grand, curved staircases, one to their right and one to their left, led to an upper level. The Alkoryns talented craftsmanship with wood most certainly showed in the fine interior. The man-sized statues gave the lobby room a very royal air.

"Your rooms are just up here," Annard said, gesturing in a welcoming manner, "and, madam, our finest ground level room for you and your husband, as you requested.

"Thank you very much." Cresadir shook his hand and he gave her the room key. As the others made their way upstairs he passed them their keys too. "Our young servant shall bring your bags."

"No, that's not needed," Cresadir replied sharply, thinking of the unusual cargo they had.

The hotel owner seemed surprised, but remained well-mannered. "Yes, madam," was all he said.

Miah, Daimeh and Oeradon arrived at the top of the spiral staircase and were greeted by a young, pretty girl, wearing a modest but fitting maid's outfit. Oeradon smiled and winked as he passed her. She blushed coyly.

She took them all to their rooms, and before leaving them,

said warmly, "Please, if you need anything, just ask."

Before Daimeh had the chance to shut his door behind him, Oeradon ran up the corridor and asked, "Daimeh, do you want to go take a look around the town?"

He slowed his pace.

"I saw a nice looking place just down the road," he said, recalling the lovely girl he had seen in the window.

"I'm tired, Oeradon. It's been such a long day and tomorrow will be a long one too."

Daimeh slumped his shoulders.

"Oh come on, drink with me. You'll feel relaxed in no time, I promise."

He patted Daimeh's shoulder.

Daimeh exhaled.

"Fine, let's go."

* * *

The low-sun shone directly into their eyes as they walked down the fancy street with the three-story houses.

"I knew I should have brought my cap." Daimeh raised his hand to his eyes.

They turned right at the end of the street and headed down the main high street. It was alive with activity: people were walking in couples, a few drunken ladies were having a sing-song outside the public house and shifty-looking men were entering and exiting the gambling den.

There was a mild breeze and the strong smell of kelp weed gusted towards the two cousins.

"Do you not want a smoke when we get inside?" Oeradon asked, although he knew what the answer would be. He was a little pushy with his younger cousin.

"You ask me every time. No. I don't want any kelp," Daimeh replied, looking sternly at Oeradon. He opened the robust pub door, which was crafted from a dark-coloured, dense wood.

The intense smell of weed rushed through the opening, mixed with ales and perfumes. Daimeh squeezed past a sweaty man at the doorway who was drunk and clearly had no idea he was blocking the entrance. Once inside, he felt the floor bouncing a little as the patrons banged their feet in time with the performing band. The large, rectangular bar-room was bustling with people. All the stools next to the bar had already been taken.

Oeradon pulled Daimeh's sleeve.

"I see a few spare seats at the back there."

Weaving through the stumbling people, they arrived at a nice corner booth with a short table. On top of it was a stumpy, barely-lit candle and a few scattered glasses with dribbles of ale in the bottom.

"I'll get the waitress." Oeradon smiled as he spoke. He got up and again pushed his way through the jostling crowd.

Daimeh sat and looked out of the window. He coughed, then began fanning the smoky air away from him. He didn't quite fit into the pub scene but he always felt somewhat obliged to join Oeradon. He watched the reflections of people dancing and listened in on other conversations. He heard a couple whispering in the booth next to him about whose house they were staying at. An older man was talking rather loudly about a growth he had noticed on his foot, and a softly-spoken lady was gossiping about her neighbours.

Daimeh turned his head just as Oeradon returned. He had a lovely maiden on his arm.

"This is Lily and she wishes to be our waitress for tonight," Oeradon said, introducing the bouncy-haired, slim woman.

"What would you like to drink gentlemen? There's a food menu I can get you."

"Two pints of your finest Spiritmist ale." Oeradon ordered for the both of them.

Daimeh stood up. "Just a water for me please."

The older cousin nudged the lady's arm. "They all say he's the sensible…" He looked directly at Daimeh then raised his voice. "Boring," he said, before lowering his voice again, and finishing, "one."

So mature, Daimeh thought.

"But I know what you like, miss." He kissed her cheek and she giggled coyly.

Oeradon sat down in his chair.

"How do you do it?"

Daimeh always wondered how it was that Oeradon was able to immediately befriend every woman he met.

"I've charm, I don't sit at the window staring out of it."

"Hmmm, I don't believe you'll meet the right girl in a place like this."

"I'm not trying to meet the right girl," Oeradon replied, with a wink.

The young lady returned to their booth with one glass of water and a pint of ale. She smiled at Oeradon flirtatiously.

"So, I'll meet you outside when you're finished," Oeradon said, seductively raising his eyebrows as he spoke.

The waitress giggled and replied, "M-hm" before walking off. There was a slight silly squeak in her voice.

"What? We're staying here all night?" Daimeh asked, sounding unimpressed.

"Yes, get comfortable," Oeradon replied. "And thank you, for venturing out with me tonight."

He smiled.

"At least it's a change of scenery."

* * *

A few hours had passed and the publican had announced last orders. Ten minutes later he was ushering people out.

Oeradon and Daimeh waited outside for Lily. After a few

minutes she arrived and Oeradon offered his arm ready to walk her to the hotel.

"Ready?" he asked.

"Yes."

Daimeh lagged behind them as they walked, feeling in the way. As soon as they reached their lodgings he said goodnight to them both and proceeded to his own room. As he was turning the key in the lock, Cresadir hastily ran up the stairs, carrying Daimeh's satchel. She called to him just as he was opening the door.

"Daimeh!"

He stopped and looked at her.

"You forgot this."

She shook his satchel and then passed it to him.

"Oh, you waited up?"

"No, no, I've been up – just heard you returning and wanted to make sure you had this."

"Thanks, Cresa."

Daimeh smiled and took the satchel from her.

The door clicked shut behind him, and Daimeh lay down on his bed and removed the parchment, staring at it with wonder. What did it mean? He put his head back and watched the sunlight threading through the laced decorative curtains. Slowly his eyes closed as he admired the fluffy clouds sailing past.

6

Safe Travels

Daimeh was awoken by a loud horn, which was followed by noises from the street. He must have been more tired than he had thought: he was still in his travelling clothes which stunk of sweat and kelp from the night before, and the parchment was still laid on his chest. Quickly, he got out of bed, rolled up the copy he had made of the strange tablet and put it back into his satchel. He moved the curtains aside and saw through the window a mighty ship, the merchant ship which was to take them to Aelston. Its masts were sky-high and it was sturdily built from chestnut lacquered wood and the finest woven cloth. The aft was raised slightly and there was a decorated cabin area.

Daimeh made his way out of the room and down the spiral stairs. He saw Lily exiting out of the back door, *Oeradon really?* She stayed all night, he thought as he walked out the front door.

Waiting for him outside was Cresadir.

"I was just about to come and get you, everything ready to go?" Cresadir gently called to him.

"Everything ready, except me, you mean." Daimeh smirked as he quickly ran down the steps.

"I've made sure all the cargo has been dealt with safely," Cresadir told him.

* * *

As they approached the loading bay, they watched the last cart being lowered down to the cargo hold.

"Hail there," the captain said, greeting them. "You can board through there." He pointed to a narrow ramp that led straight up to the travelling deck. "Mid-deck, we have a cabin prepared for you."

Daimeh was the first to step onto the wooden planks. The handrail was sturdy, even if the ramp did wobble a little bit. He reached the top and looked up at the three marvellous masts, the sails were fully raised and the ropes tight. He watched the seabirds hop along them as if they were branches, some even daring to land on the deck and eat the scraps of fish the sailors had left.

Continuing onto the deck and walking past the cabin, he went straight to his usual spot on the aft barrier. Daimeh watched his relatives get themselves comfy in the cabin, which was full of soft, velvety furniture, including a coffee table set with tea and an array of nibbles. Over the doorway were little, white, triangular-shaped banners of greeting, decorated with interweaved flowers. The folk at Port Draclyn certainly did not hold back when trying to impress the monarchy. But Daimeh was a down to earth kind of person and didn't care so much for the ribbons and bows. He was most content gazing out over the still, green-tinted ocean.

* * *

When everyone was aboard, the captain yelled, "Lower the sails!"

The whole crew burst into activity: the ropes were unreeled, allowing the sails to thunder downwards and the rowers jogged down to the lower deck.

Taking the helm, the captain signalled to a subordinate and called, "Let's set sail!"

The man saluted and ran to the decks. A moment later the sound of the oars could be heard as the ship began to slowly drift away from the harbour. Once the wind had caught the sails, the rowing ceased and the men returned to their duties on the top deck.

* * *

The ship steered west; if they sailed with the current it would take them just half a day to travel to Aelston, otherwise it would be a two day trip at least.

When they hit the current, Daimeh immediately noticed the change in speed. He held the barrier very tightly as he swayed from side to side. The wind had increased and was now blowing his hair across his face.

* * *

The sea was calm, emerald in colour, and completely translucent, and the sky above was cloudless. The gentle waves frothed against the ship's sides, alternately strong and calm. Port Draclyn was now disappearing into the hazy distance, surrounded by flocks of sea birds. The activity of the harbour was more visible now. There were so many boats docking and leaving the port. There were merchant ships and others carrying cargo; fishing crafts and pleasure boats also weaved between the bigger ships. The harbour showed the high level of Alkoryn craftsmanship. Daimeh wanted to appreciate it to the fullest.

Aside from the sea breeze, all he could hear was the swooshing of the sails and the creaking of the wood beneath him. Faint banter could be heard from the sailors but none of it was understandable. The sea air was so fresh it spilled into his lungs with little effort, it was very pleasurable. A perfect way to travel, he thought.

The surface of the ocean was suddenly disturbed, and a delf launched itself out of the water. A long bodied sea mammal with a stubby nose, it was as large as a small boat. They were solitary animals, yet non-aggressive to others. Its lengthy brown fur glistened in the bright sunlight. Daimeh gasped, awed by the sight. After a few moments it crashed back down into the waters.

Daimeh continued looking out over the sea in case the delf decided to show itself once more, but it did not appear again.

"Did you see that, Daimeh!" He heard Cresadir's muffled voice call.

He looked around but could not see her anywhere.

"Up here!" she shouted from the crow's nest.

He looked up at her silhouette and shouted, "Yes! It was amazing – the first one I've seen!"

Cresadir was a very adventurous and intelligent woman and a very quick learner. To further her understanding of the world she had travelled to the boundaries of Alkoryn to conduct research projects. She had seen many strange things in her time.

From her vantage point she watched Orewick, as the inland gradually appeared through the fog. Their main port was lively, packed with large cargo ships here for the metal, jewels and minerals that the mainland produced.

Cresadir watched the inland grow smaller towards the horizon as they passed; the harbour was now a few miles away, but still close enough for her to appreciate the excellent harbour design.

* * *

After a few hours of sailing, the winds changed direction and Daimeh could feel the refreshing ocean spray on his face.

"We're heading to… low… might… go inside." Cresadir was barely audible over the high wind but Daimeh understood what she meant. He didn't mind a bit of rain – actually, he rather liked the tropic steamy Alkoryn rain.

Cresadir clambered down from the crow's nest and joined Daimeh at the back of the ship. Walking past the cabin she could see the others sitting comfortably inside, enjoying themselves. Oeradon was eating small slices of crisp bread and drinking tea. He was always the first to make the most of any facilities available. He would say, "I must get my free's worth." He made her giggle inside, though she would never let her son witness it. Miah was helping Theo to drink, and seemed unaware of the change in weather.

Cresadir didn't bother to wave; no one was looking.

The clouds grew heavier as a light storm approached and the angry waves rumbled against the ship. Daimeh's face was blanched and sticky. He had never been sailing in a storm before and he felt a little seasick.

"You all right, Daimeh?"

"Yeah, yeah," he answered, his head facing towards the ocean.

"I'll go and check the lower deck; I'll be right back."

As Cresadir went down, she noticed that rain was now trickling down the steps like a waterfall.

She reached the cargo hold; it was a little soggy, but the wood was so well treated that no amount of water could have soaked through. She petted the nervous glennies then checked on the carts, which shook as the boat rocked. Most things were in order, but a few delicacies had spilled out and were now scattered over the floor. After re-ordering the cargo, she returned to the upper deck to join Daimeh.

The rain had become stronger by the time she reached the deck and Daimeh had his head up, seemingly feeling better.

"Much better now."

"Good to hear." She smiled. "The storm has almost passed; there are white clouds ahead."

* * *

They left the horizontal clouds behind them.

"It's over Port Draclyn now by the looks of it," Cresadir said, pointing back towards where they had come from. She then turned and pointed ahead of them. "We're almost at Aelston too; you can see the mountains coming into view."

The smallest isle of Alkoryn was visible on the horizon. Alkoryn's capital city was the only settlement on the island and so it was generally known as Aelston Isle. The harbour grew closer and they were able to see that not much had changed there since the year before. Daimeh looked ahead at the mountain range and could not help but wonder what lay beyond; no one had been beyond those mountains, they were known to be impassable.

They arrived at the port and the ship smoothly docked. The boarding ramp was connected to the upper deck and Daimeh and Cresadir walked off first, followed by Miah, pushing Theo. Oeradon was still getting his 'free's worth' of food.

The sailors opened the cargo hatch, then the dock workers swung the crane across and began lifting the carts from the cargo bay. Daimeh's cart wobbled for a second and he felt his heart stop. The last thing he needed was for the hidden cargo to spill over onto the deck.

The three glennies were led up from below and off the ship. Cresadir watched as each cart gently touched the stone of the dock. Cresadir and Miah tied the glennies to their carts.

The port was full of a mix of scents: food, flowers, salts, ales, as well as a faint smell of weed.

An equid-led carriage stopped next to the pavement. The equid served a similar purpose as the glenny, except it was much bigger with a long trunk that reached the ground, hooved feet and scaly skin, was off-white in colour, with a blonde mane.

The driver addressed Cresadir.

"We have escorts for your carts, I'll drive you to your father's."

Cresadir whispered to Daimeh, "Stay with your cart."

She looked up and shouted to the carriage driver.

"Daimeh will escort his own cart this year."

"As you please," the driver replied.

They all boarded the carriage and set off. Daimeh followed them through the festive streets.

7

Reunion

Aelston was a grand city, the biggest in Alkoryn, built to the high standards of Alkoryn craftsmanship. Inside the carriage everyone was silent as they began their trip through the city. Theo stared unseeing at Cresadir. Cresadir had her head back, resting her eyes and Oeradon was on a mission to clear his nose. Lovely, Miah thought, peering through the clean carriage window whilst the carriage bumped along the paved road. She watched as the merchant ship disappeared out of view and got a surprise when the sun suddenly appeared gleaming from behind it. Her eyes glazed over for a second but she quickly adjusted and turned to look at the small children standing on either side of the road who were dressed up for the festivities. They wore colourful costumes and their faces were painted to look like animals. Elegant city houses rolled into view; they were detached from one another and had arched roofs, lanterns outside and front gardens. Some were bungalows, some were three-storey houses, but all were decorated for the fete in different ways: some had made their lanterns look like stars; others had hung banners from their houses or made sculptures from topiaries.

After passing a beautiful park, the carriage slowed as they turned left into the palace entrance. It was located in the centre of the city and acted as both the political office and residence for the monarch and his close family. There was still about a mile to travel before they reached the palace buildings.

Halfway down the road they passed an immaculately white church, round in shape, and built from white marble and white-washed wood. It stood dignified and sublime, about fifty foot above the ground at its highest point. Its spire had a secondary purpose as a time-keeper.

From the church they could see the palace and after another five minutes they arrived there. Outside the palace building was a roundabout with an ornamental garden at its centre. Daimeh led the carts off to the left, and the carriage slowed to a halt outside the entrance to the luxurious palace. He rode down a small track towards the nearby stables. Arriving at the wooden building, he stopped his glenny and dismounted.

"I'll unpack this cart," Daimeh told the other drivers. Ensuring the body was still concealed; he lifted the first basket and followed the stewards, carrying it to the rear kitchen storage area.

"Yes, sir," a driver replied, hoisting a barrel from his cart. He followed Daimeh towards the back of the building.

* * *

Miah was the first to exit the carriage. Once she was outside, she gazed up at the four-storey sandstone. Tall, polished, opaque pillars stood on either side of each window and in the low sun the bricks seemed tinted with yellow. It was truly a picturesque vision. The house steward had already opened the front door.

"Please come in," she said.

Cresadir and her relatives proceeded inside.

"Your father is waiting in the banquet room ma'am," the steward told her, indicating the direction with a gesture. "The servants will take your bags to your room."

"I think we should all freshen up before our meal," Cresadir said.

"I think so too," Miah agreed.

* * *

After changing his clothes for the first time since leaving Lybas, Daimeh was ready to greet his grandfather, Ommaya. He opened the two grand double doors and entered the banquet hall, a large rectangular room, higher than it was wide, with wood-panelled walls adorned with huge landscape paintings from all corners of Alkoryn. Intricately crafted chandeliers made from black metal ore hung from the mosaic ceiling. The wall had tall, stained-glass windows which allowed ample light into the room. There were stewards standing on either side of the door awaiting their instructions. They were clothed neatly in beige.

Daimeh walked past the huge decorative stone hearth towards his grandfather.

Ommaya raised his hand and welcomed him. "Ah, there he is, my handsome grandson. Come and sit next to your mother."

The table had been laid and his relatives were already sitting down but the food had not yet been served so the table looked rather naked. There were four empty seats. One was for Oeradon, who was no doubt still styling himself, and the remaining two were for Cresadir's youngest sister, Alexi and her husband, and one chair was left vacant for the late Rodrique.

Daimeh's grandfather was sat at the head of the table. He had grown slimmer over the last year and was wearing an expensive, embroidered cloth shirt. It was loose-fitting and almost pure white in colour. In his early sixties, he was attractive for his age. His shoulder-length light-brown hair was greying in patches and he wore it parted in the centre, and tucked behind his ears. His neat goatee beard was a little greyer.

"The food will be served as soon as we're all here."

Ommaya spoke with an educated accent.

Cresadir sat to his right; next to her was an empty seat, and then Miah. Daimeh sat himself down in the free space next to his mother. His far-isle relatives were sat on the other side. Alfrit, Cresadir's older brother was puffing on a kelp stick. He was next in line to become monarch and deemed himself more important than his siblings, which further increased the tension between the two families. Cresadir, although somewhat religious, was a great

72

supporter of the sciences, whereas Alfrit's family, who were from Spiritmist, dismissed the sciences completely. Alfrit's wife and their son and daughter were sat with him and they were all dressed in robes, the traditional attire of Alkoryn's religious community.

The empty seat stood next to them. Ommaya had requested it be kept vacant as Daimeh's uncle, Rodrique, who had lived at Ridgemead, had passed away earlier that year. The current head of Ridgemead was Ommaya's grandson, Wilgard, who was present along with his sister.

There was a knock at the door, which was opened by the steward, and Oeradon finally made his appearance. He was stylishly dressed and casually walked over to his place at the table.

"Oeradon, as punctual as ever, good evening." There was a touch of sarcasm in Ommaya's words, but it was meant in only the most harmless of ways.

Alfrit's wife gave Oeradon a look of distaste: she never understood how a royal son could be so carefree, especially when her own two children were so responsible – their different approaches to parenting was another source of tension between the two families.

Through the open window the noise of equid hooves could be heard; it sounded as though a cart had pulled up at the front of the mansion. It seemed that Alexi's family, who were from Orewick, had arrived at the banquet. There were sounds of doors opening and shutting as the family entered the house. Muffled speech could be heard. Daimeh recognised his aunt's delicate tone of voice, then their baby girl, Alith, fidgeted and started to cry. He could hear his aunt comforting her. The crying grew more distant as one of the servants took her away to a nursing room.

A few moments later there was a knock on the heavy, solid wood doors. They were late and had clearly decided not to freshen up before the meal. Alexi entered the room first, then smiled at her family and apologised in a sweet tone of voice.

"Very sorry to have kept you waiting – we had an unfortunate change of wind which knocked us a little off course."

"You're here now, and that's all that matters," Ommaya said, greeting them in his usual polite manner.

Alexi quickly settled herself in her chair, and her husband also entered the room.

"Sorry, sorry," he said, hastily making his way to his chair.

Alexi inhaled the delicious smell of freshly cooked food, knowing that she had kept them waiting a little longer than they had expected.

"It's fine. Now we shall eat." Before even finishing his sentence Ommaya rang a small bell to alert the waiters that they were ready for their meal.

The first waiter brought into the room a large plate overflowing with seasoned fish.

"Fish from Bayhaven."

Cresadir smiled, proud of her village's contribution. The fish was placed under a low hanging chandelier that lit the whole table and served onto each plate by the waiter.

Another waiter entered holding a cloth wrapped around a bottle. He began filling their glasses with a deep red wine, then said, "Wine from Spiritmist."

A third waiter entered the hall holding a tray with three large bowls of green, white and orange vegetables. They had been steamed according to the traditional method, then dressed with butter and herbs

"The finest vegetables from Ridgemead."

Finally, the first waiter came back and poured a thick, creamy white sauce over their food.

"Enjoy your meal, Your Highness," he said before exiting the room.

The mature, monarch raised his glass.

"I would like to remember Rodrique, who was lost to us by illness this year. Always thinking about you, my son." His face became sad and a tear trickled down his cheek from his blue-grey eyes. The family showed their respects by falling silent. After a few moments, Ommaya broke the silence, sounding uplifted.

"We do have reasons for celebration this year. Daimeh came of age, and of course we were blessed with a beautiful grand-daughter."

He sat back down and chinked glasses with the rest of his family, then smiled and said, "Let's eat, shall we?"

"May I say a few words?" Alfrit asked quietly.

"Go ahead," Ommaya had always left honouring the spiritual world to his son.

"I would like to thank our great Aedolyn for this wonderful food. I know Rodrique is now in a joyous place with you and Mother." He paused for a moment. "This year Aedolyn has blessed us with baby Alith, a wonderful addition to the family. Thank you, our Goddess."

Ommaya raised his glass once more.

"Enjoy your food."

Daimeh took hold of the pristinely polished cutlery and cut into the fish which was cooked to perfection and topped with a delightful sauce.

"I know Alexi had some bad luck getting here. I do hope the rest of you had good travels?" Ommaya asked before taking a sip of wine.

"We had an unfortunate incident with our accommodation at Port Draclyn, but it didn't cause too much inconvenience," Cresadir replied whilst cutting up a rather large piece of seasoned fish.

The others didn't respond. Alfrit believed that his father already knew they had a safe journey. Wilgard was a pretentious, egotistical, young boy, too young to be a head. He felt silence was an appropriate response to the question.

"Oh-kay," Ommaya said, taking another sip. "Well, I'm the happiest man, knowing I eat with my most lovely family."

He smiled at Alfrit and Wilgard.

Once he had finished the first course, Wilgard changed the conversation.

"I would like to bring up the topic of our titles."

The clattering of knives and forks suddenly ceased; he had caught the family's attention.

"What of it?" Ommaya replied.

"Any further thought on it from last year?"

"You know my stance on this," Ommaya answered, patting his mouth with his embroidered napkin. "I want us to be as close to the people as possible. It was decided by my great-grandfather that we should abolish the title system."

"But I believe the people would respond to us better if they knew we also had authority."

"We're not the authorities. We're nobles, nothing more," Ommaya said, putting down his napkin.

"We do need a way to control the public though. Things on Ridgemead get out of hand sometimes."

"That's your problem, Wilgard. I suggest you appoint security to deal with it." Ommaya drummed his fingers on the table. "We have always had a low-key system. Our elders and I believed it was the best way to keep harmony in our society and it will stay that way as long as I am the head of this land."

"Yes, Grandfather," Wilgard replied, lowering his head.

The waiters returned to serve dessert and the table became quiet once more.

* * *

The monarch was the first to finish. He gently wiped his mouth, then, when the others had finished, stood up from the table, revealing that he was wearing slim-fitting leather trousers, finely stitched and dyed a light khaki colour. "I shall reside in the smoking room, please join me if you wish. I know some of you may need rest; feel free to retreat to your rooms, my children."

Oeradon also stood up.

"I'm exhausted, I'm going to go and rest."

"I'll also pass. I'd like to go check up on Theo. See you tomorrow," Miah said, and exited the dining room.

As she entered the lobby she heard Alith wailing so she walked towards Alexi's room, hoping to offer some assistance and knocked on the open door. Alexi was trying to change the crying baby's nappy.

"Hello, Alexi. Would you like some help?" Miah asked.

Alexi turned and smiled.

"Oh yes please, Miah. That would be great. Could you pass me another wet flannel?"

Miah rinsed a flannel under the tap and passed it to Alexi. "Here you go."

"Thank you."

Miah picked up the bowl of talc from the other counter and once Alexi had dried Alith, she dusted the talc over her bottom with a soft, fluffy brush.

"You know Alith was born after a blessing?" Alexi said. She loved to talk about the birth of her child.

"I heard."

"We couldn't conceive. Then we went to Spiritmist and the high priest blessed us with Aedolyn's tears." Aedolyn's tears were sacred water held in a chalice and only used on monarchs for special blessings.

Miah was not an especially spiritual person but she did believe in the miracles of the tears. Many blessings really did work.

"It's amazing. We know she watches over us, but it seems that Alith gets special attention."

Miah smiled contently. Now Daimeh was grown up she missed having a baby to look after and she had often considered having a second child with Halgar.

Alexi tied the last knot; her baby was now securely protected against any accidents.

"I believe Alith has great things ahead of her."

She picked her up and cradled her, before walking her over to the carefully-made crib.

"I'm sure she does," Miah replied.

They stroked her head and made soothing noises and it wasn't long before Alith was asleep.

* * *

The large wooden door was held open by the butler and as Ommaya entered, he bowed his head. This room was also grand and panelled with wood, and Ommaya walked towards the two armchairs which were placed in front of the tall, stone-built fireplace and separated by a small table. As Cresadir stood up from her chair, Daimeh tapped her shoulder to catch her attention.

"I'll go retrieve my satchel. Are we ready to tell Grandfather?"

"Yes, just come through when you're back," Cresadir replied.

She looked at her father, who took his pipe and sat down in his usual armchair, which had been specially made to fit his body. His daughter sat on the other chair and gazed into the tranquil fireplace for a few moments. The flames flickered and glimmered over the charred wood. Ommaya held his pipe to his thick lips; his face was somewhat wizened and he had deep wrinkles around his mouth and eyes.

Cresadir turned to her father.

"We have something we must discuss, Father," she said.

"Oh?"

"Something washed up on the shores of Galunda Bay. We

need to..."

"What sort of something?" Ommaya interrupted, taking another puff of his kelp.

"A dead body, Father. Daimeh found it. It's not Alkoryn," she explained. "We brought the body here." As she spoke her older brother and his wife came through to the smoking room, followed by Wilgard.

"The others decided on an early night since the festivities are starting early," Alfrit informed them as they found themselves seats and, sipped from their wine glasses.

Ommaya nodded at his son, then looked at Cresadir and said in a low voice, "It's in the stables, I presume?"

"Yes, Father."

He took one final draw from the pipe and laid it down on the small table, then pushed himself up from the armchair.

"Let's go, then."

Daimeh returned just as his aunt and grandfather were heading out of the back door. He walked over to join them.

Wilgard was sitting in the single chair next to Alfrit and his wife.

"So, how were your exports this year?" he asked.

He already knew that his export revenue had been the highest, but enjoyed stirring up rivalry.

"Lower than last year, but tourism increased after the addition of the new monuments," Alfrit replied, not wanting to appear beaten.

"Outstanding, they really are."

Wilgard placed his glass on the table. "Well, as you know, our largest source of revenue is tourism. We built a new courtesan house and it proved very popular," said Wilgard, smirking. He got a lot of enjoyment out of taunting his uncle.

"A courtesan house! Dear Aedolyn forgive you." Alfrit frowned angrily at Wilgard.

"We aim for different markets, Uncle, but we both provide a

service to our people," Wilgard replied.

"Excuse us."

Alfrit had had enough of Wilgard for one night; it was the same every year, as they were both very competitive. He and his wife stood up and left the room. Wilgard picked up his glass again and chuckled to himself.

* * *

Straw drifted across the cobbled pavement as they drew nearer to the stables. Daimeh arrived first and started to untie the binds on the body. He lifted the heavy sheet away, and the body was revealed, just as Ommaya arrived at the stables.

His grandfather was not repulsed, scared or shocked. In fact, he was perfectly calm and appeared excited by what was revealed. "Hmm, I recognise this creature," he said, letting out a short chuckle.

Surprised, Cresadir asked, "You do?"

"I've seen it before, in one of my old mythology books," he said, climbing onto the back of the cart. "I didn't think they were real." He prodded its tough face.

"Leave it here, we'll go to the basement library," Ommaya said, pulling the sheet back over it.

"Wait. There's also a sword."

Daimeh jerked forward and after stopping Ommaya from covering the cart, pulled it from under the body's arm.

Ommaya smiled. "So they're not just a myth either – the swords exist." He gestured to Daimeh to indicate that he would like to hold it. "Fascinating, it's as light as the myths say too." He tucked the sword back where it came from and the cargo was again concealed.

* * *

"Come, there's a basement chamber under the library. It's the only remnant of the scholarly building that used to be here," Ommaya explained.

"I see. I can't wait," Cresadir replied, excited.

8

Aelston's Secret

The door to the chamber looked old and was locked. Pulling out a key, Ommaya opened it and led them down a dark, creaky staircase. When they reached the bottom he lit a nearby lantern, revealing a modest-sized room lined by bookshelves. There was a large stained-glass window at the opposite wall, positioned there to allow light to flood down the library aisle. The light lit up the dust particles streaming through the air. The motes tickled their noses and had an earthy smell. There were a couple of small tables and comfy chairs standing between the walls of books.

Daimeh stood awestruck; looking around the mysterious room he was sure it was full of secrets about Alkoryn.

Cresadir was familiar with many of the books, as she had read them often when she was a child.

* * *

"Over here," Ommaya called, lifting up a small painting. Behind it was a metal ring, attached to the stone. He pulled the ring and a chain gradually appeared from behind the wall; making a clunking sound as it moved. Ommaya pulled on the chain and one of the bookshelves clicked open, revealing a doorway, inside which there was a derelict, spiral, stairway, leading down to the second, secret chamber. The entrance was illuminated by the light from the window, but further inside it was pitch black. Ommaya took his oil lighter from his pocket and, in a few seconds, there was a dim, flickering, orange flame burning. He cautiously stepped down the first few steps, steadying himself against the crumbling wall as he went. As he reached the first torch, he raised his lighter and lit it. It flared, slowly at first, but as more oxygen gushed down the stairs from the doorway it began burning more brightly. He continued down, lighting each torch as he went. Cresadir and her nephew followed close behind.

Ommaya glanced at Cresadir. "I never let you down here when you were younger as the ancient books are many thousands of years old and must be treated with care – not a place for children," he said as they neared the bottom of the staircase.

They entered the dusty, dim chamber, lit only by the slight glow from the last stairway torch. Cobwebs covered the shelves and corners of the ancient room and there were old illustrations of armour and weapons on the walls. Ommaya walked to the far side and lit, not a torch, but an old oil lamp.

"I recall there's an illustration of the creature you found – in one of these books here." He pointed to the left, towards the end of the room.

Cresadir reached inside her pocket.

"Oh, I almost forgot! My notes. I performed an autopsy."

She passed the notes to her father.

He opened the scroll hastily and examined what was written.

"Yes, yes, I'm sure this is the same creature."

Excitedly, he started looking along one of the dusty, neglected bookshelves. Cresadir searched the other bookcase.

Daimeh dragged a rotten but sturdy chair from under a small square table. He placed his satchel on the table and took the scrolled parchment from inside. There was an oil lamp hanging unlit just above him. "Grandfather, could you light the lamp, please? You should see this too."

Ommaya stopped his search and walked over to where Daimeh was. He lit the oil lamp, and the table top was immediately illuminated. Picking up the scroll he untied the leather thread and flattened it on the table, then began examining the writing carefully.

"I don't know what these say, but I've seen something similar somewhere before"

He turned over the paper and looked at the map. "You'll know this is Alkoryn," he started, making a circle round their homeland with his fingers. "But this place," he continued, pointing to the top of the map. "I don't know."

"Got something here," Cresadir said, holding an open leather-backed book. It was crusty and red in colour and there was dirt dried into the cracks in the leather. She walked over to the table.

"*Encyclopae...*" she read, but the rest of the title was not legible.

"*Encyclopaedia of Alkoryn Mythology,*" Ommaya said, completing the title for her. "That was the one I was looking for. I estimate that book is over three thousand years old."

He tapped the table.

"Careful with it."

He was rather attached to his old books.

Cresadir placed the large book carefully onto the table and pointed to the open page.

"That's it isn't it?" she asked, indicating an illustration of a creature very similar to the body they had found washed ashore. The beast wore only a loin-cloth and was running on all fours through a desolate landscape.

"Let me see."

Ommaya pulled the book closer and turned the next page, looking for a description.

"Hmm, the body you brought to me appears to be a creature from the mythological race known as the rhajok'don. The description doesn't say much."

He moved his finger down the text and read out a few lines: "The fable says... a rhajok'don arrived on Spiritmist... it was presumed to have been a villager punished by the Goddess and condemned to live as a monster. The beast was killed out of fear and the body cremated."

He moved down a few lines.

"The rhajok'don were never seen again."

Ommaya looked down at the timestamp, then gasped: "era 1:350. Over three-thousand years ago."

Puzzled, Daimeh looked from his aunt to his grandfather.

"We thought this creature was a myth; if it's not, how much of this isn't a myth either?" Daimeh asked. He began turning the pages, skimming through story after story.

Ommaya stepped back and began stroking his goatee.

"There's a movement on Spiritmist," he began, but then hesitated, as if unwilling to say anything more.

He turned, pacing up and down before sighing.

"You're my family, of course I trust you," he said, as if answering an unvoiced question. "Some of the religious scholars started to apply science to explore the world. This movement – which your uncle has been trying to stop for some time now – goes against the scriptures which are the basis for our beliefs."

He rubbed his chin.

"It would seem they're trying to rewrite our religion."

Cresadir stepped forward. "They believe we live on a planetary land mass which is revolving around the sun."

Ommaya frowned.

"Cresa? You're part of this movement?"

She bowed her head, looking a little ashamed.

"I started it," she began, then lifting her head she continued. "I'm a scientist and so are you."

She caught her father's hand.

"I believe in having an open mind, dear – I'm not a scientist," Ommaya answered, removing his hand from hers. "I'm the Monarch of Alkoryn..." he continued, lowering his head and looking back at her. "But I'm also not willing to deceive myself when the evidence is in front of me." He turned the page back to the illustration. "This is not a myth, it is lying dead in my stables. There's a dark world somewhere... somewhere very close to us."

"We've been monitoring the movement of the sun from different places around Alkoryn."

Cresadir pulled a blank piece of paper out of her bag and crumpled it into a ball. She pointed to an area on the ball, a little north of the equator.

"Alkoryn is here."

She crumpled up a second piece of paper, making a ball slightly larger than the last one. "This is the sun." Holding the second ball and spinning it she showed them how the sun moved through the sky.

"That look familiar? It's how our sun moves."

She pointed to the side away from the sun.

"If our sun never sets, their sun never rises. The bottom of the axis is the darkest place on this world." She pointed to the illuminated side. "This also means there's a place on this world where the sun moves in a small halo in the middle of the sky."

At that, Ommaya seemed to have an idea and began searching through the books around where the encyclopaedia had been found.

"I remember reading something about an ancient land in one of these books… here."

He pulled out a second book and ran through the pages. Seemingly by accident, he came across something.

"This text looks to be written using the same characters as the script you brought to me."

Continuing to flick through the pages, he found what he was looking for. "Here it is in Alkoryn. There are stories of an ancient land to the north, where there is an immense civilisation with great powers."

He looked up at Cresadir.

"Our Goddess resides in the Golden Lands," he said, reciting a phrase from the religious texts. "The Golden Lands? Could it be?"

He looked back down at the page.

"More of this writing, what does it all mean?" he pondered. "Should we travel to these lands?"

"We can't leave Alkoryn," Daimeh said, joining the conversation. "Don't you remember the stories? There is only danger beyond our borders."

"Daimeh's right. I've been to all the edges of our land and there's no path through. Many have died trying to reach the world beyond. The presumed lands to our north are hazardous to travel through. There are towering peaks, mountains of lava and pools of acidic chemicals. I also saw some creature in the distance. One minute."

She began flicking through the pages of the encyclopaedia, guessing there would be an illustration of it there.

"Here," she said, her finger smacking down on a drawing of a strange flying monster. "Those too are beyond Alkoryn."

Could that be the winged giant from the fable, Daimeh wondered.

Ommaya ran his hand through his hair. Picking up a chair that had been propped to the wall, he sat down at the table.

"This must all mean something."

"Wait," Daimeh said, turning over the scriptures paper and looking at the map once more. "I remember there were four small symbolic details, starting from Alkoryn. I didn't know what they meant, but I have an idea. This isn't just a map of the lands. It's a way through to the ancient civilisation."

He pointed his finger at each symbol as they dotted their way through the impassable lands.

"Look, you see what I mean?"

"My goodness, Daimeh. I think you're right!" Cresadir said joyfully. "What does each symbol mean, though?"

Ommaya picked up the second book once more and returned to the page with the symbolic characters on it.

"They look similar to these," he commented. "They're keys, four keys we don't have."

"We must find these keys. We need to go to this land, Father. I believe it's our destiny."

Cresadir sounded optimistic and insistent.

"It's out of our hands. We've nowhere to look," Ommaya replied.

Daimeh turned the parchment over again. "Yes we do. We can decipher the script."

Cresadir took hold of the map and examined the symbols more carefully. "Hmm, I've seen this first symbol before. It's a religious artefact on Spiritmist, and a very sacred one."

"So? We can go and get it?" Daimeh asked, looking intently at her.

"Not so easily. My brother would never allow it," Cresadir continued. "Even if Father asked him, we still wouldn't be allowed to take the artefact."

"I'll talk with him tomorrow," Ommaya promised.

Just as he finished his sentence a commotion was heard from upstairs. Something was smashed and there was the muffled sound of a man's deep voice, shouting, followed by irregular footsteps and then a women's voice.

What's going on, Ommaya asked himself. This was certainly not a usual occurrence.

"I'll go check what's happening," he said

"That deep voice," Cresadir began, then paused for a moment. "It's Theo! Oh my gosh! Hurry!"

Daimeh remained in the basement but Ommaya and Cresadir rushed up the spiral staircase making the torches flicker as they ran past.

When they reached the bottom floor, the noises became clearer.

"You... go." Cresadir heard. She pointed towards where the steps were coming from and headed in that direction.

To her surprise she saw Theo, dressed in his nightwear, storming around the study, making seemingly random movements. He was stamping on the carpet and shouting, "You cannot go!" Then he would pause for a moment, before repeating, "You cannot go!" Despite this, his face was as vacant as always; he seemed like a puppet.

The nursemaid was chasing him around the room, trying to calm him down.

"Why's he saying this?" she asked Cresadir

"I don't know," she replied.

Of course, she did know, but she certainly was not going to reveal the reason to the nursemaid.

"He hasn't said a word for eleven years." Cresadir said.

This should have been a joyful moment, but Cresadir felt sad. Theo might now be speaking, but the man in front of her was still not the one she married.

Ommaya took longer to reach the room, but when he did, he was also met by Theo's ramblings. Cresadir and Ommaya looked at each other, baffled.

Suddenly, Theo collapsed to the floor and Cresadir ran over to him and helped the nurse to lift him back into his wheelchair. He immediately became as calm as he had been earlier. He fell silent and his eyes glazed over. Cresadir knelt down next to him, unable to stop herself remembering the rumours she had heard about his disappearance. She stroked his forehead for a while, hoping against hope for something more. Hoping he would come back to her – at least a little way. Finally, she had to admit defeat. Sighing she rose to her feet and, glancing at her father, shook her head, blinking back tears.

They returned to the basement library, where Daimeh greeted them.

"What was it?" he asked.

"Your uncle," Cresadir replied, still wearing a bruised expression. "He told us that we couldn't go."

"But we must," Daimeh responded abruptly.

"We will, of course we will, but... it doesn't make any sense to me. Why would my husband say this? And after so long."

Ommaya put his arm around her. "Are you all right?"

"Yes." She paused for a moment, clearly still thinking about what had just happened, then cleared her throat. "Now then, where do we go from here?"

"I think we go to bed, it's been a long day and it's very late now. The fete will commence in a matter of hours," Ommaya said. He wanted to stay and do more research, but knew it was time to prepare for the next day.

9

Missing

The events of the day had affected Cresadir more than she had thought and as she slept that evening her unconscious mind took her back to the time when Theo went missing.

Delicate, silken curtains were fluttering in the gentle wind, allowing streams of sunlight to illuminate Cresadir's spacious sleeping quarters. The bed was unmade, the sheets crumpled and she was weeping into her hands. After three tiring days her butterscotch hair looked as neglected as the bed, hanging disordered and unwashed down her nightgown.

A young, fair-haired boy, no more than nine years old, appeared in the doorway, looking sorrowful.

"I've brought you some milk, fresh today," he said, stretching his hand towards her. "Please take it."

A few moments passed before the sniffles ceased and Cresadir lifted her face. Tears were smeared over her oily skin and she ran her fingertips across her cheeks.

She stared vacantly ahead for a second or two before muttering, "You're staying strong through this, Oeradon"

"I'm trying, Mother."

Lethargically, she took the milk from his hand and placed it on the wooden bedside table before opening her arms to her son. He fell into them without hesitation. Oeradon began to sob as he buried his head into his mother's arms.

"He will... come home, won't he?" he asked, his words barely audible.

He felt his mother's hand running through his hair, listening to her heavy breathing as she held him tighter.

Settling her chin on Oeradon's crown, Cresadir felt hopelessness weighing her down.

"Yes," she finally replied. She knew that as his mother, she was expected to be strong for him, but as they both knew, he was the strong one. "Yes, he will."

Her calm reply came more from maternal instinct than from actual conviction. She knew she must give Oeradon hope.

* * *

The manor doors rattled so intensely that the whole house shuddered. Halgar was pounding the heavy knocker. A timid-looking young man answered, wearing dirty clothes blotted with perspiration.

Seeing the man outside, he addressed him quietly. "Halgar. We've just returned. I'm sorry, but we haven't found him yet."

He had a sympathetic look in his eyes as he spoke.

"Were Miah and my son part of the search party?" Halgar asked, looking desperate.

"No they weren't, why?"

Halgar barged past him and entered the main hall which smelled of sweat and grime. There were five villagers present; they had been thoroughly searching all day, as the stink made very evident. Raising his voice he addressed the assembled villagers who were packing away their things.

"Have any of you seen Miah and my son?"

The villagers stopped what they were doing and glanced at each other, shaking their heads confusedly. A tall woman wearing a long tunic and muddy trousers stepped forward looking concerned. "No, what's wrong?"

Halgar's face crumbled and he ran his hands down his cheeks. His thick eyebrows tensed and his wide grey eyes stared ahead of him. His voice breaking, he mumbled, "They're gone... they've been gone for four hours... I need to see Cresa."

Wearing a shocked expression, the woman replied, "She's still upstairs. She's not left her room for days now."

Halgar ran through the hall and hurried up the spiral staircase. Cresadir's room was the furthest along the corridor and her door was ajar, amber light beaming from the room. He pushed the door open and saw Cresadir curled up with Oeradon, asleep on the unmade bed. She was facing the door and one arm was draped around her son.

The curtains were still waving in the draught coming from the open window. He walked to Cresadir's side, then gently shook her.

"Cresa, you need to wake up," he whispered, trying not to sound as desperate as he felt. He brushed her disordered hair away from her face, and gently touched her cheek. "Cresa, Cresa, wake up."

Cresadir stirred and slowly opened her fawn-coloured eyes. Her pupils were dilated and the whites were bloodshot. Her eyelids looked slightly puffy and crusted tears were stuck to her long lashes. Her petite nose was red and swollen and appeared sore.

She groaned as she woke and opened her cracked lips. "Hrrmm... mmmrgh... w–what? Is that you, Theo?"

"No, it's Halgar," he answered, lowering his head and sighing.

He knew he couldn't tell her about her sister and nephew: she was in too much distress as it was. He tried to comfort her, saying in an affectionate tone, "I'm just checking on you, go back to sleep."

A draught gusted through the room, blowing her hair back over her face. Halgar turned around and closed the window, then drew the curtains before tucking Cresadir in. Oeradon was still fast asleep next to her.

There was a rose-coloured chair at the back of the room covered with cushions. Halgar sat down and watched over Cresadir and her son. He could hear the villagers downstairs leaving the house; they would go to their homes to rest and would return for another search in the morning. Halgar felt helpless, waiting for Cresadir to awaken from her slumber.

* * *

The rear door was open when Miah arrived at Cresadir's, so she let herself in.

"Cresa," she called through the empty hallway, looking left and right. "Cresa…"

Halgar bolted down the stairs to meet her.

"You're back," he gasped, his voice weak. "I thought you were gone too…"

He ran towards them and took them both in his arms, relieved to see his family. He never wanted to let go. A broad smile swept involuntarily over his face.

"Halgar, Daimeh's hurt. He must see Cresa immediately," Miah said, gesturing to Daimeh's foot.

"Oh my," he said, glancing down. "Let me take him upstairs." Taking his son, he noticed Miah's gashed hands.

"Oh, Miah."

Daimeh's eyes opened.

"Popa," he said, still seeming dazed.

"He went looking for his Uncle Theo on his own. He just wanted to help… he got lost in the far forest. Oh Halgar, there were tygrisa…" she whispered, tearful. "It was horrible, so horrible."

"You're safe now, but Cresa needs to see to these wounds… c'mon, upstairs, quickly." Halgar hastily escorted them both up the varnished stairs.

Oeradon and his mother were still sleeping when Miah's husband entered the room, holding Daimeh. Miah walked over to Cresadir and gently roused her from her rest. She turned towards the blurry silhouette of her sister. "Miah… is that you?"

"Yes, Cresa." Bending, Miah gently stroked her grieving

sister's cheek. "You need to wake up," she said softly, not wanting to disturb Oeradon.

Cresadir pushed herself up into a sitting position, her lethargy falling away from her like a cloak, banished by a blaze of hope. "You found him?"

Miah lowered her head.

"No," she replied. "Daimeh's hurt. We need you to look at his foot."

Cresadir inhaled deeply in an effort to get herself focused.

"Bring him over to my desk and get my medical supplies," she told Miah, lifting the sheets off her and getting out of the bed. She sat down on a nearby chair, just next to the window. Miah brought her a soft flannel, bandages and a bowl of ethanol. Halgar knelt down and gently lifted Daimeh's foot onto Cresadir's lap. The young boy winced with pain. His aunt placed her hand on his forehead, which was sticky with sweat and mud.

"No fever, hopefully no infection," she declared, then picked up the flannel and dipped it lightly into the clear liquid.

After gently cleansing the dirty, scabby wound, she could see that the stalk had pierced the arch of Daimeh's foot.

"The puncture wound is, thankfully, not too deep, it's inflamed, but..." She delicately squeezed a drip of ethanol over the broken skin. "I don't see any obvious signs of infection."

She reached for the white bandages.

"It could have been a lot worse – you're a lucky boy, Daimeh," Cresadir said, beginning to dress the wound.

"There you go. I don't want you using your foot too much for the next few days. Is that clear?"

She smiled reassuringly at her nephew.

"Thanks, Aunt Cresa," Daimeh answered, before falling silent for a moment. "Cresa?"

"Yes."

"I only wanted to help," he said, in a sorrowful tone.

"I know you did, Daimeh, and I thank you for that."

She hugged him.

Miah placed a hand on her sister's shoulder.

"There was no sign of Theo. I'm sorry Cresa," she said as she neatened her sister's straggly appearance, straightening her hair and wiping away her tears.

"The search was thorough, I fear the worst."

"Miah, I think I'm ready for the worst," Cresadir replied, her expression sad and heavy. "Father's scriptures say they never come back."

Her dry, swollen eyes filled with tears again.

"Every few hundred years an Alkoryn vanishes and is gone forever." Sorrow overcame her and she covered her face with her hands

"We don't know yet. Please, Cresa, don't lose hope." Miah cuddled her sister, trying to comfort her in her distress. She was exhausted, but her only concern was for her family.

"We'll stay here tonight and keep an eye on you and Oeradon," Miah said, taking Cresadir's hand and guiding her back to bed.

"Tuck yourself in – I'll get cosy on the chair."

"Thank you, Miah, for everything."

A grateful smile crossed Cresadir's face as she lay back in bed.

"I'm taking Daimeh to the guest room to rest," Halgar stated, lifting his son into his arms.

He stood looking at her for a moment before confidently declaring, "We'll find him."

* * *

The early sunlight sparkled against Bermel's window. As so often, he was sat on his balcony. The Cyan Ocean was calm and a mild breeze was wafting the salty scent of the sea over the bay. He leaned forward and tied up his forest shoes, preparing to lead another search into the forest. Ready, he stood up and gazed across Galunda Bay.

In the distance, Bermel caught sight of a short, well-built man, staggering towards the village. *Theo*? He launched himself quickly over the balcony fence into the warm shallow water below and sloshed along until he reached the dry sands.

Theo's feet dragged as he wandered towards Lybas, driven more by instinct than anything else. His face was filled with confusion and fear. He was still wearing his sleeping clothes. These were elegantly-made, but were now completely ruined. Theo's entire body was covered in a shiny, clear oil that reflected the sunlight. He swayed down the beach. He had clearly fallen at some point and there was sand caked to his arms, legs and hands. He was completely unaware of Bermel sprinting down the bay towards him. He could hear someone calling, but was too dazed and bewildered to even recognise his own name.

"Theo... Theo!" The sound grew louder in the half-crazed man's ears, but he recognized it not.

Bermel reached the lost man relatively quickly, although the frantic sprint had left him with a stich in his side and gasping for breath. Theo's dark, coffee-coloured eyes were totally vacant and dead to the world. As soon as he was close enough, Bermel grabbed Theo's sticky, grainy hand. Theo's hair was greasy and slick, and there was oil still dripping from it. His mouth was open, possibly in shock, and his face was expressionless.

"Theo, you've been gone for four days. Where were you? Your family has been so worried about you."

Theo just stared vacantly through Bermel, as though he wasn't even there.

Bermel shook him hard in an attempt to wake him from his seemingly semi-conscious state. He slapped his face.

Finally, Theo seemed to rouse. "W-w-wha-what?" he stuttered.

"You've been gone for four days. Where were you?" Bermel

repeated.

"I d-du-don't... I... don't... remember."

10

Trouble At The Fete

It was the morning of the fete and the Alkoryn people were up early.

Cresadir knocked on Daimeh's door.

"You up?"

She heard rumbling from inside, and then the door opened.

"Yes, just."

"I wanted to give you the shell, you can present it yourself."

"Thanks, Cresa."

She handed him a lace-covered box with a delicate bow on top. Daimeh opened it and saw the beautiful shell from Galunda Bay set amongst leaves.

"It looks lovely," he said before closing the box.

"I'll see you outside," Cresadir said as she took her leave.

* * *

Miah had been one of the first to awake that day. She was in the kitchen stirring her home-made spiced porridge when Daimeh entered.

"Morning, Mother," he said, yawning.

"Up late?"

"Yes. We told Grandfather... about everything."

Daimeh was unsure how to break it to her that he was about to travel away from his home. He hesitated.

"And?" Miah glanced at her son. "Daimeh, I know when you aren't telling me things."

"Err," Daimeh said, searching for the right words. "Aunt Cresa and I, we're going away... travelling."

"Oh? For how long?" Miah asked, worried.

Daimeh paused again. "We don't know." He tried to explain in more detail. "The map... we believe it shows a route out of Alkoryn."

"No, no, no, that's impossible, son," Miah insisted. "Everyone knows the lands beyond Alkoryn are impassable."

"That's the thing. They're not, or so we think. There's an artefact at Spiritmist. We believe it'll help us find a way across the borders."

His mother stopped stirring the porridge and sat down at the kitchen table. She looked into Daimeh's eyes, her face sad.

"You're my only child, is this so important that you need to leave your family? To leave Lybas?"

"Mother, I'm not a child anymore. Remember that seven-year-old who went off to search for Uncle Theo all those years ago – I still want that adventure."

The porridge began to bubble over. Daimeh rushed over to it and lowered the heat. He put his arm around his mother who was close to tears.

"I'm afraid for you, for both of you," she sniffed, leaning on her son's shoulder.

"We'll come home. I will come home to Lybas, I just don't know when it'll be." He also began to get tearful, but he continued. "My mind's made up. I must do this. It's something I've been waiting for my whole life."

Miah knew her son well and knew there was nothing she could now say to make him change his mind. She wiped her tears, trying to appear strong and supportive for him, although inside she was crumbling.

"I understand, Daimeh," she said, grasping his hand in hers. "Just promise. Promise you'll come back to us."

"I will," Daimeh said, embracing his mother lovingly.

* * *

They left the house and walked into the glorious courtyard gardens. Only prestigious members of society celebrated in the royal landscape gardens. The warm high-sun air washed over them. The gardens were full of the sound of singing birds, laughing, screaming, children playing and chatter from the guests.

A perfectly-manicured lawn extended as far as the eye could see, bordered by huge bustling trees, closely planted to ensure complete privacy. The trees were decorated from top to bottom with sparkling baubles, which were so big that they could be seen from the mansion's rear court.

Daimeh and his aunt walked down the solid stone steps towards the multi-coloured festival tents, which were really more like canopies with veils instead of walls, there to keep out biting insects. Inside, there were a few small tables with jugs, beakers and glasses of alcoholic drinks on them. To the rear of the court there was a small platform, on top of which was a three-man band playing jingling melodies. There was a long banquet table covered with a delightful selection of foods from the four states, as well as carved wooden ornaments crafted especially for the festival. The table was overflowing with fruit, nuts, roasted meats, cooked vegetables and sauces. The chairs were immaculately crafted and matched the table and ornaments. There was a show stall area where all the gifts presented to Ommaya would be displayed. They were surrounded by colourful plants and shrubs. Opposite this was a second stall where produce from the different villages was laid out for guests to help themselves.

Ommaya was sitting in the centre chair, dressed elaborately. Daimeh was sat two seats further down. Contrary to etiquette, Daimeh had put an elbow on the table and was resting his head on it. He nibbled at the delicious food feeling bored, just like every year. His reluctance to participate in the festival was all too evident.

"Daimeh, remove your elbow please," Ommaya asked.

Daimeh did as his grandfather ordered, whispering to him, "I just want to make progress with the script."

Ommaya whispered back, "I know you do."

"Can I go to the basement and do more research?"

"Absolutely not. The fete is an important event. Just try and endure it please." Ommaya also wanted to do more research as soon as possible, but he was obliged to be present at the fete.

* * *

Miah had gone to mingle with the other guests and was now awkwardly dancing next to the bandstand. She tried to make small-talk with some elderly people next to her, who were also bobbing to the music.

"Very nice this year, isn't it?" she said.

"Pardon, dear? The music's a bit loud."

Miah shouted over the noise, "Very nice this year!"

The old lady replied in a gruff, but pleasant voice.

"Oh yes, it's lovely – especially the baubles. Ingrid loves the baubles, don't you?"

She nudged her friend.

"Hmm?" the second lady responded.

"I say, you like those new baubles."

"Yes, I believe they make them over on Spiritmist using some new-fangled technique."

"I see," Miah replied, nodding.

The band suddenly quickened the pace and Miah began to clap along.

"Oh, I like this one."

The same tunes were played almost every year, with a new one added only now and then.

"We're not so interested in the music. We just came along for the gossip, although the decorations certainly are eye-catching," the elderly lady said, chuckling to herself.

Ingrid leaned over to Miah.

"Did you hear about Wilgard and his tangle with Salnia?"

"Yes, unfortunately. That boy's just too young to be the head of Ridgemead," Miah replied.

"Oh, I was hoping for an elaboration," Ingrid said, cheekily.

Miah stopped dancing and clapping. "Well, I don't know about the specifics of the relationship, but Ridgemead needs a strong head, especially with all those pubs and drinking. The problem will only get worse now."

An elderly woman joined the conversation. "All those young hooligans over there, yes. I hear there's even some vandalism and crime."

"I didn't know that, perhaps it's time for my father to have some words with young Wilgard," Miah replied, taking her wine glass from the little table next to her. "It was a pleasure speaking with you both. I best go sit up there," she continued, pointing at the long table where Ommaya and Daimeh were sitting, "and pretend I'm someone important. Bye."

She laughed and, smiling, walked away.

"Bye, dear."

* * *

In front of the banquet table there was a square stage and on it were dancers, who were moving to the melodies played by the band, symbolically representing the growth and production of the land's resources. The monarch joyfully applauded their performance.

Cresadir sat next to her father, her legs crossed. Theo was next to her and she was feeding him with a selection of food from the table.

After watching the dancers for a while, she addressed her father saying, "Alfrit is on his own over there. I'm going to confront him."

"This is not a good time, Cresa."

"It wasn't a question, Father."

She stood up and marched towards Alfrit. She glanced into the tents as she passed them, and at one she stopped, gasping.

"Oh, my."

Inside, she saw her son in a compromising position with one of the waitresses.

"Oeradon, please, not here." Oeradon immediately pushed the girl aside, looking embarrassed.

"Mother, hi-hi," he said in a high-pitched voice. "Good fete, isn't it?"

"Yes." She pointed to the pretty young maiden. "You, go do your job."

She turned to Oeradon. "And I think you should get yourself up to that table, we're giving the gifts soon."

"Yes, Mother," Oeradon replied, and off he went.

Cresadir proceeded on towards Alfrit's tent. He was sipping red wine when Cresadir marched in.

"Alfrit, I need to ask you something."

She picked up a glass of wine for herself as she entered.

Alfrit viewed his sister with contempt because of her pursuit of science. "What could *you* want from me?" he snarled.

"That artefact, the one you keep in Aedolyn's Promise," Cresadir explained. "It's of use to me."

He laughed.

"Oh, so you've decided to return to our religion?"

"Not exactly," she answered. "I believe it's of scientific value."

"Stop this, sister!" Alfrit was clearly annoyed by his sister's words. "That artefact is the oldest relic known to our civilisation. You know its value to our religion. I'm *not* going to just *give* it to you. For you to do whatever blasphemous experiments on it."

He waved his arms around angrily as he spoke.

Cresadir also raised her voice. "Look. *Brother.* I *need* that artefact for something much more important than your preten-tious, measly worshipping of some make-believe goddess!"

"How dare you!"

Alfrit slapped Cresadir across her face with the back of his hand.

Cresadir threw her wine at him and stormed out; as she exited she noticed a few eyes looking in her direction. Ommaya was one of those nosy, peering people, and he looked very disap-pointed by his children's behaviour. Cresadir kept eye contact with him for a few moments as she walked, and shook her head. Ommaya entered Alfrit's tent, wanting to understand what had happened.

"Urgh, I need to change," Alfrit said, dabbing at his shirt with a handkerchief.

"No, you *need* to tell me what just happened!" Ommaya demanded.

"Father, didn't you see what she did? Wine – look, this top is ruined," he fumed, holding out the front of his shirt. "She dared to ask me to remove the artefact from our most sacred temple and hand it over to her; what did she expect my reaction to be?"

Ommaya breathed in deeply before answering. He knew he risked completely alienating his son and his family if he was seen to support Cresadir and Daimeh's expedition. He had to seem unbiased in front of his son. He chose his words carefully.

"You know I've never liked these public disagreements," Ommaya began. "I understand that the artefact is important to both of you. I'd like to find a compromise, my son..."

Alfrit interrupted. "A compromise! No! It will not leave the temple. You can tell her that from me." He dropped his voice to a whisper, "As she's your favourite." Raising his voice again, he continued, "I'm not naïve; I know you support her sciences, especially considering all the attention she gets, like every year – don't think everyone has ever noticed!"

Ommaya was not pleased by his son's lack of composure. He

pointed a stern finger at him before replying.

"One – I do not take orders from my son. Two – I saw you strike your sister, so she was perfectly within her right to *ruin* your shirt. Three – yes I value the sciences, but this does not mean my faith isn't strong!"

He lowered his hand. "I can see that nothing productive will come of this conversation, I'll get back to my duties." He lifted the flaps of the tent and strode regally away.

* * *

Ommaya returned to the table, sat down and crossed his arms. Cresadir sat next to him, her eyes red. "He won't budge on this," she whispered to her father.

"No, he won't. We're going to have to do something a little underhanded if you're to go on your journey."

"You mean steal it?" Cresadir asked.

"Borrow it, yes."

Ommaya smiled and chuckled. He stood up and applauded the entertainment once more. Sitting back down he continued, "My son may not want you to take it, but he cannot stop me from wanting it displayed on this isle, to, you know, reintroduce spirituality to Aelston. Trust me, we'll get that key. We'll plan how, tonight."

* * *

The music stopped and an announcer strutted onto the stage. Daimeh left the table to prepare himself to present his gift.

"Evening, ladies and gentlemen. I am happy to announce that the gift-giving is about to commence. Please take your seats and remain quiet for the duration. Thank you."

He bowed and left the stage abruptly.

The band started playing a slow tune and the presenters lined up, ready for their cue.

The announcer raised his voice and introduced the first presenter. "From Orewick, presented by the lovely Amele, are the finest jewels, cut to perfection."

Amele approached the table and handed over the diamonds.

"Very beautiful. Thank you, Alexi."

"Presented by Edion are replicas of the outstanding new Aedolyn statues which decorate Spiritmist's unforgettable skyline."

Edion passed the monarch the replicas.

Really, Alfrit! More rubbish I have to display, Ommaya thought, before saying politely, "Thank you, Alfrit."

"From Ridgemead, presented by Lalia, are ten barrels of exquisite wine from the year 1479"

Ommaya held back a sigh. So predictable, the same gift as his father.

Lalia removed a velvet sheet revealing the stacked barrels.

"Thank you, Wilgard."

"And finally, from Bayhaven, an immaculate and rare monea shell, presented by its finder, Daimeh."

The announcer clapped.

Ommaya's youngest grandson approached the banquet table and leant over towards him, passing the delicately decorated box.

His grandfather accepted the gift and opened it. His shoulders relaxed as he looked at the magnificent shell.

"Perfect. Thank you, Daimeh."

He stood up and, leaning forward over the table, gave Daimeh a loving hug.

"I'll cherish it."

11

The Theft Of Spiritmist

A few days after the fete...

Ommaya pushed the crude little boat away from the shore. It was now midday and time to put their plan into action.

"Don't worry, I'll deal with the aftermath." He chuckled. "Safe journey, my dear."

His daughter took the oars and raised the small sail. She waved back at her father as she set off for Spiritmist.

* * *

After a day's sailing, the current took her straight to the western side of the island. Cresadir arrived at the harbour, which was not especially busy. Spiritmist only had a small population, as only the most devout were allowed to reside on the island. She could already smell the candlewax and incense from the harbour. When she was near enough to the docks, she tossed a rope ashore and called for assistance from a passer-by, an old man dressed in a white gown. He tied the rope to the nearest bollard and helped her out of the wobbly boat.

"Hello."

"Hello, I'm Cresadir from Bayhaven."

"Oh ma'am, excuse me," he said, bowing. "I wasn't expecting a visit from you."

"Indeed. It is a little unscheduled. I'm just here to see my brother," she lied.

"I see." He nodded twice.

"Well, you know your way around," the old man said, signalling with his hand in the direction of the main road. "Enjoy your stay."

Apart from this polite man, there was no one else in sight as she walked towards the central temple of Spiritmist.

* * *

Her naked feet brushed sand over the cobbled street and she listened to chanting coming from inside tall, intricately carved white buildings. A narrow road ran around the buildings and they were interspersed by many marble fountains sprinkling beautiful clear water upwards. As she walked towards the central terrace the sculptured shrubs gradually fell into the shadow of the towering monuments of Aedolyn, which could be seen from the sea. Cresadir continued through the garden and past the large ornamental pond at its centre, until she came to the cardinal temple with its imposing central ovoid dome and magnificent colonnaded shrine. Aedolyn's Promise, the temple that made Spiritmist special was awe-inspiring to look at. She casually strolled up the front steps, ready to greet the temple guardian.

When she reached him, she politely raised her hand and said, "Afternoon. I'm Cresadir from Bayhaven and I'd like to enter the temple."

"Hello, ma'am. We've not seen you on Spiritmist in quite some time."

"Er yes, I lost my way spiritually for some years after what happened to Theo. But now, I want to reconnect to Aedolyn."

"Your brother will be very pleased to hear that." The aged congregant smiled, letting her in.

* * *

The inside of the large, religious building was like a small city in itself. Though the oldest construction on Alkoryn, it was so well maintained it looked newly built. Cresadir remembered that the doctrine even said it pre-dated Alkoryn settlement.

She walked down the central aisle, which was illuminated by light streaming through the windows high above. There were two storeys of arcades on either side with murals on their walls. One of the pictures depicted the business and legal transactions that used to take place there before Aelston became the capital city. Others showed initiation ceremonies and images of Aedolyn visiting her devotees.

The corridor led directly towards the dome room. Inside, she found a magnificent monolith, three times higher than the roof of the corridor and tapering to a narrow point at the top. Carved from marble, it had engravings of vines cascading down its four sides. The monolith was intended to represent the rays of the sun descending to earth. Cresadir stood at the monolith for a short space of time, appreciating the smell of incense and the sound of scripture being recited. It was a perfect moment.

* * *

A single bell chimed, and soon she heard gentle, echoing footsteps coming from her left. A distinguished man walked out of the chancel chamber wearing a hood. His head was down and his hands were cupped. He walked towards Cresadir without looking at her. He passed her as if she wasn't there and walked straight to the nave opposite, then turned left, and passed through a door leading to the meeting room above the arcade.

A meeting. Luck was on her side.

Cresadir watched another two worshippers slowly walking down the right nave; one had a grey beard tucked into his robe, another wore a washed-out red collar and looked like an apprentice. They were both heading towards the meeting room. Minutes later another two dozen devotees entered the arcade door.

Cresadir thought quickly. The place would be almost empty.

This was going to be easy.

The heavy door closed and it echoed through the dome room. It was time to move. She hastily tiptoed down a corridor to the exhibition area. It was clear. Only the monarchy heritage was able to visit the temple, so aside from the guardians, security was low. She approached two tall doors, set with windows. Through the glass she could see the radiant artefact. It was protected by a glass dome and had not been touched for centuries. She reached for the handle and silently clicked it down, opening the big door as quietly as she could and entering the room.

Her feet glided along the smooth, white stone floor. She moved gracefully towards the only thing in the room, wanting to be respectful in her attitude to the artefact. It was in the shape of a lemniscate with many curving tubes intertwining. Its polished surface reflected even the dimmest of light. Its shapeliness and symmetry displayed its absolute perfection.

The object caused Cresadir to feel suddenly overcome with guilt. How could she do this? Disrespect everything her brother lived for, everything she used to live for. A single tear ran down her cheek.

Motionlessly gazing at the artefact, she felt completely lost.

Images of the rhajok'don's body, the symbols on the map and the scripture flashed through her mind, obscuring her thoughts. She had been waiting for this her whole life. She knew what she had to do. She couldn't back away now.

Cresadir raised her hands towards the pristine display dome. Holding the bottom firmly, she lifted it slowly upwards. Small particles of dust rushed in and the artefact was exposed to air for the first time in a long while.

She placed the dome on the masonry display table. The clink of the glass reflected outwards and Cresadir looked around anxiously, checking if anyone had heard. Detaching a small satchel from her waist, she lifted it up to the relic and quickly slipped it into the bag before re-attaching it to her waist. Once she had settled the dome back down, she walked briskly back towards the doors. An elderly man was shuffling through the aisle, from one arcade to the other. She quickly dodged to her right and hid by the tiled wall. Once she was sure he had gone, she dashed down the corridor, around the obelisk and then slowing to a reasonable pace, she departed from the temple.

"He was in a meeting; I'll make an appointment next time," she said to the guardian in a composed manner before leaving.

"I see. We hope to see you soon," he answered, smiling warmly. "Good day to you, ma'am."

Cresadir hurriedly walked towards the dock. There was still no one around. It was so much easier than she had expected.

The rudimentary boat wobbled as she boarded it. Once settled she pulled the rope free from the mooring, and drifted away, back to Aelston.

* * *

One hour later, Alfrit stood looking into the exhibition room. He looked at the open doors, then the glass dome. He saw the missing amulet and his chest tightened.

"What have you done, Cresadir? What have you done?"

12

Tropical Haven

"All set?"

"Yes, Father," Cresadir replied shortly, fiddling with the amulet around her neck.

Ommaya affectionately placed his hand on Daimeh's shoulder and guided him to the two-man sailing ship. "The equids are on board, as well as your needed provisions." He looked at Daimeh. "And so is your sword."

"Good-bye, Grandfather. We'll be back."

Cresadir followed Daimeh up the ramp and went straight to the bridge while her nephew went below deck to man the oars.

Cresadir waved to her father as the ship floated away.

"Good luck!" he shouted.

As the ship gathered speed, Daimeh rushed from below and let the sails down. Their exciting journey to the far north had begun.

* * *

The ocean was calm and the glorious sunshine bounced off the ripples. Cresadir, who was on the bridge manning the wheel, was half-blinded by it, and had to pull her woven hat over her eyes.

Daimeh was below deck checking on the equids. He untied the one which would be his mount and led her up to the upper deck via a sturdy wooden ramp. He strolled slowly up and down with her, circling around the sizable chestnut-coloured ship. Then he re-tied her to the mid-sized crow's nest and headed back down to get Cresdair's equid.

* * *

Later that day…

Daimeh was slouched on deck, examining the detailed map. The location they were looking for was west of Orewick and away from any centres of population. The symbol was marked on a ridge near a cliff face.

"Cresa, you got the bearings for here?" He turned the parchment around and pointed to the location.

Cresadir glanced over her shoulder. "Of course, Daimeh, I've been there before."

"Really?" Daimeh asked.

"Yes, Daimeh. Didn't I tell you about my expeditions when you were a boy?"

"You did, but I was young. I thought you'd only gone to the forest."

Cresadir chuckled.

"Just after your uncle came back to us…"

"I remember that night – I had such a sore foot," Daimeh interrupted.

"Yes you did, it took a while to heal. Anyway, I nursed Theo day and night, but I could never stop wondering where he had gone. The feeling built up until it was unbearable and I felt an urgent need to travel, to find answers – not just for Theo, but for our people generally."

"I remember my mother lived at yours whilst you were away."

"She did," Cresadir replied. "I asked her to care for Theo for a while as I would be absent."

She smiled.

"Your mother was worried and didn't want me to go. You know the way she is."

Daimeh nodded, smiling.

"M-hm."

"But one day, she realised it was something I had to do and

agreed to what I was asking. I went to every corner of Alkoryn, since I never really believed that it was impossible to leave this land. The myths were just that, after all." Cresadir turned the wheel before continuing. "I never found a way past, but I did see beyond."

"What do you mean?" Daimeh's interest had been piqued and he sat up straight.

Cresadir lifted a nearby mop and jammed it into the ship's wheel.

"That should keep us on the right track," she said, then sat down next to Daimeh. "Pass me the map over, would you, please?"

He gave her the map and she rested it on her palm so they could both see it.

"Well," she continued. "First I travelled to the south over the oceans."

She ran her fingers over the map, indicating her journey. "I went as far as I could but our boats were just not strong enough for those waters and I had to return. But I did notice that there, the sun was lower in the sky than I had ever seen before. I could only surmise that the further I went south, the lower the sun would get."

"Interesting. Then where did you go?" He looked directly into his aunt's eyes, his interest heightened.

"I returned to Lybas a few weeks later and stayed there for a few days, then I headed to the north-eastern landmass."

She showed Daimeh the area on the map.

"There was very little there. Impassable cliffs and jungles, home to many deadly creatures, including tygrisa."

She paused for a moment before sighing. "It was a dead end."

"What did you see beyond?" Daimeh asked.

"Wait, I'm getting there," she said, pointing at the map again.

"Here's Orewick, as you know. I travelled through the mining villages and continued north. I walked through the savannah for weeks, stopping at every waterhole. The sun was higher than I had ever seen it before. Everything looked promising. But then came the desert. In the distance, far to the north, I could see volcanic mountains. That's when I saw it."

"Saw what?" Daimeh's eyebrows rose, intrigued.

"I saw something flying above the mountains. It was the most amazing creature I had ever seen. It must have been huge, probably even bigger than the whole of Lybas. And its colour was striking – even from the distance I was at I could see that it was a very bright blue."

"Wow, unbelievable."

The hairs were standing up on the back of Daimeh's neck

"And that's when I realised that there was more out there. But, at exactly the same time I realised that to the north was a death trap."

Her shoulders dropped and she sighed again.

"Did you ever go west?" Daimeh asked, keenly interested.

"Yes I did, to the mountains you can see behind Aelston. I travelled there. But they were so high and I could get no higher than a few hundred feet, no matter how much rope I had."

She gave Daimeh the map back.

"We simply don't have the technology to scale those mountains."

"Then you went northwest, I take it?"

"I did. To the northwest of Alkoryn is a bay between two cliffs. A tropical haven which was preserved for its beauty. That was why we didn't colonize there," Cresadir explained.

"It was similar to the northeast – impassable high cliffs and dense jungle. However, I didn't spot any deadly creatures."

"Oh, well that's a relief."

"And soon we'll be there, and we'll finally see what's beyond."

She gave Daimeh a quick cuddle before folding the map and packing it away.

"I'm tired. Do you mind if I have a nap?" Daimeh asked.

"Of course not. I'll keep watch in case we reach the mainland."

* * *

A few hours passed…

"There they are!" Cresadir shouted, standing up suddenly and pulling the mop from between the spokes of the wheel. Daimeh abruptly woke up and stood up to see what was happening. She checked the sun.

"The map please, Daimeh."

He passed it to her and she glanced quickly over it.

"Yes, over there. Can you see?"

She pointed towards a ridge between two cliffs.

Daimeh raised his hand to shade his eyes before answering.

"M-hm, I can see the small oasis too," he said.

"We'll be there in no time."

* * *

An hour later they were nearing the cliffs. The jewelled sand of the small bay glistened like a guiding light.

Daimeh steered the ship and Cresadir climbed up to the crow's nest, trying to locate a good area for landing.

"Daimeh!" she called.

He poked his head out of the bridge and looked upwards.

"Yes!"

"That way." She signalled towards a smooth patch of sand. "If you could beach us there, it would be perfect. I'll raise the sails."

"Got it!"

The ship slowed and began to drift towards the sandy bay. There was a grinding crunch as it hit the beach, the curved underside digging into the wet sand. It shook from the impact and Cresadir toppled from side to side, holding onto the crow's nest very tightly. Daimeh had the wheel to support him. Then, it stopped abruptly.

Cresadir scaled the mast incredibly quickly, as nimble as a small monkey, and Daimeh immediately went below deck, intending to open the sealed side door of the hold, where the cargo was stored. As soon as she reached the moist sand, Cresadir removed the map from her rugged backpack, followed by a compass. She quickly worked out the exact direction in which they had to go and started to walk slowly towards the grassy dunes.

Daimeh was guiding the fully-packed equids off the small ship. They seemed unscathed by the impact and were very compliant. He mounted one and led Cresadir's equid over to her.

"This way – it's not far," Cresadir said, mounting her own equid. They started to ride through the dunes towards the cliff face. In front of them were dense tropics full of activity. Berries poked through the long grasses which hid most of the under-growth. Plump, ripe fruits dangled down from the branches of the many trees, all competing for sunlight.

As they approached the last of the dunes, the plants began to obstruct their path. The air became increasingly clammy and was saturated with the smell of over-ripe berries. They trotted towards the vividly-coloured, sweet-smelling plants, inadver-tently disturbing some local wildlife as they went. Several times leaves rustled under the flowers, followed by short, high squeaking.

Half an hour later they had almost reached the cliff face and could clearly see the thick vegetation growing from the rock and cascading down its side. Small streams carved their way through, washing over the flourishing, dark green leaves.

"It's beautiful, Cresa."

Daimeh was awestruck by the sheer fertility and scale of the nature.

"It's certainly a pleasure to see this sight again," Cresadir said.

As she spoke she felt the amulet warm against her skin. She pulled it from under her loose top and noticed that it had begun to pulsate and was glowing golden.

"Look!" She pointed, scrambling quickly down from her mount.

"Look," she said again.

Daimeh jumped off his equid and walked over to Cresadir. She turned around.

"Wow, it's glowing!" Daimeh said.

"Yes, it's slowly pulsating as well."

She paced a few steps forward and the amulet began to pulsate more quickly.

"It's guiding us. We're close to the first symbol," Cresadir declared.

They continued their hike on foot, leading the equids behind them.

"I've been here before and I never found a way through these cliffs, and believe me I searched. This is so exciting."

Cresadir could not help bursting into laughter. It sounded a little eerie, but she could not stop.

The amulet had begun to flash so rapidly that it was almost permanently glowing.

"It must be here," Cresadir said, gesturing to some grey crumbling rocks that had fallen from the vine-entwined cliff side.

"I don't see anything," Daimeh replied. "Wait."

He heard the indistinct sound of a falling stone. Listening attentively, he heard it bounce off the rock pile, then fall further.

"There – did you hear that?" he asked.

"Yes, there's something behind this rubble," she answered, looking at the map. "And the symbol is just behind there too."

Daimeh went ahead to scout, but he had no idea what he was looking for. A doorway? A cave? A tunnel? He unsheathed his sword and started poking around amongst the debris, managing to loosen some of the smaller stones as he did so.

"Cresa, we need to dig here."

"I'll get the axes," Cresadir replied, hurrying to retrieve them.

Daimeh started hacking at the surrounding undergrowth, then at the vines poking through the rubble. Cresadir returned with pickaxes and they both started digging.

* * *

After two more hours of exhausting shovelling, they had still found nothing.

"Maybe this isn't our destiny," Cresadir said, sounding doubtful.

"Don't give up. Let's keep going. Why does that glow if there's nothing here?" Daimeh asked dejectedly.

"Let's dig more towards the east, the stones seem to fall further in that direction."

* * *

Three hours later, the low sun was upon them. The loud tittering and chirping of earlier in the day had faded to a low chatter and Daimeh could hear the faint trickling of water.

"It goes further down here," he mumbled exhaustedly.

Daimeh continued hacking away at the stones; Cresadir cleared away the dislodged rocks as he went.

Finally, through the dim light that came through the canopy of the trees, he saw something. It seemed to be the top of a massive octagonal doorway. It was perfectly smooth and there were no visible means of opening it. Daimeh could make out part of an engraved design, but the rest was invisible behind more of the rocks.

"There's a faint glow down there, but we need to move these rocks first," Daimeh said, sounding discouraged.

They were both so tired already and at such a late stage in the day the thought of shifting a huge pile of boulders seemed like too much.

Cresadir shook out her dirty, sweaty clothes, then continued hammering the rubble into easily moveable pieces. Daimeh spooned the smaller pieces of gravel, which were easy to dislodge, out of the hole they had dug.

"There! Look! There it is!" He saw a slight gleam through the gaps in the rock. It was unreachable and seemed buried deep below.

"Come on – we're nearly there."

They kept digging, revealing more of the doorway. As they got lower down the rocks became easier to crumble. Only one rock remained and it seemed cemented to the symbol, the light shimmering around the edges. It was almost as if it was magnetically attracted to the shining light.

"Break this last one, Daimeh. It's covering the symbol."

Daimeh lifted his pickaxe and with all his remaining energy he smashed it down onto the stone. It crumbled and fell down to the pile of debris. Daimeh brushed the dust aside and there it was. The symbol from the amulet was engraved into the cliff face, pulsating in synchronicity with it.

Cresadir collapsed to the ground in relief, laughing.

"Haha, we actually found it," she said, as if she hadn't believed they would. "Fascinating, look at it." Looking at the door, she felt unable to believe her eyes. "No Alkoryn made this."

She stood up and brushed dust off the surface.

"The gloss, the pristine smoothness. The material used, it's nothing I've ever seen." She leant forward and swept her hand slowly over the engravings. But she was exhausted and almost immediately slumped back down again.

"Cresa, pass me the amulet."

She unhooked the chain and stretched over to hand Daimeh

the gleaming key. He held it firmly in his hand and removed its chain. Kneeling on the rock pile, he moved the glowing amulet towards its counterpart in the door. They slotted together with ease. The glow spread through the rest of the door's engravings until they were all illuminated. Cracks appeared in the door, and the stone in the centre was thrust backwards; the amulet split into five pieces and the pieces retracted with the door. As the door opened, bright, orange sunlight spilled into the naturally formed cave. Cresadir and Daimeh looked awestruck by the magic that had just taken place in front of them. They stared at each other astonished. Daimeh's jaw hung open.

"Come on," he said, already clambering over the rock piles.

13

Stickiness

Cresadir hauled herself onto her feet and reminded her nephew that they had to go to get the equids. She walked back towards the animals, then tucked her pickaxe onto the carrying bag, grabbed the equids' reins and came towards Daimeh in the doorway.

He jumped down from the rocks and taking his equid from Cresadir, guided it carefully over the rubble. Cresadir and her equid followed.

The small cave darkened as they tunnelled further. The whistling wind in the trees outside made echoes and insects hummed around the stalagmites. There was a musty smell of decomposition and animal excrement. Daimeh took a step forward into a stagnant pool, one of the many on the dirt floor. Cresadir rested her hand on the slimy moss wall for an instant, then cautiously followed. The door slid closed behind them and Daimeh flinched and turned to the only light in the cave, which came from the golden engravings. In the centre of the door was the amulet, somehow reformed and now hovering in front of its mould as if magnetically repelled by it. It held its distance about one inch from the door. Daimeh grabbed it, replaced its long chain and passed it back to Cresadir. The glow coming from both the symbolic necklace and the keyhole immediately ceased. They were in total darkness and the space would have seemed completely empty had it not been for the echoing drips, the warm moist air and the chattering of insects. They could also hear water dribbling down the stalactites and small animals scurrying through the lichen-covered pools.

"I've got a light," Cresadir said suddenly.

She fumbled around in her backpack and found a small, flint

and oil lighter. She flicked it alight, then unpacked the oil lamp and lit the wick. An amber glow began emanating from it. It did not light the way ahead very effectively, but they could see at least a few steps in front of them. Slowly they began to walk into the darkness of the desolate cave.

* * *

After what seemed like a few minutes of walking, they reached an unusual junction where another cave appeared to intersect with theirs. The rock in the other was not crumbling and igneous but from a much darker sediment. The light from their lamp glinted off the smooth tunnel wall. Daimeh tapped it and found that it was hard and almost completely smooth, except for protruding grooves which went vertically all the way around the circle. It was as if it had a hardened protective layer on it. There were no pools, stalagmites, stalactites or vegetation.

As they walked into the middle of the space it became apparent that the caves were formed into a perfect circle with a diameter of about eight feet. There were now four ways to go: back the way they came, left or right through the new cave which seemed more like an artificial tube, or forwards, continuing through the naturally-formed cave.

"Which way?"

"I don't know, Daimeh."

Cresadir swivelled around and held the amulet up in front of her. She took a step into the natural cave ahead. There was no response from the amulet. She checked each cave in turn.

When she took a step into the darkness of the cave on the right the amulet lit up again and started to slowly pulsate.

"This way," she said and began to walk into the perfectly cylindrical passage that led through the cliff, leaving Daimeh to follow with the equids.

Initially, faint sounds from the other cave could still be heard as they advanced into the newer cave. But with each step the sounds got dimmer, until, eventually, there were no sounds at all to be heard. Whatever the wall covering was made from, it was soundproof.

They had been walking for an hour when the amulet began pulsating more quickly again. They continued walking, without knowing how far they had to go.

Suddenly, Cresadir tripped on one of the ridges.

"Ow."

She dropped the lamp and it fizzled out, leaving them covered by the heavy blanket of darkness. The only light came from the glowing amulet.

Daimeh gasped and guided himself to his fallen aunt.

"Are you all right?"

"Yes, I'm fine," she answered, blindly tapping her hands against his. "But we need the lamp."

"I'll go look."

As he moved out of reach of Cresadir there was a low echoing rumble in the distance, then a slight vibration. Daimeh froze in his steps and the equids quivered, making distressed noises.

Cresadir inhaled sharply.

"What was that?" she whispered into the darkness. "Quickly, find that light!"

There was another vibration, which made the lamp clatter loudly.

"I've nearly got it," Daimeh said. He nimbly walked over the trembling ridges and grabbed the lamp, then sat himself down next to the wall. He tried to light it but the vibrations were making it increasingly hard. The juddering stopped and stale air whisked through the tunnel as a louder rumble encapsulated them. Daimeh took this opportunity to light the lamp.

Now they could see that there was something large behind them. It moved closer, and the ground quivered beneath it.

Slowly emerging from the veil of darkness was an immense

creature. The equids immediately panicked and pulling free of Cresadir, they ran ahead into the murkiness.

"We've got to go," Daimeh said hastily, seizing her hands and jerking her to her feet.

He stretched out his arm, wanting to illuminate a little more of the creature. He saw a bony jaw and a cream-coloured, translucent mouth with teeth protruding from it. The shape filled the entire passage. It looked like a worm of some sort and as it got closer the smell of stomach bile became stronger.

"Oh my goodness! Run, Daimeh!"

Cresadir tightly squeezed her nephew's hand and they both ran, taking care not to trip over the rough terrain of the tunnel.

"It's moving very slowly. We can outrun it, Cresa, watch your pace."

* * *

After they had been jogging for some time, the noise of the worm began to diminish and they slowed to a walking pace.

"You think it'll catch up?" Daimeh asked.

He checked the oil lamp then looked at his aunt.

"It will. We need to get out of this tunnel." Cresadir had a basic knowledge of how smaller worms behaved, but whether that would be much use with a creature of this size she did not know.

Up ahead, they could see another four-way junction and as they got closer they could hear the equids snorting in a disgruntled manner. They were hiding in the left, naturally formed, cave. Cresadir and Daimeh rested there.

"Interesting that the worm doesn't touch these caves," Cresadir said, slapping her hand against the knobbly stone wall.

"These walls are solid. Perhaps it can't gnaw through them and instead finds weak spots in order to make its own passageways."

"Sounds plausible," Daimeh replied.

Cresadir examined the sediment under the hard casing. "Yes, you can see this is more of a mushy soil, it seems watery, so…"

She was interrupted by a low trembling.

"The worm's coming this way," she said, and sat down by the wall. "But I don't believe it's interested in us."

"And you want to test this theory *now?*"

The lamp rattled as Daimeh held it tighter.

"Trust me," Cresadir replied in a soothing voice.

The tremors increased and they knew that soon the worm would appear in the cave. Cresadir took the lamp and glanced around the corner.

"It's nearly here, stay calm," she whispered.

They could hear a slimy squelching as the creature got closer. There was a clacking noise; the worm was instinctively snapping its jaws as it wiggled through the cave.

Daimeh and his aunt pressed themselves firmly against the mossy wall, pulling the equids as close to them as they could. The worm slowly moved past them, ignoring them. They watched its body segments pushing and pulling against each other until it reached the cave ahead.

"See, it just wants to gnaw on new moistened rock for nutrients," Cresadir said, sounding relieved. "We should follow it, eventually it will tunnel out of the cliff."

They moved out of their hiding place and stepped into the now mucus-covered cave. It didn't have a face as such, and its tail was indistinguishable from its bulbous body. Fresh sticky slime was under their feet and their shoes kept getting pulled into the sludge.

"Daimeh! Careful you don't get this on your skin – you saw how solid it gets."

"I know," he said, and he yanked his shoe free, protecting his hand with his shirt.

* * *

They continued onwards for hours, moving at the worm's pace, following it along caves, sometimes even going through the ones they had already been in again. They often heard other worms rumbling from another part of the cave system. Lifting their shoes from the sticky tunnel floor only made them more exhausted, but they knew they could not rest. As they walked the glow of the amulet sometimes ceased, but it would always reactivate after a while. Daimeh and Cresadir felt disheartened by their lack of progress and were frustrated that they didn't know when their fruitless treck would end.

* * *

Another hour had passed and the amulet's pulsations had again quickened. They could hear the faint sound of trickling water and rock being crushed.

"Hear that? We're heading out I think!" Cresadir said excitedly.

"Thank goodness, I'm not sure how much longer I can keep walking through this stuff," Daimeh replied, puffing.

The worm had slowed down even more, the sound of its grinding jaws became louder and echoes could be heard from what they assumed was a natural cave ahead. Eventually, the noise of rock crumbling stopped and the worm sped up its pace, now moving faster than they had seen it move since they began following it. As it crawled and wiggled its way out, sunlight began to flicker into the cave, together with a rush of fresh air, dry and gritty on the tongue.

"Nearly there," Cresadir spluttered exhaustedly, wiping her forehead. At first the whistling air was cooling but as their clothes dried, the torrid heat quickly became apparent. "I think it's a desert up there."

"Our flasks are nearly empty," Daimeh said, shaking the water-bottles. They could both hear that there was only a dribble inside.

"I can see a steep rock face just out there," Cresadir said, pointing. "I hope we're in a canyon, if we are, we shouldn't be far from water."

The cave exit eventually cleared and they walked out into a narrow, shadowy gorge. To their relief there was a steady stream flowing through the ravine and along its edge were a few sprouting sprigs of vegetation. The worm sploshed across the stream and started burrowing into the next wall of rock, leaving its tell-tale trail behind it.

The amulet was still slowly blinking. Cresadir turned left and it slowed still further.

"We need to go right," she said, unrolling the map.

Daimeh was busy whacking his shoes against the ground.

"I want to get this stuff off first."

"Good idea." Cresadir paused and thought for a moment. "Actually, we should rest here tonight."

She walked away from the cave exit and put her backpack on the ground, then took the carrying bag from the equid. She removed a large, soft blanket, woven by Miah, and laid it on the sandy ground.

"Going to help?" she demanded of Daimeh; it wasn't really a question – he didn't have a choice.

Daimeh helped her to set up a small campsite and once he had finished he walked the equids to the stream to clean the sticky sludge from their hooves. When he returned to the serenity of the campsite, his aunt was lying down in the shade.

"Aunt Cresa?"

"Yes, Daimeh."

"Do we really know what we're doing?" he asked.

"I have my doubts. We've no clue where we're headed," she answered, crossing her legs. "But we're curious about this map and where it might lead."

"What if it leads somewhere dangerous?" Daimeh asked.

"It might."

She sat up.

"We have to expect anything that may come."

"I feel so unprepared for this," Daimeh said, bowing his head as he sighed.

"Don't worry, we're as prepared as we can be. We're explorers – the first real Alkoryn explorers," she reassured him.

Then she asked another question, "Tell me why you're here, Daimeh?"

"Well…"

He looked at his aunt.

"My heart has been full of adventure my whole life and when I found the body and saw the map, it lit a spark."

His face shone with passion as he spoke. "Travelling to foreign lands. I knew it was just a dream, but I think I followed it through quite well."

"Indeed you did," Cresadir replied, smiling warmly. "I admire it, I wish I had had your tenacity when I was younger. Maybe I felt held back by my duties, I don't know."

"Cresa?"

"M-hm."

"What do *you* think we'll find?"

She chuckled.

"Hmm, let me think," she said, clearing her throat. "I simply want to see beyond Alkoryn, and that's what I'm doing. When I was young I was very religious and the idea that Aedolyn existed somewhere excited me so much. As I grew older, as you know, my ideas about the world changed, as a result of my father's influence. I was the only one he could relate to, and that was because of our common interest, science."

Her voice deepened, taking on an edge of sarcasm. "That was most likely why the rest called me his favourite."

Resuming her normal tone, she continued, "At that point Aedolyn seemed no more real to me than the possibility of riding on the clouds. So, I started experimenting – looking at things through powerful glasses, mixing and boiling available alcohols. I taught myself basic maths, and began dissecting dead animals. I know – a bit grotesque for a young girl!" She smiled. "Then I met your uncle and moved to be the head of Bayhaven, then we had Oeradon."

She looked contemplative. "My duties took over. I was now a head and had to take care of the wellbeing of the inhabitants of Bayhaven. The science got left behind. Then your uncle went missing and everything changed."

She paused for a few moments before continuing.

"What happened to your uncle upset me so very much that I almost broke completely, and the rest you know."

She searched in her satchel for something to eat, and, finding an apple, began to nibble on it.

"To answer your question – what I think we'll find…"

She paused and thought for a moment.

"Answers… answers to the questions I've always had. I believe we're heading to the place they call the Golden Lands, and whether this be for religious or scientific reasons remains to be seen. But if the old books are right, we have nothing to fear from this place."

"I'm looking for answers too." Daimeh smiled. "I'll get a bite to eat now, then go to bed."

"All right, Daimeh, sleep tight."

* * *

In the morning, after Daimeh refilled their leather water pouches, he fed the equids. They both mounted up and set off through the ravine. After trotting for an hour, Cresadir saw a glint in the distance, and looking closer, noticed a small bunker built into the cliff face ahead. The glint had come from light bouncing off the bunker's chrome door. Pointing, she drew Daimeh's attention towards it.

"What?" he asked, squinting, looking in the same direction. "Oh. Yeah."

"We should take a look."

The door was also uniquely etched like the one at the cave entrance. The amulet was shining brightly and so was an engraved symbol in the centre of the door. It was the same shape as the amulet they held.

"We need to be here," she said, putting the key in the lock and opening the door.

They entered a bizarre, tiny room. It seemed to have liquid walls, made from some kind of molten, metallic fluid. They stood still for a moment, confused, and then Daimeh saw a small transparent container in the middle of the room. Inside, there was a second talisman, and an unusual device, oblong in shape and hand-sized. It was the same material as the tablet he had found at Galunda Bay, and had the same smooth edges with nothing visible on its face.

The amulet around Cresadir's neck ceased glowing and the other one began to pulsate gently.

"Should I smash it, Cresa?"

"Yes."

Daimeh unsheathed his sword and swung it down onto the thin glass, which shattered easily.

Cresadir removed the first key from its chain and put it safely into her backpack. She threaded the new amulet onto the chain and put it around her neck. Daimeh picked up the smooth tablet and pocketed it. They left the small room and continued through the ravine.

14

Gargantuan

As they reached the mouth of the canyon they saw that the stream splashed over the edge, forming a waterfall. Steam was rising upwards from the steepness of the drop. They could see they were on a cliff-top and that the ground below was volcanic. The landscape seemed unnatural, as if it had been dropped from the sky and embedded into the ravine, destroying all the cliffs.

Daimeh ran to the edge.

"There's no way down!" he called, his voice echoing.

Turning back, he caught a glimpse of something odd. There was a short crack in the cliff face, and from it a metallic liquid was trickling – similar to what they had seen in the bunker.

"Come here! I found something!" he shouted to Cresadir.

They both watched as the liquid streamed far down into a basin below.

"Um, what do we do?" Daimeh asked, folding his arms.

"What about the black object you picked up?"

"Hmm?"

Daimeh casually took the device from his trouser pocket.

"Let's see," he said, staring at it.

He touched the surface and one side lit up, illuminating all the symbols.

"Just press a few," Cresadir instructed, a touch of impatience in her tone.

Daimeh began tapping the symbols. The first few did nothing, but then he touched one which activated another screen, which showed just two dots.

"Let me see that," Cresadir requested, eagerly.

"No, Cresa, I can do this!" Daimeh snapped at his aunt.

He pressed his forefinger down on each dot separately. They

both vibrated. *Hmmm?* He tried holding his finger on one; this just made it vibrate without stopping. Then he slid his finger over the surface and a surprising thing happened.

"Oh my goodness. The liquid's moving!" Daimeh shuffled backwards, his voice suddenly high-pitched.

"Oh, now that is interesting," Cresadir said.

He placed one thumb on one dot, and the other thumb on the other dot, then ran his thumbs over the surface of the tablet. The object vibrated faster or slower depending on where his thumbs were. He looked up, but kept moving his thumbs. The liquid formed random shapes as he did so. He directed the vibrations so they grew faster, and the liquid began making a more familiar shape. A stairway.

"It's working. It'll show us how to get down."

"I know, Daimeh."

He slid his thumbs around until the vibrations became more intense. A more complete stairway formed, stretching down to the bottom of the cliff. The shaking stopped and the mysterious object became calm once more, but the steps downward remained.

Placing the tablet into his backpack, Daimeh said, "Let's move."

They pulled the equids close and cautiously began to make their way down the flowing, metallic liquid staircase.

* * *

The sun had peaked in the highest part of the cloudless sky and was boiling with heat. This was the highest they had ever seen it. They mounted their equids and began to trot along the hot, soggy soot. The black volcanic terrain was barren of any vegetation and stank of sulphur, making the equids cough.

"It's all right, honey; I know you're tired," Daimeh said, lovingly patting his equid's mane.

The sound of rubble and ash crumbling could be heard as they traversed the ground, and the amulet continued to glow, seeming to direct them towards the largest volcano in sight. They passed bubbling, steaming, lava pools. Little scurrying lizards popped their heads above the small rocks, then, seeing the riders, leapt down into their burrows.

Daimeh exhaled sharply as they came nearer to the volcano.

"We can't get too close to that."

"We'll get as close as the heat will let us. If we're lucky the amulet may change the direction."

* * *

Daimeh took a swig from his water-bag as they approached the volcano. The heat had intensified and the symbol was still directing them to go closer.

"Hmm, it's going to be impossible for us to get closer," Daimeh said apprehensively.

"We must be missing something," Cresadir replied, and as she spoke an enormous creature flew out of the top of the volcano. Daimeh and Cresadir stopped dead in their tracks, their eyes widened and their faces drained of blood. The amulet had by now become fully illuminated.

"It's the beast I saw from a distance on my last travels," Cresadir gasped. "Oh no."

The immense animal, with a wingspan the length of Lybas, soared in circles above them. They were the size of insects in comparison. Its body was a deep cerulean blue, fading to a bright turquoise at the extremities. They immediately started galloping in the opposite direction; they knew they couldn't outrun it, but they had little other choice.

"Don't run."

A thunderous voice from above spoke to the fleeing Alkoryns. "Don't run," it repeated, sounding almost soothing.

"Huh," Daimeh said, halting his equid and turning around. "Cresa, it's all right. I think."

Cresadir stopped too.

The huge creature made one last circle in the bright sky, then began to descend towards them.

There was a booming sound as it landed, its human-like hands and feet opening small fissures in the ash-covered ground. Daimeh and Cresadir nearly fell off their mounts from the shock. Once the vibrations had stopped they jumped down to greet the creature, which was lowering its head down to their level. Its face was gigantic, but its features were not much different to those of a person. It had big, deep-set eyes with white irises, a broad, flat nose, and a wide mouth.

"Don't fear me, my purpose is to serve you," the creature told them, its low, rough voice making the earth rumble.

"What?" Cresadir was surprised. "Who asked you to serve us?"

"I was sent here to defend this land, but then I received word that I had another purpose here." It snorted. "I have something for you."

"Am I the only one confused here?" Daimeh asked, sitting down on a nearby rock.

Cresadir turned to him.

"I'm not sure either. It would seem this... fellow... has been expecting us."

The enormous creature rose up onto its two legs and shuffled its left foot towards them.

"Take a look."

Warily they approached the big toe; it was the height of a man. The skin was thick and coarse and a dirty teal in colour.

"Look under the nail," it said.

Cresadir climbed up, holding onto the cracked edge of the nail and then pulling Daimeh up after her. The nail was as solid as granite and caked in sooty mud, and the foul smell of mould rose from between the toes.

"Look there, it's glowing."

Daimeh pointed to an area just near the cuticle.

The amulet was now shining without interruption, and it was clear they were in the right place. Cresadir immediately went to the glowing area, her neckpiece seemingly pulling her towards it. She dampened a cloth and wiped away the grime revealing a keyhole the same shape as her symbol. She magnetised them against one another as she had done before and the glow began to spread towards what looked like a panel on the surface of the nail. There was a sudden mechanical noise and the panel began to rise upwards until a small, transparent cube was revealed. The third key was inside.

"What's happening? This can't be real," Daimeh said in disbelief. He stood up, rubbed his face and began to pace back and forth, his arms waving and tensing.

"I don't believe this thing is organic," Cresadir said, touching the cube's immaculately smooth surface.

"I'm not even going to ask."

Daimeh felt overwhelmed by the magic, if that's what it was, and jumped down off the toe.

Cresadir detached the third amulet and the second ceased to radiate. She attached it to the chain and put it around her neck before carefully sliding down.

She was very curious about the huge creature. "What was in your toe wasn't natural, where are you from?" she shouted up to it.

It stood up proudly. "I have one memory of being somewhere blue. I think it was my mother's womb, so I can assure you I am real. My other memories are of this place and defending it." It sighed before continuing. "I had a vision, in which I was told that visitors would come to this land and that I was to give you whatever was in my toe and show you a message."

"A message?"

"Yes, I'll show you," he replied, placing one hand either side of the two adventurers.

"What are you doing?" Cresadir asked.

"Wait, and you'll see."

A deep golden glow appeared at the tip of each of the creature's fingers and thumbs. After a few seconds, rays began to shine down onto Cresadir and Daimeh. A small, octagon room was appearing around them. In it was an elegantly styled chaise longue, an engraved wooden cupboard and a beautifully crafted chair, carved from a rich sepia-coloured wood, marbled with knots, and polished to a fine lustre.

"I've seen enough," Daimeh said almost walking through a complete wall before it fully visualised. The walls were smooth and painted a sandy rust colour. There was a single painting, showing a lustrous green land, full of vividly colourful plants; a brilliant blue sky was overhead, and the scene was lit by bright sunlight.

A blurry image of a person also began to appear. After a little while they could see that it was a woman with wide, round eyes, a soft flame colour.

"Welcome, Alkoryn travellers," she said in a sultry voice.

"Hello," Cresadir replied, disbelieving the evidence of her own eyes. She didn't understand how she could be talking to an illusion.

"You've found the clues I left for you. It was my intention for you to send my message to a place called Amunisari," the strange woman explained. "The people are the most gracious of any I have known, but I must warn you not to trust the council, who are corrupt."

She walked behind Cresadir, and reappeared on her other side.

"There's one more symbol for you to find, and that will grant you access to the citadel doors. This gargantuan will take you to your next destination. May your travels be safe."

As soon as she had spoken her final words, the three-dimensional scene vanished in a second, but Cresadir was still surrounded by the gargantuan's two great hands. After a few moments, the hands lifted; looking around, she saw Daimeh on his equid, ready to travel further.

"We're supposed to travel with this creature," she called to him.

"No!" Daimeh replied, adamant; he turned his equid around and began to ride off.

"Waaaaait." The roar came from above as the towering creature knelt down and placed its open hand onto the ground. "I'll take you, then you can rest."

"Oh – no, no, no," Daimeh insisted.

"Come on, Daimeh – it'll take days off our journey," Cresadir urged.

She had already instructed her equid to board the creature's palm, but it was too high up for it to reach by jumping. She dismounted and climbed on.

"I'm going. I can meet you there," she said, then continued, smirking. "I'll need to leave the equid though – maybe she can be company for you."

"Damn it, Cresa," Daimeh said, following her cautiously.

Cresadir clapped her hands at the equids and pointed back the way they had come. She shouted, "Shoo!" The equids reared and ran in the opposite direction.

Daimeh felt sad about leaving the equids behind. He hoped they found somewhere safe to go.

The creature suddenly clutched onto the two of them with its chunky fingers and they flew upwards.

"Whooooooooaaaaaa!"

Daimeh's stomach dropped to what felt like his feet, like a rock falling into water. He waved his hands all around, trying to find a good hold whilst screaming loudly.

The more the creature sped up, the more excited Cresadir got.

She began laughing uncontrollably, and shouting, "Woooo! This is great!"

She's insane, Daimeh thought.

The ride became steadier once they had reached a stable altitude. They were both very weary and settled themselves in the grooves of the creature's palm and fell into a restful sleep.

* * *

The weightless feeling as they descended woke Daimeh up but Cresadir just slept through it, completely unaware.

The creature was slowing down dramatically and the eventual landing was gentle. The gargantuan's grip on Daimeh and Cresadir slowly loosened. The sudden sunlight blinded Daimeh and the moist air almost choked him. The scent of flowers and musty earth was the first thing he was aware of, then he heard birds calling, the rustling of scurrying animals and the roars of larger ones. His eyes gradually adjusted and a jungle was revealed; it spread across a plateau.

He shook Cresadir vigorously and she woke with a start. She yelped and covered her eyes quickly against the sunlight.

"Oh, we've landed."

"It's beautiful, Cresa."

"Yes, give me a moment."

Her eyes began to adjust and she inhaled deeply.

"Amazing."

They slid off the hand and the colossal creature knelt down and lowered its head.

It pointed in the direction ahead of them. "A few hours travel that way and you will be where you need to be," it told them. It leapt upwards and opened its wings, turning around and flying back towards the volcano before Cresadir could even say thanks.

Daimeh stood and watched the gargantuan fly away, wondering what had just happened and how such a beast could exist.

"Cresa," Daimeh turned to his aunt. "Are you not affected by this?"

"What do you mean?"

"That creature? The illusion of that room you were in?" He paused. "It's like I'm living in a dream."

"Of course it baffles me too, I've so many questions that I don't think it could have answered them all." She put her back pack on. "It must all be there in our myths, except they're not myths, they're real." She looked into the direction they were headed. "We should make a move."

Before long, they realised that, on foot, it was going to be quite a trek. They filled their water-bags in the nearest stream and walked north into the blooming primeval forest.

* * *

They had been walking all afternoon, but still could see nothing ahead but more jungle.

"Is the amulet glowing? Daimeh asked. "I'm not convinced this is the right way."

"Of course it is. I do check it you know," Cresadir, replied, obviously finding it difficult to believe that Daimeh could think her so absent-minded.

Daimeh walked on ahead. After a few moments Cresadir heard a sudden 'bonk' and saw Daimeh wobble backwards and fall into the soft undergrowth.

"Are you all right, did you trip?" Cresadir asked, kneeling down next to him.

"No, I hit something."

He waved his hand vaguely.

"Go check for yourself."

Cresadir carefully walked forward, her arms stretched in front of her, scanning the jungle floor as she went. After a few seconds her hands hit something – something smooth and solid and invisible.

"What's this?" she asked, patting at it.

"It's blocking our way, whatever it is."

"I've seen the most amazing things on this journey, but this one confuses me the most," said Daimeh, who was still sitting among the leaves.

Cresadir looked at the amulet and saw that it was flashing, faintly and slowly. She walked east along the barrier and it slowed further.

"It's west," she declared, holding out her hand and helping Daimeh get to his feet.

Avoiding trees and roots, they trustingly followed the guidance of the amulet which was now glowing brightly.

"It's here; look around, Daimeh."

They both ruffled their way through flowers, ferns and roots. Daimeh was stung by a plant and pulled his hand back as fast as he could.

They searched for hours and by low-sun they had still found nothing; but it was then that Cresadir spotted an unusually thick-stalked plant, pastel green in colour and swinging unnaturally, not in time with the wind. On closer examination, she noticed the whole plant was artificial. Its stalk began to glow revealing an engraved keyhole, then the hidden amulet shone through the now semi-transparent stalk.

"Found it!" she shouted.

Daimeh rushed towards her just as she was placing the symbol into its slot. As had happened with the gargantuan, a panel appeared which rose up to form a cube. The amulet was inside.

She pocketed the now inactive symbol she had carried and gently took up the final amulet.

Almost instantly the jungle beyond the barrier vanished, replaced by an astonishing citadel set in a sandy, desolate landscape. Extraordinarily tall, its architecture was unusually daunting, featuring irregular angular panels laid into glossy, white marble walls. There was an eye-catching glass dome in the centre of the citadel and atop one of the many spires was a huge glass sphere.

Drawn to its magnificence, Daimeh and Cresadir crossed the previously blocked area without any resistance.

There was no sign of a doorway at first, but then geometric engravings suddenly appeared on the wall and an entrance opened…

One week earlier.

"Sire, there's a problem."

Ceolm, a sullen man, looked up from his desk.

"What sort of a problem?"

"Was the simulation ended without my knowledge?" the young technician asked, sounding confused. "Because it's gone."

"Show me," Ceolm said, standing up straight.

The technician walked towards a nearby wall and made a gesture with his hand. The tiles moved and the whole wall turned into a screen showing a map of a barren landscape.

"Look, Alkoryn has vanished – as if it did not exist."

Ceolm's wrinkles deepened. "Initiate 'Terminate' protocol," he said.

15

The Citadel

The doors of the grand citadel opened and two weary Alkoryns walked into the entrance chamber. Alabaster statues were positioned at regular intervals, interspersed with arched doorways, above, were two rows of balconies. The luxurious chamber was showered with brilliant lights from spotlights. A beautiful, slim, young woman was standing on the balcony from where she had a good view of the visitors. She witnessed their amazement as they entered the sanctum. Hmmm, here was a man from the lifeless lands, she thought, peering at Daimeh with fascination. Her father, Ceolm, who was also present, glanced up at her with a bitter expression. On the balcony opposite there was a well-dressed middle-aged woman.

Five men in creamy robes with sparkling platinum belt-buckles approached. Ceolm stepped forward; he looked both mature and oddly youthful. He offered his hand to the travellers, making a gesture of peace.

"Welcome to Amunisari. I am Ceolm," he said, before indicating the men behind him. "And these are my associates."

He clasped his hands before him.

"We're not accustomed to guests. However, we've been expecting you."

Daimeh stared silently into Ceolm's eyes; they were crystal blue with flecks of white in the iris. They appeared hard and insincere.

"Hello, we're from Alkoryn. I'm Cresadir and this is my nephew Daimeh – and what do you mean 'expecting us'?" Cresadir asked, suspiciously.

"Yes, thanks to our means of surveillance, we saw you approaching the citadel from quite a distance."

"I see," she replied, her eyes narrowed.

"How did you find us?" Ceolm asked.

"We were guided by this," Daimeh said, showing him the map. "There's some text on the other side, but we aren't able to read it."

At that, Ceolm lowered his hood to reveal anthracite black hair, so dark that it seemed to absorb light. Silently taking the parchment he turned it over and examined the scriptures. A look of worry crossed his face and he quickly rolled it up again, and then gave it to his assistant. He cleared his throat.

"I must see to some other business," he said abruptly, and departed from the chamber.

"Come, you need a change of clothes – your journey must have been challenging," one of the two gentle-looking men wearing stark white robes and guiding them out of the chamber said.

They were led through a vast expanse of gardens; a towering obelisk stood in the middle, similar to the one in Aedolyn's Promise, but perhaps twice its height. It pointed directly upwards, towards the sun that was beaming down on the gardens.

"Our sun moves very little from that position, it just rotates around the top of the obelisk, like a halo," the second guide told them.

The gardens went on as far as the eye could see, encased in a grandiose dome-like structure. The ceiling was completely see-through so Daimeh and Cresadir were able to gaze at the sun, and to their surprise it didn't hurt their eyes. The lush gardens were surrounded by walls from which shapes protruded, seemingly at random.

Cresadir gasped in astonishment, rendered absolutely speechless. The prophecy told of such a place. But to know it was real, she thought, losing her balance slightly. Daimeh quickly grabbed her hand.

"Aunt Cresa, are you all right?"

He had noticed a marked difference in his aunt since her arrival.

"I'm wonderful," she replied.

Teardrops gathered in her eyes. She had been searching for this oasis her entire life.

"I'm better than wonderful," she said, then fell silent once more.

* * *

Elisaris, the enchanting young woman Daimeh and Cresadir had seen on the balcony, was now walking down a spiral stairway towards the ground floor. Reaching the bottom, she found that the two guides were showing the Alkoryns to their rooms. She walked under the archways and behind a column, watching the visitors intently but discreetly. She observed Daimeh thanking his assistant. So polite, she thought.

Daimeh caught a glimpse of Elisaris out of the corner of his eye and turned his head to watch her. She was so delicate and graceful that it seemed like she was hovering over the smooth floor rather than walking. She maintained eye contact with him from a distance before walking under another archway. Daimeh felt an overwhelming sensation of warmth inside his chest. He had never before seen such a beauty – she was angelic. His heart quickened, and he knew he had to meet her.

* * *

Having thanked his escort, Daimeh entered his room. The oval chamber was elegant and spacious with relaxing cream walls. The light reflected of an enormous glass enclosure, revealing colourful deep-sea animals, none of which Daimeh recognised. Through an archway, he could hear the relaxing sound of water flowing. It was surreal after the arduous journey he had just endured. Looking around, he noticed that white robes had been laid out on the luxurious bed. He strolled through the archway and was greeted by an astonishing bathing room, colourful flowers and lush green plants contrasting with white walls. The water flowed down a wall into the bath, glistened like sapphire. In a trance-like state, he undressed and stepped into the bath. The water was oily and the dirt dissolved from his body. It was the perfect temperature; sunlight glared down through the glass ceiling, slightly dimmed and refracted. Daimeh took this opportunity to look at the sun without shielding his eyes. He watched a heavenly cloud pass overhead, white and perfectly fluffy, prisoner of the wind. Listening to the relaxing ripple of the water, he drifted into sleep. Had he really found paradise?

* * *

Daimeh woke gradually to angelic chanting. He felt incredibly refreshed; although he was sure he had only been asleep for a short time. He rose from the water and looked around for a towel. It was then he realised that the air in the room had almost immediately dried his skin, leaving it immaculately soft – softer than it had ever been.

He walked under the arch into the bedroom and picked up the clean robes from the bed, then wrapped the amazingly soft fabric around his body. The gentle chanting was still continuing and he could feel it calming his soul, so he lay self-indulgently on the bed for a few more minutes. A bell sounded and the see-through image of a citadel resident appeared on a curved section of the wall. Daimeh was completely taken aback: this seemed like magic.

A young man spoke to him in a pleasant, gentle voice. "Good morning, Daimeh. Please, join us for some breakfast."

Morning? He had obviously slept for much longer than he had thought. He walked towards the doorway, which opened for him, and the man he had seen on his wall stood in front of him, ready to show him the way.

* * *

Daimeh was led through the gardens by the young man. He couldn't see many people about. The citadel was obviously built for a powerful civilisation, and yet appeared to have only a small population.

"Here it is," his escort said, abruptly stopping before a door.

Unevenly-shaped triangles set into the wall began glowing and the door slid open, revealing another radiant room. There was a large, oblong, alabaster-coloured table in the middle. Ceolm sat with his wife on one side of him, and the astonishingly gorgeous young woman Daimeh had seen earlier on the other. Cresadir sat opposite them and he could see a lovely pearl-covered chair waiting vacant and ready for him. But to him, everything except the beautiful woman was a blur. He watched her take a bread roll from the centre of the table. Her hair was golden amber with light blonde highlights and soft; it cascaded down her shoulders and bounced a little as she moved. Daimeh stood in the doorway for a few moments longer than he should have before walking to his chair.

"This is my wife, Eleanor," Ceolm said, then turned to indicate the woman Daimeh had been gazing at. "And this is my daughter, Elisaris."

Elisaris looked up coyly, watching Daimeh settle into his seat. She waited until her father had initiated the pleasantries before greeting him individually with a nod of her head. "It's my pleasure to meet you," she said in a delicate voice.

Daimeh was magnetised by her two-tone blue eyes, aqua at their centre but darker around the rim of her iris. They were large and round – the most captivating eyes he had ever seen. She returned his gaze for a moment before smiling and returning her attention to the food. Daimeh had been too distracted to take any food. He felt lost in his own world and time. It was as if everything around him was moving faster and the only people unaffected by it were himself and Elisaris.

Ceolm's voice jolted him out of his trance. "You may eat, Daimeh."

"Er, yes, of course," he mumbled, seeing that his aunt was already tucking into a full plate of food. Noticing that his palms were a little sweaty, he took a roll of bread for himself.

Elisaris giggled under her breath, but Daimeh was unaware of her amusement. His nervousness was obvious to her as he stumbled over his words, but she found it adorable.

Listening to the morning conversation she delicately ate her food, glancing periodically at Daimeh. Cresadir and Ceolm were conversing about their journey to the citadel.

"Yes, we're a very secretive civilisation," Ceolm answered, before quickly changing the subject. "So, tell me – excuse me if I'm prying..."

He paused for a few moments, thinking.

"How did you come by this map?"

Cresadir put down her fork before answering.

"A rhajok'don brought it to us."

"Brought it?" he asked, trying not to sound too eager.

"Well, his body washed ashore at the Galunda Bay," Cresadir explained.

"And how do you know of the rhajok'don?" Ceolm asked, listening intently for her answer.

"My father, the Monarch of Alkoryn, has a basement library from ancient days, when the scholars occupied the capital. There are books and manuscripts going back thousands of years."

Ceolm tried to hide his deep curiosity, but Cresadir could see his eagerness. Choosing his words carefully, he asked "So, your people, the Alkoryns... you say, do they know of the Amunisari and this citadel?"

"No, traditionally we worship a Goddess known as Aedolyn, who came from the Golden Lands, but I always thought they were only stories."

She laughed. "I never believed it would be a real place."

"Well, I've not heard this place referred to as the Golden Lands for quite some time, but as you can see we're very much real," Ceolm replied, nodding and smiling.

"So what is it that you do here?" Cresadir asked.

Ceolm was a little taken aback by the question but he felt there was no harm in answering.

"We research in order to better educate ourselves. We also mine a crystalline substance to power our technology."

"I'm quite the scientist myself, although not quite at your level," Cresadir replied with a smile. "Since being here I've also reconnected to my religion. You won't mind if I say that I see you as deities?"

They were deities, Ceolm thought. "Of course not," he agreed.

"Sire, you're needed."

A pleasant voice summoned Ceolm from the breakfast table.

He dabbed his mouth with a cloth and poured Daimeh another glass of exquisitely fruity juice, then stood abruptly.

"I'm very pleased you've visited our citadel. But, bear in mind that we don't leave our walls..."

He bowed respectfully.

"Please excuse me."

Elisaris interrupted, pushing her plate forward as if finished. "We didn't even know about you. We were told the lands beyond the walls were uninhabitable."

She stopped speaking for a moment, looking closely at her father as he hurried from the room.

"Clearly, they're not."

She seemed a little upset and stood up, her robe flowing.

"I must leave now, thank you for a lovely breakfast."

And with that, she also left the table.

"I'll leave you two to finish. Go where you please – I'm sure there's much for you to see here." Eleanor smiled hospitably before following her daughter out of the room.

Cresadir immediately turned to Daimeh and smiled elatedly. "This place! Isn't it amazing? The power they have here; it's nothing I can rationally explain. My only answer is that it comes from our Goddess. I think I feel a sense of faith once more. The enchanted walls of this citadel can only be explained by the magic of Aedolyn."

Daimeh took his aunt's hand. It's true, he thought – the tablet had come from here and that was enchanted with magic. He smiled into Cresadir's eyes.

"It was a map to the Golden Lands."

* * *

Ceolm walked down a short corridor and entered a large conference room. As he walked in asymmetrical slates on the wall began to slide apart, revealing a surface onto which an image of a bare landscape was projected.

The four other members of the council were already present, sitting around the elliptical table.

"They were *never* supposed to come here!" Ceolm shouted, slamming his fist on the table. "How has this happened?"

The four others started at the noise, and one rose from his chair, saying, "Sire, we knew from surveillance that they would come."

"No, a rhajok'don brought them a map!" Ceolm said, in a harsh tone.

The council member sat down and another stood up.

"Someone wanted them to come here. One of us."

"Not one of us," Ceolm replied. "*One of the banished.*"

16

Pleasantries

After breakfast Daimeh and Cresadir took a walk through the glorious gardens which were tinted with a golden glow. They marvelled about the strangeness of the building: in the citadel, doors activated as they passed by, and when they slid closed again there was no sign that they had ever been there. The citadel was so vast and yet at the same time so empty.

As they walked, Cresadir whispered to Daimeh under her breath, "Are they all hiding? It's too quiet..."

"There is something very strange about this place," Daimeh replied, looking around in a somewhat paranoid manner.

They walked closer to the distinctive water feature, past lush topiaries. Having arrived, they both gasped at the unbelievable height of the obelisk. The tall column was surrounded at its base by water. Cresadir looked up to the top and saw the sun, which here was almost white, shining down on the water. In the blue sky, she saw a shooting star stream past, a sight that was very rare in Alkoryn. She inhaled quickly.

"A star," she said, smiling involuntarily. She watched it until it disappeared from view and then she placed her hand into the water, feeling its freshness on her fingers. Cresadir had not been herself since arriving; she seemed lost in a fantasy.

Daimeh left her staring at the water and walked around the statue, hoping to appreciate it better. When he reached the other side, he stopped in his tracks: there, in front of him, was Elisaris, sitting on an immaculate garden bench facing the aqueous monument. She peered up at him, clearly having noticed his reaction.

"Daimeh. Please sit," she said, gently tapping the bench next to her.

The young Alkoryn hesitantly walked towards her, trying to calm his emotions. "It's truly astonishing," he said. "The waterfall..."

"Yes, indeed it is," she replied, closing her book.

"...And so quiet here. Where are the people? I've only seen a handful in this huge place."

"We are not many."

She sounded troubled when she spoke.

"Excuse me," she said politely, then briskly walked away.

"Erm, bye."

It was his first real meeting with Elisaris and he felt completely bemused. He rose from the bench and walked around the waterfall looking for Cresadir. But she was gone. Daimeh looked all around but there was nobody. Just the sound of the waterfall.

"Cresa!" he called. He had no idea where she could have gone.

"Your aunt has retreated to her room. Don't worry," Ceolm said, suddenly appearing like a ghost.

Daimeh quickly turned around. "Hmm," he said.

He was beginning to feel suspicious; something did not feel right to him.

"So peaceful, is it not?" Ceolm asked calmly.

"A little too peaceful," Daimeh answered. "The scripture I gave you. What did it say?"

Ceolm expression changed.

"We don't know," he lied.

But Daimeh's suspicions were growing. "I see," he said carefully. "Well, I'll go to my room now, if that's all right."

"Of course. Relax."

* * *

Elisaris found the closest way out of the garden and then hastily walked down a long corridor towards a blue, glowing panel laid into the wall. She tapped in a short code and illuminated shapes began to shift before the panel skimmed open.

She walked through, entering the next part of the citadel. Inside was an exact replica of the vast garden. A magnificent waterfall stood proudly in the middle and people bustled around it. Some held small tablets in their hands, others had children with them. The gardens were filled with hundreds of people.

Hurriedly pushing past a couple who were chatting nearby, Elisaris brushed through the foliage, heading for the library beyond.

After opening another door with a gesture, she entered the massive library. The walls were all of equal length and multi-levelled platforms ran across the room in rows. There were no books, just thousands of screens set up on the different levels, most of which were occupied. Elisaris already knew where she was going: a secure room to the back of the library. After passing through another door she entered a little room with a single research panel inside. She tapped its surface several times and large curvy red symbols appeared. She read them to herself, *records deleted.*

It was then that she knew her father was hiding something.

* * *

The following day Daimeh had no memory of the day before and was again woken up in the bath by beautiful songs. They were familiar, but he was not sure from where. His first thoughts were about his journey to the citadel – the journey he had completed on his own. He felt proud to have travelled so far; it was a solo adventure he had succeeded at.

He got out of the water feeling more refreshed than ever after his trek. The warm air dried his skin, leaving it immaculately soft.

He walked under the archway to the main room and picked up the clean robes, wrapping them around his body. He felt how soft the fabric was, suddenly experiencing another sensation of *deja vu*.

He was sitting on the bed, listening to the gentle chanting when a bell sounded and the image of a citadel resident appeared on the rounded section of the wall. Daimeh didn't think of the magical hologram as anything new or unusual, although he couldn't remember having seen it before.

The young man spoke to him in a pleasant, gentle voice, "Good morning, Daimeh. Please, join us for some breakfast."

Morning. It felt like he had only slept for five minutes, but it had obviously been much longer. He got up and walked to the doorway which opened automatically for him. The man from the hologram stood there, ready to show him the way.

"This is my wife, Eleanor." Ceolm said, then gestured to the woman on his other side. "And my daughter, Elisaris."

Elisaris glanced at Daimeh, but there was sadness in her face.

"My pleasure to meet you."

Daimeh felt magnetically drawn to her woeful eyes. Time slowed down as the two gazed at each other for a few seconds, yet it felt like a few minutes. The moment again felt like *deja-vu* to Daimeh.

Elisaris smiled with her mouth, but there was thoughtfulness in her eyes.

Ceolm's voice jolted him out of his trance.

"You may sit, Daimeh."

"Er," he mumbled. "Yes, of course."

He sat down on the sole vacant chair and poured himself some juice.

Ceolm quietly cleared his throat. "I'm very interested to know how your journey here was," he said. "It must have been quite a challenge coming here on your own."

"It was, but I knew I needed to find out where the map led,"

Daimeh explained. "By the way, do you know what the scripture says?"

"We don't know, but I'll tell you when we've deciphered it," Ceolm answered, untruthfully. "Anyway, tell me about Alkoryn. We're all interested in your homeland."

"Well, it's a wonderful place. We're peaceful people with a flourishing culture."

He took a mouthful of food and chewed for a few moments.

"It's not as grand as this citadel. It's very different – primitive – compared to here, but just as enticing. We have talented crafters and I think even you would be impressed," Daimeh concluded proudly.

"Your homeland sounds like a very beautiful place," Elisaris said.

Her father looked at her sternly.

Seeming to notice this, she said, "Excuse me, I must freshen up" and vacated the room.

"Would you mind if I took a tour around the citadel? I'd love to see more of the architecture," Daimeh politely asked.

"Make yourself at home, Daimeh." Eleanor replied.

"Thank you, I'll take a look around. Have a nice a day, you two," Daimeh said, leaving.

* * *

Elisaris was sitting on a bench facing the glistening waterfall when she noticed Daimeh. He had again frozen as soon as he had caught sight of her. She peered up at him and politely beckoned to him, encouraging him to sit with her.

"Daimeh. Please sit."

"It's truly astonishing. This whole place," he said, sitting down cautiously.

"Yes, it is indeed," she replied in a calm tone.

"But it's so quiet here, Seems so big for so few people."

"We're not many."

Elisaris seemed mentally preoccupied, but then asked, "Is Lybas a big place?" hating herself for interrogating him. She needed to leave again.

"Not really…"

"Excuse me," she interrupted, then stood up and walked away. She could sense the bewilderment in Daimeh's voice as he said goodbye to her. Her father was waiting for her behind the door.

Elisaris whispered to him, her eyes filled with passion.

"Father, what are you doing?"

"Get inside."

He grabbed her by the shoulders and pulled her inside.

"Who are these people?" Elisaris asked, turning immediately to look at him. "I checked the records."

"You should not pry, young lady. These matters don't concern you."

"The Alkoryns were deleted from our records. They came from lifeless lands. How can this be so?"

She was almost pleading with him now, but he remained implacable.

"Go!" he ordered, pointing to the exit door. "Do not speak of this again!"

His decision was final.

As she pushed past him at the doorway, she looked over her shoulder.

"You need me, Father."

* * *

When Daimeh awoke, the last thing he could remember was arriving at the citadel the day before. He entered the breakfast room alone and the meal proceeded. Introductory questions were posed, but this time there was an extra one.

"We noticed there are symbols on the map. Do you know what they mean?" Ceolm asked. He already knew what they meant, of course, but he wanted to see if Daimeh did as well.

"Well, the symbols were actually amulets – like keys of some sort. They opened doors, allowing us to reach here," Daimeh admitted.

"Keys? Intriguing," Ceolm replied, a look of contempt in his eyes.

He knew he was getting closer to the answer he sought.

"How did you find the amulets?"

"My aunt Cresadir recognised the first one as being a religious artefact kept on Spiritmist – the furthest Alkoryn island."

Ceolm pried further. "So the amulet had been in the Alkoryn Islands for many years, I imagine."

"Oh yes, for as far back as our records go," Daimeh answered, contently buttering his bread.

"And there have not been any more amulets found in Alkoryn – more recently, perhaps?" It was a bold question given the circumstances

'Share the scripture, hide the magic.' Daimeh remembered the thoughts he had after first picking up the tablet at Galunda Bay. He immediately worried that this might be what Ceolm was referring to.

"Er... no, nothing."

Daimeh tried to lie as convincingly as he could. But Ceolm still appeared suspicious.

Finally, they talked about the flourishing land of Alkoryn once more. Elisaris said, "It sounds lovely. I'd like to see it someday." She paused, as if waiting for a reaction from her father, but none appeared to be forthcoming and she said, "Excuse me, I must freshen up" and vacated the room.

Her face grew sad as she walked through the corridor; she knew she had to keep up the pretence until her father had got the information he was after.

"May I take a look around the citadel? I would love to visit the obelisk," Daimeh asked politely.

"Please, go ahead," Ceolm replied.

"Thank you. Have a nice day," Daimeh said, exiting the room.

Once he had left, Ceolm rose from his chair.

"She won't listen," he said to his wife.

Eleanor put her hand on his.

"Please. Don't condemn her."

"I can't promise anything."

* * *

One week later, Elisaris had just left Daimeh on the bench. She could still hear his bewildered goodbye in her ears. Every day was the same – there was seemingly no end to the deceit. The door opened, and, as usual, her father was waiting on the other side. This no longer startled her.

"How long must this go on Father? I can't do this to him. He's not a toy," she told him, but her sympathetic words fell on deaf ears.

"You know this is a necessary procedure," he replied precisely.

"I don't agree with it," Elisaris stated.

"Do not disagree with me, my daughter," he replied sternly.

Elisaris bowed her head and replied, "Yes, Father," sounding obedient but dignified. She allowed her father past and continued on her way.

The door closed behind Ceolm and he approached Daimeh, as he did every day.

Ceolm gazed at the monument for a moment, then addressed Daimeh. "This morning, you mentioned a basement library in Alkoryn. I'd love to hear about the knowledge that's stored there."

Daimeh thought it seemed like an odd question but he

answered anyway. "The library's located under my grandfather's palace. Apparently it dates from ancient times, when scholars occupied the capital. There are books and manuscripts going back thousands of years. He kept it secret for a long time, we only found out about it just before our journey here. We used it to research the rhajok'don and the symbols."

"It sounds like a very interesting place indeed."

"Any news on what the scripture says?" he asked.

"We don't know," Ceolm answered; lying to Daimeh became easier with each day that passed.

"I'd very much like to know when you decipher it," the young Alkoryn replied, fooled by Ceolm's calm demeanour. "I'll go to my room now, if that's all right?"

"Of course. Relax."

Ceolm nodded goodbye.

* * *

Later that day, Daimeh took another stroll through the citadel. Entering the garden he walked over to the waterfall statue and saw Elisaris sitting on a bench.

"Hello again, Daimeh."

"The waterfall's amazing," he said, nervously sitting down next to her.

And then Elisaris said something unscripted. "I'm intrigued by you. An Alkoryn. You came from a place where there's no life."

"But, there is. There's so much life. The sun's not as high as here. Our sun moves from low to high," Daimeh explained. "Our lands, towns, and our villages – they're all prosperous."

He paused and looked into her anguished eyes.

"I don't know why you were told there was nothing beyond the walls of the citadel. Maybe for the same reason we were told that the lands beyond Alkoryn were impassable."

"You were told this?"

"Yes we were. Well, it was common knowledge, and was taught by our priests."

Elisaris hung her head for a moment.

"It makes little sense to me. I was born here and I know of nothing more than this."

But she seemed disturbed by this news, and almost immediately stood up and walked away, saying, "Excuse me," as she had done earlier. Leaving the bench and hearing Daimeh's goodbye pained her more and more.

The door opened and her father had been watching her. Raising her voice, Elisaris protested, "I can't do this anymore!"

Her father wasn't angry with her outburst, which was surprising.

"You were correct. I do need you," he said calmly. "There's something you can do to help him. The council believe we've exhausted our method of interrogation. We've decided to try a more personal approach and I'd like you to be a part of this."

"What would you have me do?"

"Get close to him; find out about Alkoryn. Find out what he's hiding."

"You won't wipe him anymore?" she asked hopefully.

"No, I won't."

He smiled at her, almost compassionately.

"Thank you, Father. I'll do what I can."

She nodded then walked past him.

* * *

Daimeh sat on the bench with Elisaris. They had been having their usual conversation when Elisaris suddenly said something quite different. "I like you, Daimeh."

17

A New Life

Cresadir was unconscious and lay on her back; a smooth, hovering slab was being used as a bed. She had tubes running into her body; two were attached to her temples.

"We've gone too far," one man said in a soft voice.

"Yes, we've lost everything," the second man said, his voice filled with disappointment.

There was the noise of chairs being shuffled and both men stood up. One of them walked to another part of the room.

"Is she ready to be woken?" the first man asked.

"Yes, I think so."

"I'll inform Ceolm that she's ready."

The second doctor flicked a few switches and all the tubes immediately retracted from her body. He picked up a needle and approaching Cresadir from the side, jabbed it into her neck.

"We'll need to give her a few minutes," he said.

* * *

She opened her eyes slowly, but found she only had two blurry slits to see through; her eyelashes obscured her vision and her head was throbbing.

Bright light filled the room and she blinked a couple more times. As her eyes widened, she saw two blurry figures looming over her. Where was she?

Eventually, she managed to gather enough strength to sit up. She rubbed her eyes and as her sight cleared, she could see she was in quite an advanced room with white walls and filled with medical apparatus; above her was another operating device. The smell of chemical substances tickled her nose.

"Do you… know… w… you are?"

She had trouble focusing on the man's voice; her mind was still dazed and blank and the words slipped in and out of her consciousness.

"Who am I?"

The doctors peered across the bed and conversed together as if she wasn't even there.

"It's worse than we thought."

"Well, she's useless now," the more distinguished-looking man said. "She'll probably be bani…"

"She's not useless," they heard Ceolm's voice say. He had been stood in the doorway since she awoke.

"She's perfect for our biogenetics research. We'll integrate her into our society, give her a life, a job… and monitor her."

He stepped into the room and walked over to the sitting woman. She was so hazy she had no clue what was happening.

"Where am I?" she asked, her voice trembling, but no one there cared about her fear and confusion.

"Please… where am I?"

Tears began to fall from her sad eyes; she suddenly looked like a child who had lost its mother.

Ceolm reached his hand out and touched her chin, gently stroking her jaw with his fingers. "Don't worry, dear."

He turned to his associates and ushered them away.

"Get her some clean clothes and her own residence. Make her feel that she's safe and cared for."

"Yes, sire," they replied, leaving the room.

Ceolm stayed with Cresadir. Brushing her hair to one side, he told her, "You're like family to us and we'll help you to re-adjust after this amnesia."

Cresadir smiled at him.

"I don't remember you."

"You will in time."

* * *

The hovering bed hummed soothingly, making echoes through the smooth corridors. She was gliding through the empty passageways.

"You need some more decorations, and a few paintings and plants wouldn't go amiss," she said to the nurses by her side. It seemed somewhat out of place.

The younger nurse giggled, then she giggled again at the sound of her own echoing voice.

"Er, yes, I think you're right." The older nurse replied. "I'm not sure if Ceolm would agree. He likes to keep these areas clear."

"Your residence is just up here," she told her, pointing to the door ahead which immediately slid open. They walked through it and into the living area. Everything was pure white, from the lamp shades to the carpets. *Don't they get bored of white* she thought and then felt confused.

"This isn't my room," she said.

"What? Of course it is."

"I would never have it looking like this," she said.

"Well, you've just recovered from an awful accident. Give it time," the nurse said, in a reassuring tone, as she had been instructed to do.

The nurses aided her to her feet and as she stepped down she felt a luxurious carpet against her soles. *Mmmm.* She wiggled her toes through the silky strands before shuffling, refusing offers of assistance, towards the enticing, comfortable-looking settee. As she sat down she admired the long rectangular windows set into every wall. They showed off the flourishing outside world; she could see beautiful gardens and a glistening lake, with amphids, animals with incredibly long legs, hopping into the water. The settee moulded itself to her body and she felt incredibly relaxed. There was a smooth-edged table in the middle of the room with an unusual looking, see-through, aqua-coloured cube on its surface. She was too tired to investigate further, instead she lay down on the sofa, looking at the lovely aquarium, watching the exotic fish swim in-between vibrant green leaves. Her eyelids began to get heavy.

"There'll be someone to see you soon," the older nurse said before leaving the room.

* * *

When she opened her eyes, the living room was filled with tranquil music. She sat up, determined to have a look around. Standing up she began to pace around the room, and as she did so, a door slid open, leading into a beautiful bedroom, also oval in shape. In there she saw a very large, round, bed was fitted to the wall; it was in a capsule and could only be reached through an entrance hole. A cosy cubby hole.

There were some clean, simply-designed bedroom units alongside. She reached out to open the first drawer but it glided open before her hand had even touched it. The drawer contained a small device: a rectangular prism. She picked it up and found that it had a hard, shiny casing: aqua, a similar colour to the cube. She walked back through to the living area and held the prism next to the cube. They were magnetically attracted, and the cube absorbed the prism. It began to flash, slowly at first, then quicker; then it projected outwards a three-dimensional image of herself and a male stranger sat next to each other on a sleek metallic park bench. He was very youthful in appearance; she guessed he was in his twenties. After a few moments the image began to move: the man put his arm around her and kissed her on the cheek.

"I love you," he said.

A second clip played. It showed the same man, who was now sitting on the settee with his feet up, watching projections from the cube. "Don't forget our appointment today," he called over to her.

"Just let me take the video," she replied from out of shot.

Then a third clip played. It showed the two of them standing in front of the obelisk in the gardens. She was cradling a new-born infant.

"Oh my," she said out loud. Was that baby hers?

Just as she was about to move on to the next video, the communication system activated.

"Hello, Ceolm here. May I come in?"

She stood up and walked towards the door. It opened, and Ceolm came in and calmly sat down. She followed him over to the settee and sat down next to him.

Ceolm noticed the cube was active.

"I see you've been doing some catching up."

"Yes, I'm confused. I seem to know the man in the video, but he's a stranger to me." She looked away awkwardly, feeling ashamed that she could not remember the child. "Do I have a baby?"

"Yes, you have a child, she's safe in the incubation chambers. Incidentally, that's where you work," Ceolm confirmed.

"What's she called?"

"Kiara."

"And the man?"

"He's your husband and he's called Tristan," Ceolm replied.

"He's my husband?" she asked, sounding surprised. "But he's so young. I would never."

He cleared his throat. "There was a spark between you two and I know he loves you very much."

"Why haven't I been able to see them?" she questioned, curiously.

"We thought it would be best if you had some time to rest, to allow you to adjust yourself before we reintroduced you."

She sighed and let her eyes wander around the room.

"This is so much to take in."

She sighed again, more heavily.

"I think I'm ready to see them." She stood up and straightened her clothes.

"I'll go and get him," Ceolm said before leaving the room.

* * *

Tristan stood outside Cresadir's door. He paced back and forth, then scratched his short, gently pointed, nose, rehearsing in his head what he had been instructed to say.

"Cresadir," he would begin. "Oh my goodness, they finally let me see you."

He practised how he would walk up to her; he wanted to seem non-threatening and yet loving, like he had really missed her. Maybe he could add a little emotion, some tears?

"All right," he said with confidence.

He activated the communication system and asked if he could enter. Cresadir allowed him in – it was his residence too, after all. He gestured for the door to open and hesitantly walked in.

His plump lips smiled and he quickly advanced towards her. He held out his arms.

"Cresadir. Oh my goodness, they finally let me see you."

He went to give her a hug and a kiss on the cheek, but Cresadir backed away, raising her hands defensively.

"I don't know you," she said, looking a little frightened.

"It's fine, my love," he answered, stopping in his tracks. "I've missed you so much."

His face became sad and he forced tears from his almond shaped eyes. His crystal-blue iris's stared longingly at Cresadir, but he began to edge backwards, away from her.

"I'm scared. It's Tristan, isn't it?" she asked quietly, sounding distrustful.

"I am, you don't need to fear me," he replied calmly.

"Where's my daughter?"

Cresadir only cared about her baby. Tristan was an inconvenience to her.

"She's safe. We can see her later," Tristan said, looking towards the settee. "I'm going to take a seat if that's all right?"

"Er, yes, of course."

Cresadir stood cautiously at a distance and watched him sit down.

The comm activated again and this time it was Ceolm.

"Sorry to intrude, but it's time for Cresadir's first treatment."

Cresadir slowly walked to the main door and it slid open for her. "I'm ready."

Ceolm gestured towards the hovering bed, she lay down and the nurses began pushing her along the empty corridor.

* * *

When they arrived, Cresadir realised it was the same room she had woken up in. She vaguely recognised the instruments. Ceolm asked her to stay lying down and the nurses began to prepare a long tube for her, which was attached to the machinery above. She also felt a pressure against her temples as something was placed onto her head. Don't be scared, she told herself. A slender doctor entered the room, dressed in white trousers and a neat matching shirt.

"This will only take a few moments and won't hurt," he said, activating a virtual screen and tapping at some symbols. The tubes lit up and the devices on her temples began to softly vibrate.

"Another ten seconds," the doctor notified them in a calm, soft voice.

The pulsating intensified then abruptly stopped.

"There we go."

The instruments were removed from Cresadir and she sat up.

"What sort of therapy am I getting?" she asked

Ceolm chose his words carefully. "You're receiving a serum to try to reverse the effects of your amnesia and we're stimulating your brain with additional neurotransmitters."

"I see."

It meant little to Cresadir.

"We'll see you tomorrow for your next treatment," the doctor said.

"Yes, all right," she replied before they escorted her back to her room.

* * *

Gleaming sunlight pierced the rectangular windows, illuminating areas of the carpet. Cresadir stood by the central window, peering out at a glorious evening. She could see a luscious palm forest and a couple strolling together over the succulent green grass. Another young man was sitting by the clear, light-blue pond. She wondered why everyone wore white.

The time for sleeping was approaching. Confused, mistrustful and frightened, Cresadir contemplated her day. She was living with a stranger and had a baby she could not remember ever having held and a job she knew nothing about. How could she move forward from this? She gave a signal for the windows to darken.

"Do you want me to sleep on the settee?" Tristan called to her.

"As you wish," she replied, not caring.

Tristan quietly excused himself and went to get some blankets. Cresadir just stood and watched him go. When he returned she paced into the bedroom. "Goodnight," she said as the door slid shut.

* * *

All night Cresadir twisted and groaned. There were sweat marks on the sheets and they were crumpled up from the constant movement.

Suddenly she jolted awake, shouting, "Darkness!"

Images of symbols rolled before her eyes for a few moments before dissolving. She recognised the symbols, but she did not know from where.

Seconds later Tristan ran into the room.

"Lights on," he ordered, and the room was immediately dimly lit by fluorescent lights.

"What happened?" Tristan asked, sitting down on the bed next to her and sounding genuinely concerned.

Cresadir shrank back.

"It was just a bad dream. I'm fine," she said.

"You shouted 'darkness!'"

"There were these symbols I recognised, but I've never seen them before."

"I see."

He edged closer to her and began stroking her face.

"I can stay with you if you like?"

She paused for a moment, looking into his eyes, at the tiny white specks near the pupil. She almost agreed, but instead nervously answered. "No."

"Thank you for your support, Tristan," she said. "I appreciate it."

He lifted her hand and kissed it.

"Anytime, my love," he said before gesturing for the lights to switch off and leaving the room.

18

Lost Souls

Meet me after breakfast at the garden bench...

Daimeh was woken by the sound of a woman's voice

"Elisaris?" he called.

He got out of bed and was dressed and ready before his escort arrived. Right on time the polite image appeared.

"Good morning, Daimeh. Please join us for breakfast."

* * *

He arrived in the breakfast room on his second day, feeling more acquainted and relaxed. He calmly chose a light selection of food from those displayed on the table, then sat down.

Elisaris was flirtatiously eyeing Daimeh and when their eyes met, she shyly smiled at him. Daimeh smiled back, but then blushed embarrassingly. He was trying to act normally but just appeared clumsy. Elisaris giggled under her breath.

Ceolm was the first to speak.

"Morning, Daimeh. Did you sleep well?"

"Morning, everyone. Yes I slept wonderfully, thank you," he replied, smiling warmly at Ceolm.

Elisaris gently brushed a lock of her bouncy hair away from her face before eating.

"That's good. Sleep is the essence of life I think."

Elisaris's mother, Eleanor, continued the conversation. "May I ask? Do you miss Alkoryn, any family there?"

"I am excited to be here, but I do miss my family a lot, and the homely village we have. I'll be back there in no time, I'm sure," Daimeh replied, confidently.

"No need to hurry," Elisaris said, her voice wobbling a little.

"I'd love to hear about your family," Eleanor said politely.

"They're a fantastic family! My mother, Miah, is so caring and generous, too much so for her own good. My father's a hardworking, honest man, he keeps to himself a lot."

He took a bite, chewed a little, and then continued, "My Aunt Cresadir, our head of Bayhaven, is a fascinating person. It would take me a day to describe her," he giggled.

"And I have a cousin, who is Cresa's son; he's pretty useless to be honest, and he knows it. He loves his lute and I think deep down he too is a very loving person... Then there's my uncle – he disappeared for four days when I was a boy. He hasn't been the same since his return and now he's catatonic and in a wheel-chair... Oh, and my grandfather – I can't forget him. He's a great, honourable man and Alkoryn's Monarch. I've more family members on the other isles, but I'm not particularly close to them."

Ceolm swallowed, clearing his throat quietly.

"I'm sorry to hear about your uncle, but I'm most intrigued by your Aunt Cresadir."

"I think I miss her the most. She helped me to prepare for the journey here, gave me all the advice I needed, and sailed me to the first location on the map. She's well-educated and travelled a lot after Uncle Theo came home."

"Where did she travel?" Ceolm asked inquisitively.

"Oh, to the borders of Alkoryn. Although she couldn't go any further, she always believed there was more out there," Daimeh answered, continuing to munch his food.

There was silence for a few minutes.

"Your aunt, what did she know about these lands here?" Eleanor asked, joining the conversation again.

"Not much, only what the scriptures told us."

Daimeh chuckled. "It seems you'd rather she was here than me."

Ceolm smiled. "No, of course not. We're very pleased to have you with us." You'll prove very useful to us, he silently added.

Daimeh glanced at Elisaris and she looked at him before quickly looking away. He noticed she was interested in him.

"Thank you for breakfast. I'm thinking of going for a walk," he announced, standing up.

"Good-bye," Ceolm courteously replied.

"Enjoy yourself," Eleanor said in a soothing tone of voice.

Elisaris remained silent but locked her eyes onto his, which Daimeh found most alluring.

* * *

The beautiful gardens were an idyllic place to have a morning wander. Daimeh strolled calmly about for about an hour before considering what to do. He contemplated checking the bench, then realised it was just a dream, before deciding he would check it anyway.

He passed the great monument and there she was, sitting on the bench.

"Daimeh, I've been waiting for you. Breakfast was an hour ago," she said as he approached.

"Wait a minute. What?"

"Yes, I told you to meet me here after breakfast."

Daimeh didn't want to mention his dream. Maybe it was a coincidence?

"It's all right, Daimeh. I used thought projection," she explained – as if he knew what that was.

"Erm, yes, of course – thought projection," he answered slowly, nodding his head sarcastically.

Elisaris giggled. "Come sit with me."

He sat down, leaving a small distance between them.

"I learnt it from a very young age. Only the counsellors and their families may use it," Elisaris said, trying to explain the phenomenon.

"But why?"

"I don't know. I always believed it was so the council could better control their subordinates," she said, then added, "Oops, I really shouldn't have said that."

"Control. I see."

Elisaris quickly looked around then turned back to him, smiling nervously.

"Anyway, I brought you here for another reason."

"Oh, what was that?" he asked.

"I've been watching you, Daimeh, and you interest me greatly. A mysterious man emerges from the derelict world, devoid of life."

She stroked her hair behind her ear and looked into his deep, peridot eyes, tinted with yellow close to the pupil.

"I admire you for finding us."

Daimeh looked away, embarrassed; he wasn't quite sure how to reply. He just sat in silence. He knew what he wanted to say, *"And I admire you, a magical maiden in the lands of our Goddess."* But he did not dare.

Elisaris's gentle, bubbly voice broke the silence. "A little shy, I see."

His cheeks turned a light red and his eyes darted around, trying to focus on something other than the delightful lady sat next to him.

"You're very lovely," she said.

She knew what she was doing and Daimeh felt even shyer and more uncomfortable. Then, thankfully, she changed the subject.

"Would you like to see something amazing? Something that I bet you've never seen."

She placed her hands on her knees as she spoke.

"I'd love to." Daimeh gave a relieved grin and stood up.

Holding out her hand, she followed suit.

"This way," she said.

He stared at her hand for a moment before nervously reaching for it. His anticipation was immense. Time seemed to slow down as he touched her soft skin.

He composed himself before replying, "Let's go."

* * *

Elisaris led him along two balconies before they ascended a spiral staircase until they reached a paper-thin glass door. It opened and they entered a small, featureless room, which began to move upwards. After a few minutes of elevating, they arrived at a small viewing platform. All around them was the sky, and nothing else.

Daimeh inhaled deeply and his jaw dropped; he remained completely speechless for a few seconds.

"I knew you'd like it."

"It's magnificent!"

Daimeh felt overwhelmed by the view, lost his balance and quickly sat down.

"So high. So clear. The sky worshipping the sun." The advanced thin glass was protecting his eyes and so he looked directly above his head at the outstanding brilliance of the Golden Land's sun; the aqua sky seemed to cascade down like a waterfall.

Elisaris sat closer to Daimeh than was comfortable for him, but he didn't say anything. She let her hair down and it loosely fell over her shoulders.

"I think a few clouds would not go amiss," she said.

"Yes, I think so too."

They sat silently for a few minutes and then Daimeh leaped to his feet.

"Look! Look!" he shouted, pointing at the sky. "A shooting star! They're so rare in Alkoryn... And another!"

He laughed. "Amazing."

"This was the main reason I brought you here, we get so

many of those."

She paused, contemplating her next sentence.

"I'll let you know a little secret."

"I won't tell," Daimeh replied

She stood up and whispered into his ear, "They're not shooting stars."

Daimeh looked at her, confused. Not stars?

"Let's dance!"

Taken back by her sudden openness, Daimeh wasn't quite sure how to reply and just stuttered, "Er, I don't dance too well." He hesitantly stood up.

The small size of the platform they were standing on made him somewhat nervous. But Elisaris took his shaking hand. It was a little sweaty but she didn't mind. She guided his other hand to her waist before moving gracefully from side to side. Daimeh didn't move much at all. He was simultaneously happy and terrified to have her in his arms.

They danced for the rest of the evening under the sublime, serene sky.

* * *

Meet me today in the sky sphere...

Daimeh woke and got dressed quickly. He didn't feel like breakfast. He just wanted to go to her.

* * *

After breakfast he ran towards the sky sphere and caught up with Elisaris on the stairway.

"That thing you do," he said, waving his hands around her head, "it's really effective."

Elisaris chuckled; she had a big smile on her face.

They sat on the platform as they had done the day before.

After a while Elisaris received a prompt from her father – *ask him about the artefacts.*

She sighed and hung her head.

"Are you all right?" Daimeh asked.

She composed herself.

"Yes, just a little dizzy from the…"

She gestured towards the spiral staircase with her fingers, "…the spirals, they get me sometimes."

There were wispy buoyant clouds in the sky, fuzzy at the edges. The fuzzy, bobbly shapes were recast again and again by the blowing of the wind, each time into a new flossy delight.

Breaking off eye contact, Elisaris asked Daimeh.

"Do you still have those artefacts with you?"

"Yes, they're in my room," he replied, a little bewildered by her question.

"May I see them?" she asked.

"I guess so."

* * *

The door opened smoothly and they proceeded into Daimeh's room. The glistening wall display always looked attractive on entering.

He went to his bed and picked up his backpack.

"You do know there's storage here," Elisaris said, waving her hand at the far wall where a door appeared.

"Oh."

Chuckling to himself, Daimeh emptied his backpack onto the bed.

"And tables."

"All right, all right; I get it." He smiled.

Daimeh searched through the contents of his luggage and selected the four symbols. They were lying next to each other, immaculate and interweaved, each with a marbled, shiny surface and a different design.

"On my way here, each guided me to the next one by glowing," Daimeh explained.

"I see; they're fascinating," Elisaris replied, awestruck.

"Oh, there's also this," he said, picking up the technological device and showing her.

"This is interesting, and not from this land – we don't use these darker materials." Elisaris picked it up and read the symbols out loud.

"The key will guide you, but the harmony will take you."

She pressed all the symbols, but only the one which said 'harmony' did anything. "What does it do?"

"We had to move around the dots until a liquid metal stairway appeared.

"Oh, you have to tune it to the right frequency for the transmuting liquescent to morph," she said, as if this was common knowledge.

"Er, yes... I think," he answered, without any idea of what she had just said meant.

"The artefacts look like they were made here. I don't know how you had one in your temple."

She packed the backpack and put it on the table top before sitting down on the bed.

"Sit with me," she said, holding out her hand. He sat a comfortable distance from her as he had done on the bench.

"I'm more intrigued by you with each day that passes," she said, turning to him. He didn't move, just nervously looked ahead of himself, breathing irregularly.

She moved her hand over the sheet and softly touched his hand. Daimeh continued to look ahead.

She gently stroked his high, angular cheek with the back of her hand, trying to be as delicate as she could. His lips were nicely-shaped, she thought, but she could see from his lack of eye contact that he was a little afraid.

He couldn't do it. It wasn't that he didn't want to; he just felt that he wasn't ready.

She edged herself closer to him, but he immediately stood up, looking uncomfortable.

"What's wrong Daimeh?" she asked thoughtfully.

"I-I'm not used to this," he said, pacing around the room.

"Then let's talk some more," she suggested.

"I think it's probably a bit late. But we can meet again tomorrow."

* * *

The next day, when Daimeh arrived in the garden, Elisaris was already waiting on the bench.

"Good morning. I'm sorry about last night."

"Don't think anything of it," she replied.

He sat a little closer to her than the day before.

"I like you too, Elisaris," he said. Finally, he thought, I've told her.

"I know you do," she said with confidence. She projected a message to him – *I'm falling for you.*

"Should we go and look at the clouds again?"

"That would be lovely," Elisaris agreed, with relief.

They stayed there all day in perfect tranquillity, looking at the glorious sky, and then returned to their rooms.

19

Land Of Eternal Stars

The next morning was a peaceful one and Daimeh slowly woke up, smiling. He heard Elisaris's voice echoing in his head – *"Today I want to show you the library."*

He got out of bed, dressed himself and went to meet Elisaris on the bench as usual.

* * *

When Daimeh arrived, Elisaris was sat there, looking as graceful as ever. He sat down next to her.

"How did you sleep?" she asked.

"Wonderfully – spending time in the sky sphere relaxes me so much," he happily replied.

"Yes, it does have that effect," Elisaris said, leaning in as she spoke

"So, the library?" he asked.

"Yes, follow me."

She took his hand and together they stood up and walked through the vibrant gardens. Near the back were tall trees with thick trunks and dark olive-green leaves, teardrop-shaped and glossy. An animal with vivid yellow and pink feathers perched on a nearby branch and squawked. Despite its loud voice, it was small in stature.

Daimeh didn't recognise the species. "Wow, what is that?" he asked.

"Beautiful, is it not?" Elisaris answered.

"He's an Aves."

To Daimeh the Aves looked like a bird but with a feline-like face, tiny in size.

"We breed them here. They're feathered mammals native to our homel—" Elisaris stopped abruptly, realising she had said too much.

"Homeland?" Daimeh queried. "Where are you from?"

Elisaris appeared flustered, and hastily answered, "Far from here."

But Daimeh realised that she was trying to deceive him.

They continued walking towards the far edge of the vast domed gardens until they finally arrived at the furthest door. It opened, and beyond it, they saw the magnificent library. Daimeh had never seen such a chamber before. The room was divided by four aisles; between them were hundreds of monitors, stretching up towards the ceiling. Looking up, Daimeh lost his balance. Elisaris grabbed his hand.

"This way," she said, leading him towards a little room at the back. "I have access to the archive hub."

"Why are we here?" Daimeh queried.

"Do you not wonder about the rhajok'don that washed ashore?" she asked, her expression enthusiastic. "I know I do, I heard one lived with us many years ago."

"Of course I want to know about the rhajok'don," Daimeh replied excitedly. "How did he get here?"

"Maybe he travelled, like the other one."

Elisaris tapped into the records using the nearby monitor, and rolled back the date.

"I think it was about this time," she said.

She pushed a symbol and numerous other symbols appeared. They projected out of the hub and then remained static around her head, one symbol always a little in front.

"This is it."

She nodded and the first archive opened. She began reading.

"What? Three millennia ago. Subject A01... Subject?"

"Doesn't seem like he was living here of his own free will," Daimeh replied.

"No."

She continued reading out loud, "Taken captive on Era 1:345."

Elisaris sighed.

"We took another species captive."

She hung her head, ashamed of her people.

Daimeh put his arm around her.

"Don't worry. You're not like them. This was many years ago."

Elisaris sighed before continuing, "He complied with us and through interrogation we were able to establish his birthplace, as well as what degree of potential threat remained from the banished."

Daimeh interrupted her. "Banished? Who are they?"

"They're criminals of the worst kind. We banish them to a place called Stygia."

"Where's Stygia?" he asked, becoming more curious.

"A place far south of here, towards the Land of Eternal Stars."

"My aunt always said there were dark places in this world. I never believed her, until now."

"What?" Elisaris said, a hint of anger in her voice. "We performed genetic engineering on this poor soul too."

"What kind?"

"Splicing, cloning, memory extraction, implants, mutations... everything."

Looking disgusted, she read on. "There were mixed results."

She tapped the symbol next to the text and there was a red flash.

"I can't access them."

"It's probably for the best," Daimeh said, pointing to a symbol which hadn't flashed red. "What about this one?"

Elisaris tapped it. "It's the results from the rhajok'don's memory implant, and more information about his time at Stygia. It would seem my people wanted to find out why they lost surveillance of the banished."

She read on. "I was in the fields raking kernels when I heard them approaching. I looked through the fallen trees and that's when I saw them: a band of mounted men, maybe two hundred strong, approaching my tribe's encampment. I charged back, reaching the camp just as the army of men arrived. They wore unusual armour and had weapons at their sides – they were soldiers. The villagers were overcome by fear; we all ran inside the huts, but they were no defence against these men. We were choked out by the purple smoke and they demolished my home, leaving the huts reduced to piles of rubble. The mounts encircled us, their weapons drawn; we cowered before them. They took the women and children first, then chained the rest of us.'

Elisaris skipped a few lines before continuing. "The slave camps were overcrowded and depressing. We were stripped naked and kept in large fenced-off areas. Our excrement mixed with the oily, muddy ground, we were chained and given very little space to move. One of my tribe would be taken away each day and when they came back they weren't the same."

"Maybe being here with the Amunisari was a blessing, considering where he came from," Daimeh said.

"Yes," Elisaris agreed, sighing. "But it wasn't right. It should never have happened."

"It seems there are a few secrets dwelling in this place."

"There certainly are," she said, looking down at the glassy floor. She was silent for a moment as she contemplated what to say next. The discussion saddened her so she took a deep breath and changed the subject.

"I think we need some entertainment," she said, and tugged Daimeh to follow her. "There's a hub just below us."

She led him outside the archive room to a small elevator, similar to the one at the sky sphere. It hummed as they travelled downward.

When they reached the bottom they entered an empty, perfectly square room, with liquid metal walls; its floor and ceiling looked identical to those of the small bunker in the ravine.

"This is the metallic liquid."

Daimeh recognised it straight away.

"The transmuting liquescent," Elisaris said.

"Why don't you just call it T-Liq? It's so much easier to say."

Daimeh never understood the long-winded way the Amunisari spoke.

"It's not our way to call it such a thing," Elisaris replied, sounding confused.

She began wondering about it herself. There were a few things about her people which she had taken for granted, but since meeting Daimeh, she had been forced to ask herself many questions: questions regarding their white gowns, their language and their pursuit of perfection.

"How does it work?" Daimeh asked, stroking the solid wall.

Elisaris raised her voice to activate the system, "Begin!"

Symbols appeared on the wall in front of them.

"It just says, 'Welcome to the Lower-01 entertainment hub,'" she informed him. "Elyon," she said, apparently to the wall.

The liquid morphed again, forming three-dimensional moving objects. Unusual-looking purple mushrooms began to grow upward, slowly turning murky in colour before becoming black. They stood as tall as trees. Dull purple moss started growing up from under Daimeh's feet, followed by wavy, thin grass stalks, also purple in colour.

He walked backwards towards the door.

"I'm not sure if I'm going to like this."

"Relax," Elisaris said, holding out her hand. "It's fun."

On the ceiling, the image of a hyacinth-coloured sky appeared: silky violet clouds streamed across it.

"It gets better."

As she spoke, the underside of the mushroom became a luscious pink and fluffy pink bobbles started to appear from the grass. They were little animals, round, with two small ears; their faces were hidden behind fur.

Daimeh gasped with astonishment.

"It's amazing... and colourful," he said, then bent down and picked up one of the little creatures. "And cute." The little thing emitted a high-pitched beep, then jumped off his palm and bounced off across the moss. Daimeh slowly moved forward, worrying that he would step on them. They're not even real, he thought.

"They're fine," Elisaris said, dancing forward. "They move out of the way."

The beeping balls rushed away from her feet moments before they touched the ground.

The skyline broadened and more mushroom trees sprouted. Succulent, sweet aromas drifted down from the trees and mixed with the scent of musk coming from the ground. As the creatures continued to hop around the smell of musk intensified and small glittering speckles appeared in their fur.

"I didn't think your people liked colour."

"We do in our free time. We need to work in white as it stimulates our neurotransmitters, ensuring focus and well-being," Elisaris explained.

"Of course it does."

When Daimeh was baffled by something, he tended to just agree.

Elisaris ran ahead of Daimeh and peeked at him from behind a black trunk.

"Where are we?" he asked her, standing on tiptoes, as if this would help his voice to project further.

She revealed herself from behind the mushroom and called back to him.

"Elyon. It's a world..." She paused for a moment. "It's a fantasy world popular with our people."

"I see," he replied, noticing her sudden pause.

Daimeh ran through the grass laughing, stirring up as much glitter as he could. When he had caught up with Elisaris he stopped awkwardly; he was too nervous to show her any affection and she noticed this.

"Let's sit in the grass," she said, taking his hand and lowered herself to the ground. He followed her lead and sat down next to her.

"It feels like magic, does it not?"

"It is magic," Daimeh replied, convinced.

"Of sorts, yes."

She rested her head onto his shoulder and Daimeh raised his hand to stroke her hair.

The next moment, time stopped for Daimeh as she turned her delicate head to his. He gazed upon her gorgeous, melting, elliptical blue eyes, huge, both in size and in the emotion they showed. He was captivated.

"Elisaris, you're magical."

"Daimeh," she said softly, almost whispering. "I think I'm falling in love with you."

She began stroking his neck. Daimeh felt his heartbeat quicken and he started to shake ever-so-slightly.

She was so beautiful, he thought, as he watched her eyes glance across his face and down to his neck. He felt an urge to touch her and lovingly stroked her hair away from her eyes. Then he lightly glided his hand from her temple to her cute, rounded chin. He closed his eyes and his face slowly drifted towards hers. Their noses touched. Elisaris gently caressed his with hers. Daimeh felt as if his nose was on fire in that moment, and it tickled intensely.

He exhaled slowly, then, as he breathed in, he brushed his nose against hers, moving closer to her full lips. She moved nearer to him; their lips were now so close that their skin was tingling, which only intensified the anticipation.

Their lips touched and he kissed her delicately; it felt like a puff of wind. The sense of connection was heavenly. Elisaris returned his kiss, then embraced him.

20

Colours

"Morning, Cresadir. I let you sleep in, but it's time for your treatment," Tristan said, buzzing the comm to the bedroom.

Cresadir was already awake, but was still resting. Her nightgown was sweaty from the night before and clung unpleasantly to her body. She felt strange and her muscles were tense, but her head was clearer than previously. She pushed herself through a gap in the canopy and stood up. Quickly removing her gown, she casually walked towards the bathroom area and it immediately began to steam. She gestured at the wall for a mirror and one appeared. As she stared into it she noticed something unusual had happened to her face. She stretched her skin and it bounced back with more vigour than usual. What was happening to her? She ran her fingers over her crow's feet which appeared to be diminishing. She thought she looked great. She pouted and saw that her lips were plumper than they used to be; the skin on her face was tighter as well – she looked ten years younger. She continued to peer into the reflective surface for a few more moments, until she heard talking in the living room. Ceolm had arrived. Cresadir hurried from the bathroom and got dressed.

Tristan shook Ceolm's hand. "Morning, sir. She's just getting rea…" He was interrupted by the bedroom door opening.

"Morning," Cresadir said.

"How are you today?" Ceolm asked softly.

"I feel much more refreshed and more focused," Cresadir answered, nodding and smiling. "And the anxiety isn't as bad."

"That is good to hear," Ceolm said. The treatment was working, he thought.

He smiled back at her, then said, "Come, the treatment room

awaits."

Two nurses, the same ones as the day before, stood by the door, together with the hovering bed. Cresadir sat on it and was escorted away.

* * *

They arrived in the room they had been to the day before, and this time the procedure was over in five minutes. Standing up, Cresadir thanked the nurses.

"I can walk fine now," she said, then asked, "How long will I have to have this treatment for?"

"For as long as it takes," Ceolm replied.

"What's the goal? For me to have my memories back?"

"Yes, of course, Cresadir. That's what we all want." The deception came easily to him. But only the memories we give you, he thought.

"I'll head back to my room then."

"Wait, today we'll show you where you work," Ceolm informed her.

"The incubation chambers?"

Cresadir remembered it had been mentioned the day before.

"Yes."

"May I return to my room to change my clothes? I'll meet you in five minutes."

Ceolm nodded in response.

* * *

Cresadir rushed back to her quarters. Tristan was inside, on the sofa. Cresadir thought he was there a lot and a bit lazy.

He acknowledged her presence. "Back so soon – quicker than yesterday."

"It gets easier," she said.

She hurried to the bathroom and called for the mirror to appear. Scrutinising her face, she saw it seemed to have become younger still. She looked in her early twenties and she wondered how she could be looking younger. It was beginning to worry her. She walked back through to the living room. "Do I look different to you?" she asked Tristan.

"You look just as you did when we met."

"Why am I getting younger?"

"It's a result of the repair work. The accident triggered a genetic change in you and it reactivated the ageing process." Tristan explained.

"I see."

She hesitated.

"Then when *did* we meet?"

"Twenty years ago. I'll never forget. You were working at your first job as a junior lab assistant." He smiled lovingly at her.

Cresadir raised her voice in shock, "Twenty years ago?"

He sat up from his slouched position and addressed his wife. "Yes."

Her expression wobbled and she raised her hands over her nose. She took a short, sharp breath in and mumbled under her breath. "I d-don't remember any of it." She only just managed to get the words out before choking up.

Tristan immediately went to comfort her. He put his hand around her shoulder, trying to sound sincere.

"Cresadir, Cresadir, my dear. That's what the treatment is for."

She burst into tears.

"B-but I'm not even myself. I don't like all this white, yet I must have been fine with it before."

"You loved this home before the accident."

She inhaled deeply, trying to calm herself.

"You keep saying accident. What accident did this to me?"

"It was at work. You were connecting the neural links, but

there was a malfunction and the power had not yet shut down. As you slotted the tubes together there was an electrical surge and you were shocked with the neurological signals. That damaged your brain, wiping your memories and causing you to age."

He held her tight.

"But we're fixing it. You can even go back to work from tomorrow."

Cresadir's crying had ceased and Tristan helped her over to the settee. He wiped her tears away and kissed her forehead.

"I love you, Cresadir."

His training was serving him well.

* * *

Ceolm arrived and let himself in.

"Are you ready, Cresadir?"

"There was a small incident but she's fine now," Tristan replied.

"Yes, I got a little upset. Shall we go?"

"Yes," Ceolm nodded, offering his hand and inviting her to join him.

The corridor entry opened and they stepped into the grand gardens where many people were going about their daily business. Most seemed in a hurry, talking into the air, holding small pad-shaped devices in their hands.

The obelisk glistened so brightly that the sun's beam caused a rainbow to appear behind the cascading waterfall. It was beautiful.

They walked slowly along the left edge of the enormous enclosure, next to the wall. Cresadir very much admired the oasis, noticing that there was even an artificial breeze which made the leaves and plants sway from side to side. One poor spider was being blown around and was dangling on a piece of web like a needle on a thread. Cresadir aided the struggling spider back onto the leaf.

"You like nature?" Ceolm asked, having noticed what a caring person she was.

"I love nature, the natural order of things and the fact all animals are equally evolved, each having their own speciality. We're no more advanced than a spider on a web."

She went into specifics to a greater deal than Ceolm had expected and this worried him. The Amunisari thought themselves above all animals.

"You seem particularly knowledgeable about the subject," Ceolm said.

"It seems to me that the knowledge is innate. I don't know why I think the way I do. But it would appear the accident spared one part of me at least."

"Yes, indeed."

That would have to be addressed, he thought, as they continued on their way.

* * *

A strange young woman kept glancing at Cresadir through the trees. There she was again, trying to act casual, tapping her fingers on her thin virtual pad. The woman glanced at her again, and this time she caught Cresadir's eye, then she squeezed the pad and it shrank in her hand before she disappeared through a doorway. Was she just becoming paranoid, Cresadir asked herself?

"We're nearly there. Just the next door on our left."

Ceolm waved his hand and an opening appeared. The walls of the incubation chambers were painted white. Cresadir was so tired of white. Against the walls were dozens of booths with large incubation chambers embedded inside. Hoses and pipes, for use in injections, were connected to the big cylindrical test-tubes: blue, bubbly liquid could be seen oozing through them. Inside each chamber was a suspended infant, none of whom were more than a few weeks old.

"Where's my baby?" she asked anxiously.

A physician approached; she looked to be in her twenties, although age meant very little to the Amunisari.

"Cresadir, welcome back – it's so good to see you." She took Cresadir's hand and clasped it between hers.

"This is Olivia, she works with you. She's the senior medical professional in this department," Ceolm explained before leaving them.

"Hello," Cresadir replied hesitantly.

"Your daughter's this way, in Chamber 17."

Olivia led the way through the desks. Each desk had a cube on it, displaying information charts. Medical assistants scurried back and forth between the charts comparing statistics and monitoring their patients.

When they arrived at Chamber 17 Cresadir stared longingly at her daughter, her face filled with joy. Olivia tapped a few buttons and the large test-tube activated. Making a swirling noise, it extended from the booth then changed its position so it was horizontal, before sliding into the prepared hovering unit. The gelatinous goo drained from the cubicle, rousing Kiara. She waved her arms around, stretching her small fingers. A moment passed and a short whimper soon turned into a wailing cry.

The chamber enclosure slid open and Olivia reached down to carefully remove the invasive tubes before picking her up. She cleared away the remaining gel with a small towel and handed Kiara over to Cresadir.

Cresadir cupped the baby's head in her open fingers and held up Kiara's hips with her other hand. Slowly she brought her close, cradling her baby against her chest. She was much lighter than she had expected. Cresadir gazed with wonder into Kiara's eyes; they were a creamy yellow with an undertone of pale tan.

"She has your eyes," Olivia commented, smiling.

"Yes," Cresadir replied. Gently, she rocked the child, trying to settle her.

"Shh, there now, Mother's here."

Her voice was soothing and compassionate. Kiara's cries became quieter; quite soon she stopped wailing and simply babbled.

"How long can she stay out?"

"Just a few more minutes, I'm afraid."

* * *

Cresadir's heart sank. Olivia was waiting with her arms outstretched, but Cresadir continued to hold onto her baby. She didn't want to give her back, but she knew she had to. Something broke inside of her when she handed her baby back. She wanted her with her. Holding Kiara carefully, Olivia walked back to the incubation chamber. Cresadir's feeling of loss intensified as she watched them take her child away. She tried to distract herself by glancing around the room once more. She didn't know the machines, yet she worked here. The prevailing white irritated her and her attention began to wander. After a few moments she noticed a tub filled with a thick, yellow-brown liquid. Wood. A random thought came to mind. She wanted her room to be wood.

Olivia returned.

"Would you like me to show you what you'll be doing tomorrow?" she asked politely.

"No, I have an odd question," Cresadir said.

She hesitated and then went on. "Where can I get some wood?"

"Excuse me?" Olivia asked, tilting her head. "That's an obsolete resource."

"Oh I see," Cresadir answered, looking around the room, apparently thinking. "May I take this then?"

She pointed to the tub.

"In fact, with our technology, can you synthesise a mixture of these colours?"

Olivia was still bewildered. "Er, yes we can... may I ask what for?"

Cresadir's reply was short and to the point. "I'm bored of white," she said, snatching the tub and hastily walking away.

Olivia stood in the doorway, baffled.

"Wait, don't take that, it's waste!" she called, even though she knew Cresadir didn't want to hear.

* * *

As soon as Cresadir got to her room she opened the tub and dug her hand into the coloured paste.

"Cresadir?" Tristan asked, confused by what she was doing.

"White. I'm tired of white."

She slapped a handful of sticky faeces onto the wall.

Tristan stood up abruptly.

"Urgh! W-what are you doing? It stinks."

"This home needs to be wooden," Cresadir answered, adamant.

Something suddenly occurred to Tristan.

"I need to go," he said, rushing out of the room.

Cresadir hastily and passionately painted the walls; the distress with her baby had affected her more than anticipated and she seemed to have temporarily lost her mind. The paste slopped onto the floor and all over her gown, yet she was so focused on the walls, that she didn't notice the smell and the mess she had made.

* * *

Rushing to alert Ceolm, Tristan and Olivia met in the corridor outside his office and entered the room together.

"She took a waste unit and she wants me to mix her a wooden colour."

"She's at home now, splashing it on the wall."

Ceolm stood up.

"What?"

"She remembers, sire. We need to give her emergency treatment," Tristan advised.

"I agree. I'll contact the medical officers."

Before tapping the table comm, he asked Olivia, "The clone, did she accept her?"

"Yes, it was a very special moment for her," Olivia replied, trying to hide a smile.

The comm buzzed. "We need you at Cresadir's room, now." Ceolm ordered.

* * *

The door opened, flushing the ripe smell of baby excrement out into the corridor. Tristan rushed in first and the medical staff followed.

Cresadir was smudging the edges as much as she could and spreading the pigment thinly to ensure as much of the wall as possible was covered.

"Cresadir, we're here to help you," Tristan said, running over to Cresadir. He caught hold of both her arms from behind.

"Get off me!" she shouted, panicked, shaking Tristan off her.

"This needs to be wood! Wood!" she screamed. She focused on the colour... and wall panelling seemed to appear before her.

"Look at it; it's beautiful."

Aided by one of the nurses, Tristan jabbed a needle into Cresadir's neck and she immediately flopped to the floor unconscious.

"Quickly, get her back to the lab," Ceolm ordered abruptly.

The second nurse pushed the hovering bed into the room and helped Tristan to lift Cresadir. Once she was on it, they steered her back to the genetics lab.

* * *

Cresadir woke with a terrible feeling of nausea. She had been cleaned up and her clothes had been changed. Sitting up, she saw a young adult sat at the side of her bed.

"How are you?" Elisaris asked.

"You're the girl who's been watching me," Cresadir whispered through dry lips, squinting distrustfully.

"Yes, I am. I'm not supposed to be here, but I had to see you," Elisaris answered. She gently placed her hand on Cresadir's. "I wanted to tell you that Daimeh is all right. He's safe for now."

"Hmm?"

Cresadir appeared puzzled.

"Who's Daimeh?"

"I feared this."

Elisaris's expression tensed and she lowered her head.

"They wiped you clean."

"They're giving back my memories."

"Those are not your memories," Elisaris replied. "I've said too much, they'll be monitoring me."

She bent low, whispering, "I'm very sorry, but I must put you to sleep, for a long time, it's the only way I can protect you."

"What do you mean?"

"It'll last a few months – give me enough time to free Daimeh and yourself."

"What're you talking about?"

Without answering, Elisaris discretely and quickly injected a large amount of medication into Cresadir's arm, I'm so sorry, she told her silently. Immediately Cresadir descended into an artificial sleep.

Elisaris had one final task to do. She must implant her with the knowledge of the council. She lifted Cresadir's head and under cover of puffing up a pillow, she quickly injected a device into the nape of Cresadir's neck.

When Cresadir awoke, nothing would be a secret anymore.

21

Love Thwarted

Bobbles covered the two lovers, but when Daimeh awoke they scurried away in the blink of an eye – all except for one, which remained perching on Daimeh's head. He carefully picked it up and held it in his hand. It chirped and bounced off.

Elisaris lay by his side, spooning him; glitter was sprinkled over both of their bodies. He watched her sleep for a few moments before softly kissing her on her delicate cheek. Her eyes opened slowly, but when she turned to look at him, she sat up suddenly, surprised.

"Oh, we're still here." She laughed.

Daimeh chuckled with her. "It would seem so."

"Perhaps we should head to our quarters. It must be getting late now," she said, standing up and brushing the glitter off her clothes.

"Before we go," Daimeh began, then paused and pondered for a second. "Could you show me Stygia? The Land of Eternal Stars."

Daimeh was unsure whether he should have asked the question; it seemed an unusual request.

Elisaris stopped shaking her clothes.

"Yes, but why do you want to see that horrible place?" she asked, continuing to brush away the last of the glitter.

"I'm curious."

"All right."

Elisaris raised her head and shouted, "End!" in a sharp tone of voice.

Elyon melted away around them and they found themselves standing in the large, empty room once more. She cleared her throat and shouted, "Stygia!"

The floor began to wobble and the metallic liquid began to morph into peculiarly-shaped trees, they leaned sideways and had large, thin, sheet-like leaves which were a deep shade of teal. Curious trees continued to sprout, but the ones further away from Daimeh and Elisaris were increasingly smaller in size. The ground below them was sloppy and oily, covered with dried, dead leaves and luminescent glowing fungi.

Daimeh trudged through the sticky mud.

"Uurgh."

He sniffed the air. "It smells so musty."

"Yes, I told you it wasn't nice."

"But look."

He pointed upwards.

"There's glitter in the sky," he said, then looked behind him. "And… no sun."

He span around once more to make sure.

"Where's the sun?"

"There's very little sun here, it never fully rises, and is mostly under the horizon."

"The same reason we always have a sun?" Daimeh asked, remembering what his aunt had said about the world orbiting the sun.

"Yes," Elisaris answered, nodding.

The trees were obstructing his view so Daimeh plodded through the mud to a clearer view of the sky.

"And, I've heard of stars, but I never thought there would be so many."

Elisaris followed him.

"And there are many more still, we just can't see the furthest ones away."

The bottom of her gown had become soggy from the mud Daimeh noticed.

"I'm sorry about your dress."

She looked down.

"Oh worry not, the transmuting liquescent will clean that up," she said, smiling. "Shall we go?"

"Yes, I think I've seen enough of Stygia for now," he replied contentedly.

"End!" she shouted, clearly and sharply.

Stygia liquefied around them and they were returned to the metallic room. They took the elevator up and then parted ways.

"I'll meet you tomorrow? At the same place?" Daimeh asked hopefully.

"Of course," she replied, then added, "my love."

She hugged him tightly before walking away.

* * *

Daimeh arrived at his quarters and disrobed. His bed was perfectly moulded to his body shape, and he quickly got comfortable and fell asleep with ease.

* * *

Dyak bats were squawking in Lybas and the sun was at its lowest point. The day was perfect. Daimeh was stood in the village centre, under the canopies. Nobody was around; he looked slowly to his left, then right. She sat on the steps of his parent's house, looking sultry, and graciously waved to him. He went to her and sat as close as he could, placing his hand in hers and softly squeezing it.

"Did you use projection to get us together here?" Damieh asked calmly.

"Yes, I did. It's the only way that I can avoid him seeing me."

"Seeing you?"

"My father's watching us, Daimeh. He's trying to manipulate you. I'll protect you, I promise."

She placed her hand on his shoulder and gently ran it along

his neck. He wasn't nervous; the dream had relaxed him.

"What does he want?"

"You've information he wants. It's been an interrogation the whole time."

Daimeh shrank back from her. "What? You've been spying on me?"

Elisaris lowered her head.

"This is all a lie?" he asked.

"No! We're not a lie! Let me explain," she said, reaching out to him. "Alkoryn vanished from his observation and he wants to know why. Whatever the reason is, don't share it. Not even with me. You understand." Her voice was passionate.

Daimeh immediately thought of the oblong tablet he had left in his larder at Lybas. That must be the reason.

"Are you trying to trick me with this magic? This projection?"

"It's not magic and I'm not tricking you," she said. She bowed her head for a moment, then looked up and gazed into his eyes. "Despite him using me. My feelings for you are true, Daimeh."

He could see from her eyes that she was speaking honestly.

"For some reason I believe you. It's why we're here."

He took her hand again.

"I am being sincere," Elisaris said, resting her head onto his shoulder.

* * *

Ceolm was sitting at his desk when an alert appeared on the screen in front of him. He answered hastily, but in a confident, commanding tone.

"Yes."

"We had a glitch whilst monitoring last night," a technician said, sounding hesitant.

"Go on."

"Elisaris's projection activated, but we had no surveillance of it." He sounded frightened.

"What?"

Ceolm stood up suddenly and thundered his palms against the wall.

"She's deceiving me – my own daughter!"

"We also have this footage." The footage of Elisaris putting Cresadir to sleep projected onto the screen. "She's sabotaged our experiment."

"This will not go unpunished," Ceolm said angrily, clenching his fists tight. "At least we can still continue the treatment whilst Cresadir is asleep."

"We can?"

"Yes, not as effectively, but when she wakes up she'll be much more compliant. Maybe my daughter has done us a favour."

Ceolm sat down and tried to relax.

* * *

Daimeh was woken from a satisfying sleep by Elisaris's caring tones – this time not her projected voice, but her real one. Daimeh sat up quickly; he felt full of energy. A hologram of Elisaris was standing in the corner of the room.

"Morning. I'd like to come in," she said sweetly.

Daimeh rose from his bed and gestured for the door to open.

Elisaris pounced on him and passionately squeezed him. He could see she was excited about something.

"We must escape from here. We could live in Alkoryn, under its protection. My father wouldn't know, I'll reform the amulets so that they can protect us too."

She sounded hopeful, but Daimeh wasn't convinced it was possible.

"You're sure we can do this?"

"I know —"

She was interrupted by red lights flashing in Daimeh's room.

A hologram of Elisaris's father appeared.

"My own daughter disobeyed me."

His stare was intense. Two members of the security forces had forced the door open and now ran into the room.

"Take her away!" Ceolm ordered.

Elisaris ran behind Daimeh and clung to him. "No. No, Father. Please don't do this."

"And take him too."

Ceolm pointed at Daimeh and the guards seized him and pulled him from Elisaris's hold.

Two more guards entered the room.

"You did this to yourself, Elisaris," Ceolm told her; holding himself upright and stiff, his shoulders squared.

The two guards held her arms firmly and began to drag her out of the room. She resisted as much as her strength allowed her to, grabbing at the walls and the doorway.

Before she lost sight of Daimeh, she screamed, "I'll find you, Daimeh. They will not take this from us."

"She knows nothing of what she speaks," Ceolm said coldly.

"They have Cresadir! I've seen her. They've done something to her—"

Ceolm slapped his daughter harshly across her cheek, drawing a little blood.

He waved to his guards. "Bring him to me."

The screams grew more distant, and then suddenly stopped.

"Where are you taking her?" Daimeh demanded, struggling against the guards who were restraining him.

Ignoring his question, Ceolm raised his hand towards Daimeh's forehead, intimidatingly. He cupped it over his brow and a golden spark pulsed from Ceolm's wrist into Daimeh's head. Daimeh felt the warm pulsation affecting him and his muscles weakening. Unable to resist, he dropped to the floor. He remained conscious for a few moments more, enough time to shed a few tears.

22

Memories Are Never Gone

Behind the blue-hued glass, Elisaris placed her hand on the flat surface and ran it down the exterior.

"I'll free us both, I promise," she said, her voice consumed with sadness.

A condensation outline appeared around her hand. The only noises were that of the bubbling of fluid and the technician going about his business.

Inside, Daimeh hung seemingly lifelessly. The tube he floated in was filled with a crystalline liquid and golden streaks were cracked into the glass, like little frozen lightning bolts.

Elisaris was still pressing her hand against the glass when her father entered the purging room. This was a somewhat nondescript room with mostly empty walls, one screen and a few bland benches. The main feature was the glass tube: It ran from the floor to the ceiling and had many other smaller tubes connected to it.

Ceolm approached from behind and stood by her side, looking at the helpless Alkoryn.

"You know they're not our equals. You shouldn't see them as such," he said.

"I love him, Father. I'll never forgive you for your lies," Elisaris replied, her pent up emotions detectable in her voice. "Why do you tell us there's nothing outside these walls?"

"It's no one's concern. This protocol helps maintain the status quo in our society," he replied. "We don't lie to our people. We protect them."

"Protect them from knowledge of what? That they too are being manipulated, or that our council are barbaric?"

"What you do to the Alkoryn people is immoral. You observe

them like pets. You manipulate their lives. And I think most members of our so-called civilisation would agree with me."

"Our people will never know, no matter what you try to do," Ceolm answered, confidently. "We need to manipulate their environment and their genetics to better understand cultures and how they evolve. We need to do it to enable our race to evolve – you know this. We seek perfection."

"We're not an evolved race. It's wrong!"

"And there's nothing you can do about it."

Elisaris removed her hand from the glass and turned to look directly at her father.

"Sadly, I know this to be true. Your methods of manipulation go beyond anyone's understanding. But I'll tell you this, I will not give up, Father. You'll never have me on your side."

"I don't object to that, but I'll never allow you to be with this boy either."

"Or I'll be purged? Our genes are protected remember," Elisaris said, her voice full of anger.

Ceolm leant down to her and said firmly, "I'm condemning you. All your access privileges to the examination citadel are now removed."

Elisaris pushed her father away.

"At least let me stay with him until you take him from me."

"Very well." Her father turned and departed from the room. Elisaris placed her hand on the glass once more and stared at her trapped love. She heard a few quiet clanking noises behind her as the technician, Isak, placed what he was holding on the bench. Hearing him approach, Elisaris turned around.

"Excuse me – I overheard what was said between you and your father. I sympathise with your feelings. I've watched the Alkoryns grow and their community develop over many years," Isak said, pausing to take a deep breath.

"Go on," she encouraged him.

"It was just a simulation, or so I thought. The council asked me to simulate the evolution of cultures," he explained. "Then one month ago, when the simulation of Alkoryn was wiped, we were no longer able to monitor them."

"All records of the experiment were deleted too," Elisaris added.

"Then, when Daimeh and Cresadir arrived at the citadel, I realised the truth."

He looked at Daimeh in the stasis tube.

"The council believe Daimeh knows why we're not able to watch his people anymore," Isak continued, placing his hand on her arm. "I can help you."

"You're one of the trusted few?" Elisaris asked, hopefully.

"Yes – Councillor Salvador, my superior, needs my technical knowledge. We can use this to our advantage and get you both out of here. That's all I can do. I don't have the means to expose what's going on to the public, and I don't want to be banished."

He put his right hand to his temple.

"Once you're free I'll purge myself. It's the only way to keep you safe."

"You'd do this for us?" Elisaris asked, her eyes grateful.

"I'll do what's right," Isak replied.

Elisaris hugged him tightly and whispered in his ear, "Thank you, so very much."

"I'll meet you in your chambers two hours from now. We'll discuss the plan."

Isak gestured Elisaris towards the door.

"You must go now."

She smiled at him as she walked out. Her father was outside the door and escorted her to the room where she would live from now on.

* * *

Two hours later Isak knocked on Elisaris's door.

"Come in." She beckoned whilst sitting on her bed.

Isak entered, removing a strange book from his robe.

"We'll use this."

"How does it work?" she asked, curious.

"We need to acquire some of Daimeh's genetic material – skin, hair, anything," he explained. "Then I can fuse his DNA to the yocto-mechanics in this book. Yocto-mechanics, as you know, are tiny particles of easily manipulated energy."

He showed Elisaris the symbol on the front.

"Then he'll need to bind the book to himself. A small sample of his blood will work." Isak showed her where the incision on the forefinger was to be made then pressed the marked symbol.

"His memories will return to him and we can progress with the next part of the plan."

"The stasis chamber! Get some DNA from him there!" Elisaris said, grabbing his arm and standing up.

"No, that's not possible. The purging chambers are self-contained and sterilised. Nothing can leave those chambers. Only the purging pulses are used. We also have drone assistants who are responsible for placing him back in his bed."

"And I'm condemned to this side of the citadel. I can't get what's needed," Elisaris commented, her face sad.

"Don't worry, Elisaris. We need a more subtle approach. Tomorrow, for Daimeh, it's his first day here again. And I have an idea." Isak looked into her sorrowful eyes and smiled reassuringly before saying, "I believe we can do this."

* * *

The Amunisari staged the scene as it was when Daimeh first arrived at the citadel, placing his sleeping body in the bathing area.

Gentle music awoke Daimeh. Feeling refreshed, he got out of the water and allowed his skin to dry. After dressing, a young man with a pleasant, gentle voice spoke to him.

"Good morning, Daimeh. Please join us for some breakfast."

* * *

A vacant chair was waiting for him by the breakfast table. Opposite him sat Ceolm and his wife.

"My wife, Eleanor," Ceolm said, gesturing to his wife.

"My pleasure to formally meet you." She smiled. "Please, eat."

"Thank you, the food does look incredibly tasty," Daimeh said before taking a couple of pieces of ripe fruit.

Ceolm quietly cleared his throat before speaking. "I'm very interested to know how your journey here was – it must have been quite a challenge?"

The conversation proceeded along its usual path. Ceolm asking questions and Daimeh doing his best to satisfy his host's curiosity as to his home.

"Well," he said, rounding off the morning's discussion, "it's a wonderful place, and a peaceful one. We have a flourishing culture."

He got to his feet. "Would you mind if I took a tour around the citadel?"

"Make yourself at home Daimeh…"

* * *

As he walked among the alabaster columns, Daimeh noticed that a man kept peering at him. Daimeh remembered him from when he first arrived. He was one of the men who had stood behind the council; he had been peering at him curiously then as well. The inquisitive young man stepped down from the canopy and approached the young Alkoryn.

"Wonderful to meet you," he said, seeming intrigued by

Daimeh. "May I touch you?"

"Er... yes," Daimeh replied, confused but politely acqui-escing to him and lifting his hand. "I don't understa..."

Daimeh stopped mid-sentence as the man took his hand and carefully examined his shoulder. There was nothing to be seen.

"Fascinating. Thank you. Good day," Isak said, beginning to walk away. He could sense Daimeh's confusion and knew he was watching him go. He tried to act as casually as he could. Daimeh continued on to the water feature as he did every day.

Later that day Elisaris met Isak in her room.

"I couldn't get what we need. I'll try again tomorrow," he said, pursing his lips.

* * *

Two days later, Isak again bumped into Daimeh as he was making his usual after-breakfast tour of the Citadel.

"Oh, I'm sorry. And I feel very privileged to meet you. I do hope you're enjoying your stay here."

He took advantage of Daimeh's distraction to look for a hair. He noticed one stuck to Daimeh's shoulder.

"It's beautiful here," Daimeh said, still a little startled by the way Isak had walked into him.

Isak patted Daimeh's shoulders and sneakily took the hair.

"No harm done. Enjoy your day."

He walked away casually; his acting skills had improved over the few days.

Later, he met Elisaris again in her room.

"I've finally got what we need," Isak said, pulling the single strand of hair from a small bag. "Daimeh's DNA. Now we can move forward."

He glanced at Elisaris." You have the book?"

"Yes, here."

She handed him the synthetic black book. Its back was a curve of overlapping slates, the pages were holographic, the casing was solid and there was a single symbol on the front which translated as, 'Daimeh'.

Isak chopped up the hair and mixed it in a test tube with a sticky yellow liquid. Fizzing, the mixture became golden. He hacked the room's viewing screen so he could access his files in the technical lab. A strand of DNA appeared on the screen. He tapped one more button and the screen became a holographic projection. Continuing with the procedure, he poured the golden liquid into the top of the DNA strand and watched as it drizzled through the twisting double-helix contours. Before it reached the bottom he placed the book underneath the strand and allowed the liquid to absorb into the book's symbol. It pulsed through the pages as if it was charging with power.

"Now we need to get this to Daimeh," Isak said.

"Then what?"

"He needs to activate it."

He confidently looked at Elisaris.

"I can't contact him."

"I'll do it. I can temporarily disable the surveillance. We won't have long before the council notice that the system is hacked. But it should give us the time we need for Daimeh to retrieve his memories.

* * *

The following day…

Daimeh was walking around the fountain in the same way that he did every day, when he noticed Isak sitting on the garden bench, facing the watery landmark. He was pretending to read a book. When Daimeh approached the bench he peered up at him.

"Please, join me," Isak said, shuffling along to allow him to sit.

"Hmm, do I know you? Ah yes, you were the one peering at me when I first arrived," Daimeh said, thinking out loud.

"Yes, indeed I was," Isak replied, blushing. "We've never had visitors to the Citadel before. I was maybe a little more curious than I should have been."

"Hehe, it's fine really. I'm also curious: about this place – it's magnificent. Yet so quiet."

"Yes indeed, the tranquillity is lovely." He paused. "Anyway I don't have time to chat. I must be going. Good day to you."

He placed the book onto the bench and stood up.

Just as he was about to walk away, Daimeh grabbed his hand. "Wait. Your book!"

"Keep it, Daimeh." Before walking away, he turned back and said, "Place it under your pillow."

"Thank you, I will." Daimeh opened the book, but the pages were blank. They were not paper but a synthetic flexible paper-thin glass. Daimeh did not recognise the material. The bindings were light and had a smooth texture; it had the appearance of a heavier book. Daimeh was a little bewildered by what had happened and tucked it into his robe before continuing his stroll.

He started to feel uneasy as he began to notice things he hadn't seen before. What was going on here? He walked along some open, angular corridors – all the walls looked the same and the design was the same throughout the entire building. He could only know where he was from the art and plants that had been placed in all the rooms and corridors. They were unique to each room.

He arrived at his quarters and the door magically opened for him, as it had done previously. He entered and removed the book from under his robe. Its pages made him very curious.

Why are they blank, he wondered to himself, then said out loud, "It's like the tablet. There must be words here too."

He stroked his fingers against every page. Nothing appeared.

A voice suddenly spoke through the comm system, "I have food for you."

The door opened.

Daimeh quickly hid the book under the bed sheet.

"Thank you," he replied.

The assistant walked to the wall and a table grew from it, along with a low, comfortable-looking stool. He placed the tray of food down.

"Enjoy," he said, then left the room again.

A tray of exquisite food had been prepared for him. Daimeh was not particularly hungry, but it looked delicious and he could not resist its smell. He sat himself down on the stool, feeling drawn towards the food almost involuntarily. He took a bite of the cooked meat. It tasted like nothing he had tasted before, even though he had little appetite he enjoyed the food as if he had not eaten properly for days. He was surprised, but continued eating, then took a sip of the wine. A few moments later, his eyelids were heavy, then there was a sudden blackness: his head had hit the table.

* * *

A day had passed and Daimeh's memory had now been wiped. He was in his quarters, lying peacefully on the bed; his white robe was draped over him. The chanting gave him a sense of *deja vu* although he had no idea why, as it seemed unlike anything he had ever heard before.

Suddenly, he heard the voice of a stranger from under his pillow.

"Daimeh, you must wake up – we don't have much time."

Startled, he jumped out of bed.

"What? Who are you?"

He lifted his pillow immediately and saw the mysterious book. He didn't remember it from the day before.

"I'm a friend of a friend, and you must listen to me," the stranger's voice answered, becoming more pressing. "The surveillance is down in your room."

"What do you mean by surveillance?" Daimeh asked, glancing around, suddenly paranoid.

"Never mind. Just pick up the book."

Curious, Daimeh picked up the book and opened it.

"You need to cut your finger and touch the symbol," Isak instructed.

"What? No!" Daimeh replied. "And besides, there's nothing for me to do that with here."

"Find something."

"Look, I don't know what to do," Daimeh answered, adamant.

Isak sighed deeply.

"Wait there. I'm coming to you, be ready."

"I will."

* * *

"Quick, let me in!"

Daimeh gestured for the door to open and Isak rushed in and grabbed his arm, then glanced around the room. "I can't block the surveillance technology for long. We have to hurry." Isak hastily removed the book from under the pillow. "Now give me your hand."

Daimeh was reluctant, but Isak insisted. "Trust me," he said, quickly taking a small scalpel from inside his robe. Isak seized Daimeh's hand and made a small incision at the end of his forefinger.

Daimeh winced and pulled away.

"What are you doing?" he said, watching blood trickle from the wound.

Isak gave Daimeh the book.

"Put your finger here," he instructed, pointing to the small symbol on the front.

Daimeh did as he was asked and pressed his bloody finger

against the surface. The symbol began to glow and he watched it pulsate up his finger, through the nerves of his hand and up his arm.

"Now open it," Isak said.

23

Revelations

Daimeh stared at the dense black book for a few moments, still not quite sure if he was being tricked and feeling completely bewildered by what had just happened. He slowly ran his fingers along the sleek cover and over the vivid red embossed symbol. Then, sliding his finger under the edge of the strange material, he gently opened the mysterious book and stared at the first blank page. He began to flick through, a look of utter confusion on his face.

Moving images started to appear. *Cresa?*

Daimeh's stare increased in intensity as he watched footage of their journey to Amunisari. His anger peaked when he saw her taken away. Suddenly, Daimeh launched forward and grabbed Isak's throat.

"What did you do to my aunt?" he snarled through clenched teeth.

Isak was pressed against the wall, his hands raised and shaking.

"They took her. I don't know where. I'm sorry. I'm doing all I can for you."

Daimeh relaxed his grip slightly and looked at the floor.

"You should look at the next pages, Daimeh."

Letting Isak go he continued looking at the images, breathing heavily through his nose.

* * *

The next page was a record of their first breakfast with Ceolm and his family.

Daimeh stared intensely at the following page, tears welling.

They took her away.

He turned to the next. He was eating breakfast, and he was alone.

He skipped a couple of pages. There was the plate of food they gave him each night. The next page: breakfast again. *"Tell me about your journey. How did you find us?"* They had told him about the map.

He flicked through the next pages, which showed another breakfast. More questions: *"This rhajok'don and the library. I'm very interested in this. Please tell me more"*

Another page. Another question: *"Your religion. I would like to know more about this."*

He kept turning the pages. He had been at the citadel much longer than he had thought, maybe weeks.

The later pages showed Elisaris and Daimeh dancing. Next they were in his dream, and then she was taken away too. Daimeh's face grew angrier.

Further pages: Isak was at the monument and gave Daimeh the book. *"Place it under your pillow."*

The final image: they sedated Daimeh again with food.

Daimeh was silent for a few moments, staring into space. Then he suddenly let go of the book and it dropped heavily to the floor.

"I remember everything," he said.

He sat down onto the bed, his eyes filling with tears.

"What happened to Elisaris?"

"Elisaris was condemned from this part of the citadel," Isak replied. "Daimeh, listen carefully. I need you to play along with the charade for as long as you can whilst we plan your escape with Elisaris, to the protection of Alkoryn."

"You're not coming?" Daimeh asked.

"My place is here. I'll wipe my memory and stay."

"Why's the council doing this to me?"

"You have knowledge of something very powerful. It protects Alkoryn from the manipulation of the council," Isak answered, gripping Daimeh's hand. "You must never disclose what it is, especially now. If you do, Alkoryn will be in great danger. Your culture has been compromised and there are procedures for dealing with that."

"Procedures?" Daimeh raised his eyebrows.

"Procedures you don't want to know," Isak replied, stroking the back of his own hand.

"I must go now," he said, standing up. "I'll be back with further information. Hide the book before they notice it."

Daimeh lifted his pillow and hid the book beneath it. He lay there, looking upwards at the glazed sky, still trying to digest what had happened.

* * *

Later that day, a citadel steward brought him his evening meal. Daimeh knew what was going to happen and so had left a note for himself in case he didn't remember afterwards. As expected, after eating the food and drinking the wine, he fell to the floor, unconscious.

* * *

He awoke the next day in the water of the beautiful bathing area. It was his first day in this amazing place and he looked forward to exploring. After the air had thoroughly dried his skin, he walked into the bedroom. He noticed that some paper, a piece of old parchment from Lybas, had been left on his bed. Picking it up, he realised that it was in his handwriting.

Look under the pillow and read the book. You must do this now, then visit Isak immediately at the monument.

He lifted the pillow and opened the book. A few minutes later he was sitting on the bed, sobbing.

* * *

Daimeh knew where he had to go next, and after hastily leaving his room, he ran straight towards the central obelisk. He found a nervous-looking man standing next to the waterfall.

"Isak?" Daimeh asked.

"Yes, you're here. Good. We don't have much time."

* * *

The screen activated and Councillor Salvador's attention was suddenly attracted by what was being shown: Isak and Daimeh talking in the gardens again.

"More unscheduled meetings with my technician." He sighed. "And our loss of observation of Daimeh's room last night." He trusted his suspicions. Isak was helping Daimeh, "he always seemed like a sympathiser to me."

Salvador hurried from the modest surveillance room, covered on every wall by screens, and headed straight to Ceolm's office.

"Sire, it failed. I believe Daimeh knows everything about what's going on. I believe Isak has betrayed us."

"What?" Ceolm's nostrils flared with rage.

"Take this to the next stage." He paused. "And banish Isak."

"Are you sure, sire," the councillor asked cautiously.

Ceolm stood up and thrust his chest forward.

"Yes! Of course I'm sure!"

He gestured towards the door.

"Now, do it!"

"Yes, sire." Salvador bowed and walked away.

* * *

Councillor Salvador entered the ornate gardens with two Amunisarian guards. They marched directly to the waterfall, the guards' sleek white armour rattling slightly as they walked. Daimeh heard them coming and turned around to look, then quickly grabbed Isak's arm.

"Guards. Do they know?"

"I took as many precautions as I could," Isak replied, also glancing back at the oncoming trio. "Stay calm, Daimeh."

Coming closer, the councillor pointed at the two frightened men.

"Take them both."

"No! What?" Isak said.

Isak was jerked from his position and pushed away. He frantically tried to look behind him, only to see Daimeh being dragged away in the opposite direction.

"No! Don't do this, Salvador!" Isak begged.

* * *

Daimeh was marched through a series of corridors, all identical in design. White angular tiles covered the walls, as they did throughout the rest of the citadel. The final door slid open; beyond was a room with walls of black marble. The silent guards forcefully pushed him into the fetid-smelling room and closed the door behind him. It beeped three times before the guards walked away. Daimeh waved at the door, then pushed it, but it was no good. Finally, he tried banging it with his fist. Nothing. He was imprisoned. He turned around slowly, unable to believe what had happened. As his eyes gradually adjusted to the darkness, he noticed the barbaric instruments of interrogation all around him. His face paled and he felt his hair stand up on end. These devices were not sophisticated but crude, perhaps intended to appear as frightening as possible. Daimeh backed away and leaning against the door, he slid down it. He sat on the floor, trembling and crying. He thought back to the Galunda Bay and the body that he had found washed onto the shore. Why did he have to find it? He regretted everything that he had done since that moment.

* * *

Some time passed until eventually the door slid open. Two guards rushed in and forcefully grabbed Daimeh by his armpits, yanking him over to the back wall. They dragged him to his feet, then chained his neck to a bolt fixed to the wall. Daimeh wearily tumbled to the cold floor. Finally, the guards threw a bowl of scum down for him to eat. Some of the froth spilled over and splashed onto the sleek surface of the slates. The guards stared at Daimeh intimidatingly, chuckling, before exiting the prison cell.

Daimeh refused the food and lay on his side, at a loss for what to do.

* * *

More time passed and Daimeh was awoken by a jolt at his neck. He looked up sluggishly and saw that one of the guards was releasing the chain from the wall. The guard yanked the chain forcefully, pulling Daimeh to his feet. Unwillingly he was dragged over to the first instrument of torture. This was a splintered wooden table with rusty bolts and a strange wheeled device standing alongside it. He was shackled to the table with his arms and legs outstretched and bound to its edges. Daimeh trembled, his eyes darting around the room.

Councillor Salvador entered Daimeh's cell, confidently walking over to the table, his narrow, blue eyes filled with contempt.

He looked directly into Daimeh's eyes. "You can stop this," he said. "Just tell me what's protecting Alkoryn and this will be over."

His expression was aggressive, but his voice sounded calm.

"I'll never tell you anything," Daimeh answered, his voice filling with determination.

Salvador nodded to the guard at the wheel, who responded by gradually rotating it.

At first, it felt just like he was having a stretch in the morning. Then the pain started: he heard his limbs cracking, just a little at first, then more seriously. Daimeh tried to endure the pain by holding his jaw clenched and breathing rapidly, spewing saliva with each breath.

The wheel rotated further, his tendons burned and the agony worsened. His cries of suffering echoed around the dungeon. He clasped his hands together, knowing that he had to be braver than he had ever been before. He could hear nothing but the sound of the creaking wheel.

The next turn of the wheel he felt his muscles ripping from the strain and the sweat dribbling from his hair down to his neck.

"I won't tell you," he said through his teeth, his head pulled forward.

The councillor nodded again at the guard, who unhesitatingly turned the wheel faster.

The walls reverberated with Daimeh's screams until, finally, he passed out.

Salvador quickly reached into his robe pocket. Pulling out a thin white tube, he jabbed it into Daimeh's neck. A blue light flashed and Daimeh woke suddenly. He tried resiliently to pull himself upright, but it was in vain and his screams quickly became louder than before.

"It'll stop if you tell me," Salvador said calmly, sounding almost sympathetic.

"Never!" Daimeh screeched in rage. His skin was flushed and saliva had built up in the corners of his mouth.

"All right. As you wish."

The councillor signalled to the other guard and indicated with his eyes the brutal curved sword he was holding. The guard nodded and approached the table slowly, as if he had done it many times before.

Daimeh's breath rasped and he whimpered.

"No, no, no, please."

"Tell us."

"I c-can't tell you," Daimeh stuttered, choked with tears. For a moment, he almost gave in to the torment.

The cold edge of the sword balanced on Daimeh's chest. He tensed his body in anticipation and squeezing his eyes shut he put his head back and tried to control his breathing. At first, all he could feel was a scratch, but the stinging intensified as the blade cut downwards through his flesh until it hit his ribcage. By the time the sword reached his belly, he felt as though he was on fire.

Keeping his eyes tightly shut, Daimeh shed tears uncontrollably. The agony overwhelmed him and his mind turned to thoughts of home. He remembered being with his mother as a child, watching her weave. He thought of his father showing him how to fit roofs, of running around Galunda Bay with Oeradon, of Karalyn, the girl he had liked, and his glenny, Popley, who was always so excited to see him. More tears rolled down each temple. He remembered dancing blissfully with Elisaris under the open sky.

"Enough!"

Salvador ordered the guards to stop.

Ceolm entered the room. "Anything?"

The room was still filled with the sound of Daimeh's cries.

"No, sire. We cannot break his loyalties to the people he loves."

"I know what will work," Ceolm said, his tone sinister. He left the room abruptly.

The councillor also walked out of the cell, ordering his two guards to follow him and leaving Daimeh tied to the old wooden block.

* * *

Daimeh woke to the clanks of metal chains being unravelled. No more, he begged silently. No more, please. Helpless and in pain, he could do nothing as the guards pulled him off the block and chained him to the far wall again.

The prison door slid open and Ceolm walked through.

"Now you'll tell me," he said confidently, raising his hand and revealing a gesture-activated hidden screen.

Daimeh peered at it, barely moving his head. The screen was lit up by vivid colours, but Daimeh's vision was so blurred that he couldn't make anything out. After a few moments he recognised his love, Elisaris. His eyes cleared a little and, to his horror, he realised that she was tied to a column.

"I must leave now," Ceolm said.

* * *

A few minutes later, Ceolm appeared on the screen, approaching his daughter.

Please, don't hurt her, Daimeh beseeched mutely. Aedolyn, I beg you to save us. His prayer felt like his last hope.

Ceolm removed a large knife from under his gown.

Please! No! "Elisaris!" Daimeh shouted, the veins standing out on his forehead.

Her beautiful aqua eyes gazed sorrowfully at Daimeh through the screen. He watched the movement of her lips as she spoke. The words, meant for him alone, were spoken so slowly and so clearly, "I love you, Daimeh."

Daimeh's head dropped and tears began to spill from his eyes, splashing onto the blood-stained floor. He had never had the chance to say it back to her. He lifted his head just as Ceolm put the knife to her throat.

Ceolm's final words to her were, "You brought this on

yourself."

"Father—" she swallowed, her face anguished. "Plea—urh"

With a sudden, quick movement, Ceolm plunged the blade into her throat, instantly severing the jugular. Elisaris choked for a few seconds then her lifeless head flopped forward and the blood started gushing down her delicate white gown. There was silence.

"No!" Daimeh moaned as he reached as far as the chains allowed him and screamed until nothing was left. His heart sank in his chest as his stomach churned from the emotional loss.

"No!"

His bottom lip quivered as he breathed.

"Eli!" he wailed and spluttered in agony, his words making no sense. What had they done? His shocked eyes darted about and his breathing quickened. Trying to hold in his feeling of loss, his eyebrows tensed and his eyes glazed, then he fell to his knees, staring down at the dungeon floor. Suddenly his panicked breathing calmed and slowed, until he felt as though he was in a trance, lost in his grief. A single teardrop spilled from his eye, trickled down his cheek and dripped onto the slippery, cold floor. He toppled down to the ground and lay on his side, his arm in front of him, tears flooding the floor below his face as he cried himself into sorrowful exhaustion.

Moments passed. Her thoughts echoed in his mind.

As the Amunisari prosper,
Stygia conspires.
Time is short,
As the darkness is coming...

24

Banished

There was only silence.

Her blood had seeped through her white gown and spilled slowly onto her ankle until, finally, it congealed on the pristine floor. Ceolm stood next to Elisaris's drooping body, which was pinned to the column by three straps.

Indistinct weeping could be heard in the distance gradually becoming louder. Eleanor ran into the circular courtyard and the weeping turned to hysterical screaming.

"What have you done? Why?"

Ceolm was silent.

In anguish, Eleanor cupped her daughter's head in her hands, staring into her beautiful face. Suddenly she turned to her husband and began pummelling his chest with her fists.

"Why? Why? Why?" Eleanor whimpered, her breathing irregular and choking.

Ceolm gently embraced her.

"It's all right, my love."

She pushed him away in anger.

"My daughter's dead. You killed her."

"Don't worry," he said, his voice carrying no emotion.

"Guards!"

Two Amunisarian guards approached and stood beside him. "Make me a new one," he ordered, gesturing for them to leave.

"No, no, no, no."

Eleanor covered her face with her hands. Her muffled voice said, "Clones are never the same."

"This one will be perfect, my dear."

Ceolm lifted his hand to his wife's shoulder to reassure her.

"Come, I'll escort you to your room."

Eleanor shook her head. "I'm staying with my daughter."

* * *

Ceolm confidently entered the genetics laboratory.

"How long?" he asked.

A technician waved his hand at the wall and a screen appeared. On it, Ceolm saw a man-sized test-tube filled with bubbling, clear liquid. Sparks pulsed through the pipes and tubes connected to the woman's developing body.

"The incubation period will end tomorrow, sire," the scientist replied.

"I only want her childhood memories transferred, nothing more."

"Yes, sire."

* * *

Eleanor sat in her silent room on her soft mattress, sobbing into her hands. Her olive-complexioned face was sticky with tears and her palms were wet with them. The dull bump of the hologram momentarily interrupted her endless grief.

Ceolm's voice echoed through the spacious room.

"My love, I'll introduce you."

Eleanor carefully picked up a glass of water from the glassy, marbled, table top. She didn't want to see her fake daughter, but she knew she had no choice.

The thin door slid open and there was Elisaris, looking as young and angelic as she always did.

"Hello, Mother, I was wondering if you're ready for our walk today. Remember – we planned to visit the gallery too."

Elisaris noticed her mother's tears and her reaction seemed almost automated.

"Are you all right? Why are you crying?" she asked, edging

closer to her.

"Oh nothing," Eleanor replied, sniffling.

Elisaris placed her hand on Eleanor's lap and passed her a handkerchief, watching as she sniffled sharply, then lifted her head, wiped her eyes and delicately blew her nose.

"Go now. I'll meet you in an hour," Eleanor said, composing herself.

"Yes, Mother."

Her daughter was incredibly compliant.

As Elisaris was leaving, her father entered. They passed each other in the doorway and Ceolm asked, "How's your mother?"

"She seems a little upset and she won't tell me why," Elisaris replied, in a monotone.

Ceolm approached Eleanor and she stood up to acknowledge him.

"You killed our daughter and I'll never, *never* forgive you."

She stared at him with hatred in her eyes before storming out of the room.

* * *

Fluorescent light glinted off the geometric tiles as Eleanor strode determinedly along the corridor. She walked along a second, then a third corridor, until she finally arrived at a discreet door, guarded by two Amunisarian watch men.

"I'm here to see the prisoner," she said sternly.

"Yes, ma'am."

Stepping aside, the guards allowed the door to open. Eleanor entered the black, intimidating prison cell. The torture devices were still present.

"Remove these," Eleanor ordered.

The guards immediately did as they were told and began heaving the cruel machinery out of the cell.

Daimeh was lying helpless and defeated on the blood splattered, tiled floor. Crouching, she gently stroked the side of his beaten face and he slowly woke up. He looked at her through bleary eyes.

"Huh?" he mumbled.

"I'm so sorry, Daimeh, for what's happened to you."

She bowed her head in shame.

"What are you doing here?" Daimeh managed to ask.

"I'm here to help you. I want to help you."

She wiped his grimy hair away from his forehead.

"Let's get you cleaned up and healed."

"You think this changes anything?"

The hatred in Daimeh's voice was very clear as he pushed her hand away.

"My only love is dead. You can't help me."

His anger and sudden movement had opened the deep wound in his chest and he began to bleed onto the floor. He slumped down, his feeling of loss returning. Breathing heavily through his nose, he stared into space.

"Oh we must get you healed!" Eleanor said, applying pressure to help stop the bleeding.

Daimeh aggressively pushed her away. "Don't touch me!"

"I loved my daughter too, very much," Eleanor said, lifting her head and closing her eyes, trying to hold the tears back. "Ceolm acted alone and I'll do whatever it takes to make him pay."

She stood up and unchained Daimeh from the wall.

"Please, Daimeh, let me help you get out of here."

"How would you do that?" he asked.

"The only way out of Amunisari for you is banishment to Stygia," Eleanor answered, hanging her head in shame. "It's the best I can do."

"Stygia? The Land of Eternal Stars."

She looked sad.

"I know it's not an ideal solution."

Daimeh was silent as he remembered the last words he had heard from Elisaris: *As the Amunisari prosper, Stygia conspires. Time is short, as the darkness is coming...* He thought about the words for a moment. It was a warning: *The darkness is coming...* Stygia is coming.

"I'll do it."

Daimeh knew it could be his chance for vengeance against Ceolm and the Amunisari.

Eleanor smiled.

"Then come, let me clean you and get some fresh clothes. Don't worry, no harm will come to you anymore."

She walked towards the door and gestured for it to open.

"Guards, take this young man to the medical centre."

They nodded and escorted him away, not quite as nicely as Eleanor would have liked.

* * *

Daimeh lay on his back on a bed, a screen above him. Eleanor stood over him, controlling the machine. She pressed a button then put her hand through the screen and an ethereal pen-like device appeared which fitted snugly into her hand. She guided it down Daimeh's chest and a golden, flowing liquid began to dribble onto his open wound. That done, she dabbed it around his face and onto any other injuries she could see. The machine began to puff steam onto the glowing wounds and they disappeared, leaving Daimeh completely healed.

The virtual screen vanished and Daimeh sat forward.

"Now some clean clothes," Eleanor said. She passed him some Alkoryn garments. "I was able to get the things you arrived in. Freshened up, of course. You can get changed over there."

She pointed to a concealed area.

Daimeh smiled for the first time since Elisaris's death.

"Thank you," he replied; she was earning his trust.

When he returned, Eleanor continued, "I'll convince Ceolm to banish you, otherwise he'll just kill you."

"I understand."

She tidied his apparel in a motherly way, then gave orders to the guards. "Clean his cell and get him a decent bed."

They nodded, hurrying off to do as ordered.

Five minutes later, Daimeh was escorted back to his cell.

* * *

"He's no use to us – we should just banish him. I can arrange it," Eleanor told her husband.

"For such obstruction he should die, Eleanor!" Ceolm replied, banging his fist on the table.

His wife knelt down on one knee.

"Please show him mercy. He cared for our daughter. Her heart is with him. Spare his life," she pleaded, gripping her husband's trousers.

Ceolm shrugged off his wife's pleas.

"He will die."

"I'll accept Elisaris," Eleanor finally said, holding out her hands. "I'll accept her as my own daughter."

Ceolm was silent for a few moments, then Eleanor was surprised to hear him say, "Very well… Stygia may be worse than death anyway."

Eleanor believed otherwise.

"Thank you, my husband. I'll take care of it."

* * *

After returning to Daimeh's cell, Eleanor led him to an unfamiliar facility: a lengthy corridor, split into partitions, with walls slanting inwards up to an arched roof. The walls were black-panelled, with irregular white shapes in between. In each partition was a graphite grey capsule, the size of a man and uneven in texture.

"We have one ready for you."

Eleanor pointed to a capsule on their right.

"What do I do?"

She swept her hand over the surface and it glided open making a whirring mechanical noise. Inside was a cushioned resting area.

"Get in, Daimeh."

He hesitated, his face ashen. He was fearful about what was to come. Stygia, was this what he really wanted? "I can't do this," he said, backing away from the capsule.

"It's your only choice. Ceolm will kill you if you stay," Eleanor said, stroking his arm. "I wish there was another way."

Daimeh's breathing quickened as he stared into the terrifying booth. He lifted one clammy hand and placed it on the partition, then put one foot in, followed by the other. Once inside he laid back, feeling the cold sweat running down his back and his heavy hands pulling at his arms. His lips were trembling and his eyes were damp.

"What do I do when I get there?" he stuttered, his voice shaking.

"You remove your provisions. I was also able to get the symbols for you."

She pointed to the bottom left of the capsule.

"They're tucked into a small compartment down there. The sword is in there too, for your protection."

Eleanor took a deep breath before continuing, "When you're there, I don't know what you'll find. You'll land near Kraag'Blitz, the only colony I know of."

She pulled out strapping from the inside cushions and began securing Daimeh in place.

"What about the people? They're all criminals?"

"Not all of them," she replied, closing her eyes. "My husband banished many innocent people for minor breaches in procedure."

Daimeh shook his head in disbelief.

"I'm sure someone will come to your aid."

There was a humming noise and the pod began to vibrate slightly.

Daimeh reached out and held Eleanor's hand. "Will you help my aunt?" he pleaded.

"I will," Eleanor replied.

The humming turned into loud whirring. "It's time to go."

Just as Eleanor was about to signal for the door to shut, Daimeh said, "Wait. Will I be able to return to Alkoryn one day?"

His chin trembled as he spoke.

"No." Eleanor's expression slackened with sadness before she allowed the capsule door to close with a hiss.

Inside, the capsule was completely silent apart from Daimeh's rapid breathing. The only illumination was a dull blue light between the cushions. The air was close and stale and it dried his mouth out until his tongue felt like cloth.

Vibrations shook the compact shell and he felt his insides drop suddenly, as if they were ten times heavier than his body. This was a feeling he remembered from travelling with the gargantuan. His pounding head was thrust forward by the G-force and his field of vision became increasingly grey and narrow until he finally blacked out...

* * *

The capsule skimmed across the surface of Stygia before finally embedding itself in a marshy, mud pool with a loud crash.

When Daimeh awoke, it was pitch-black. His head was in intense pain and as he fumbled to undo the straps he felt something dripping. Running his hands across his face, he realised that he was bleeding from his nose, eyes and mouth. He spluttered, falling forward out of his seat and slumping to the lower side of the pod with a thud. He wondered how he could get out of the pod, and just as he had the thought, the door skimmed open in a flash. Maybe it was timed?

He was greeted by a dark, dismal world; he could detect the stagnant stench of fetid air mixed with chemicals and smoke. Glancing around himself he saw that he had landed in a bubbling mud pool and the capsule was slowly sinking into it. Hastily grabbing his things from the compartment, Daimeh jumped free. He stood, staring in horrified shock at the surrounding land: flat, dirty ground, with small boulders scattered around and a starry sky above. He gazed at the distant speckles feeling completely insignificant. He had begun to shiver – it was so cold. He rubbed his hands roughly up and down his arms. On the far horizon he saw cliffs and when he turned around an industrialised skyline came into view. That must be Kraag'Blitz, he realized. A mass of factories desecrated the land, their towering, smoking chimneys spewing foul impurities in the form of intense chemical explosions and dense bursts of dirty grey steam.

His eyes flinched from the alien landscape, his mind running for safety to thoughts of Lybas, the home that he cherished so dearly. He had truly believed he would return one day, but instead had found himself lost in a desolate, dangerous realm, with nothing but sadness in his heart. He felt overcome by a longing for a life that was gone, perished into the emptiness of his soul.

He wanted to go home.

Glossary

Aedolyn: the primary Goddess of Alkoryn: *pron; Ed-o-lyn.*

Aedolyn's tears: is sacred water held in a chalice and only used on monarchs for special blessings.

Amphid: a frog-like animal with incredibly long legs.

Aves bird: a mammal with a bird-like appearance and a cat-like face, tiny in size and bred in the Amunisari citadel.

Avopalto: a fatty fruit that cultivates on the locyan-palm. It has a variety of uses, from sealing leaves, to varnish, ink and paint; if mixed with chalk and natural plant dye.

Delf: a dolphin-like sea mammal as large as a small boat and covered in shiny brown fur. They are solitary animals, yet non-aggressive to others.

Dyak Bats: are evening bats that dwell on cliff sides, they have a distinctive call that Alkoryn's use as time indicators.

Equid: a horse-like animal with a long trunk that reaches the ground, hooved feet and scaly skin, off-white in colour. They have white to blonde mains.

Glenny: are goat-like, herd animals with large clumsy looking ears, soft protruding snouts. Alkoryn's breed three breeds of glenny, one known as the 'kashi' with lush, thick, soft wool and leathers - the 'saable' purely for milk - the 'moxo' used as a pack animal and quality meat. They stand at about half the size of a man, with firm, sturdy hooves, and a fluffy short tail. They are most commonly cream in colour, although light brown ones have been known. Each Alkoryn child is given a glenny to teach responsibility.

Lagus: are rabbit-like animals. They are as high as a man's waist and live in mound hills. They're aggressive with two sharp incisor teeth. Their ears are too large for their heads, giving them a donkey-like appearance.

Locyan-palm: the most abundant tree in the vicinity, a thick-trunked tree with parasitic vines creeping over it's bark.

Monea snail: a rare deep-sea snail, spotted only once per year.

Phoro plant: a herb usually finely wound into incense, they are used primarily for their aroma.

Pygmy Gidar: a small turkey-like animal.

Ryndia bird: native parrot-like birds who nest in the tallest branches of forest trees. They are commonly light blue in colour, although some pink ones have been spotted. They are large in size with exquisite feathers.

Tygrisa: are slender reptilian predators, similar in appearance to a big cat, however with scaley deep green skin, they stand at about the height of a child and hunt cooperatively by skulking through the undergrowth with strong, pouncing legs and razor spiked teeth, with protruding canines. Their eyes are big, bright orange and side slanted, adapted to the lower light of the dim forest thicket, the eyes are positioned front-facing for more effective hunting. Tygrisa can open their mouths particularly wide, as they use steering hisses to lure their prey, always awaiting their next meal.

Yocto-mechanics: are tiny particles of easily manipulated energy.

About the Author

Caroline-Jayne Gleave was born in Durham, North East England and had a passion for writing at a very young age. As a child she wrote many short stories, horror, fantasy and sci-fi. The story for Scripture from the Past started fifteen years ago, when she wrote the first chapter of the book. She didn't feel she could write a whole book at that time due to her studying. She went to three north east universities and achieved a degree, a master's degree and post-graduate certificate.

Her writing really took off again in 2013 when she found the first chapter she had written all those years ago.

She hasn't stopped writing since.

COSMIC
EGG
BOOKS

If you prefer to spend your nights with Vampires and
Werewolves rather than the mundane then we publish the books
for you. If your preference is for Dragons and Faeries or Angels
and Demons – we should be your first stop. Perhaps your
perfect partner has artificial skin or comes from another planet –
step right this way. Our curiosity shop contains treasures you
will enjoy unearthing. If your passion is Fantasy (including
magical realism and spiritual fantasy), Horror or Science Fiction
(including Steampunk), Cosmic Egg books will
feed your hunger.